TRUE COLORS

Lynda Trent

W0009040

Zebra Books
Kensington Publishing Corp.

http://www.zebrabooks.com

ZEBRA BOOKS are published by

Kensington Publishing Corp.
850 Third Avenue
New York, NY 10022

Copyright © 1997 by Dan and Lynda Trent

All rights reserved. No part of this book may be reproduced in any form or by any means without the prior written consent of the Publisher, excepting brief quotes used in reviews.

If you purchased this book without a cover you should be aware that this book is stolen property. It was reported as "unsold and destroyed" to the Publisher and neither the Author nor the Publisher has received any payment for this "stripped book."

Zebra and the Z logo Reg. U.S. Pat. & TM Off.

First Printing: February, 1997
10 9 8 7 6 5 4 3 2 1

Printed in the United States of America

TRUE LOVE

"Do you really love me?" Amanda asked as she held Dakota tightly. "Do you honestly love me?"

"You know I do."

She could hear the leashed anger in his voice. When she came back from her mother's house, she never felt sure of herself and that made him angry. She knew the anger wasn't aimed at her. "You're a good person," she whispered.

"I love you. I'm not ever going to leave you."

She tried to swallow the sobs. "Don't ever send me away, Dakota. I couldn't stand not being with you."

"I'll never send you away."

"I'm sorry," she whispered. "I know you love me. I do."

"Hush," he said soothingly. He kissed her and gazed into her eyes. "I'm never going to leave or send you away. You couldn't get rid of me if you tried. Even if you chased me away, I'd only come back."

Praise for Lynda Trent and BEST FRIENDS:

"With BEST FRIENDS, Lynda Trent serves up a generous slice of contemporary life—reminiscent of Danielle Steel."
—JOAN HOHL, national bestselling author
of ANOTHER SPRING

"Lynda Trent is a talented author who always touches her audience with emotionally poignant stories."
—ROMANTIC TIMES

Praise for Lynda Trent and FAMILY SECRETS:

"FAMILY SECRETS belongs on your "must read" list. Riveting and compelling!"
—RENDEZVOUS

Books by Lynda Trent

BEST FRIENDS

FAMILY SECRETS

TRUE COLORS

Published by Zebra Books

Chapter One

"I have to go. I don't have any choice." Amanda folded a pair of jeans into her suitcase and reached for the lightweight sweater she planned to wear with it. "I wonder if Houston will already be too hot for a sweater. This time of year you never can tell." She bit her lip as she pondered.

Dakota frowned. "I don't want you to go. You know what visiting your family always does to you. You'll come back in emotional shreds and cry for days." The creases in his brow deepened as he crossed his muscular arms across his chest.

She stopped packing and went to him. "Honey, we've been through this before. It's Mother's Day. I have to go. It's our family reunion."

"Even worse. That means Grace and her husband will be there, too. Grace affects you as negatively as your mother."

Amanda stepped closer and Dakota put his arms around her. She smiled up at him. "Don't be so upset. It's only a weekend visit."

"That's long enough for your family to tear you to pieces. At least let me come with you."

"How would I explain your being there? That's one reason I have to go to the reunion. No one in my family knows you exist." She smiled and touched his handsome face. "In a few months our baby will be here and that seems rather too late for me to tell them I've met someone and fallen in love."

"Amanda, we've lived together for almost a year. We were lovers for months before that. Why didn't you tell them about me then? Why have you kept me a secret for so long?"

She sighed. "You'd have to know my family to understand that. I can't explain them."

"Try." He was still upset with her, though he continued to hold her. Dakota's mother was an American Indian and Dakota himself looked as if he would be more at home in buckskins and warpaint than in the tight jeans and T-shirt he wore.

Amanda pushed her long black hair back from her face. "Mother doesn't approve of me living in Los Angeles in the first place, much less that I'm an artist. The fact that you're one, too, would only make matters worse."

"We aren't simply artists, you know that. Soon we'll complete the canvases for our first nationwide tour. And one of the major cities where we'll be exhibiting is Houston. Our pictures will be in the paper and we'll be interviewed on TV. Don't you think someone will tell her about us? Part of our publicity focuses on the fact we're lovers."

"I know. That's even more reason for me to go this weekend. Even though Mother doesn't want me to be an artist, she keeps up with all the important art showings. She wouldn't be caught dead not knowing the latest in the arts. Besides, the Houston museum that booking agent picked for us is the one Dad helped found. She can't possibly not know we're there. I'm just glad the agency is holding back on publicity until closer to the opening."

"As much as you dread telling her, I should be with you," Dakota repeated stubbornly. "I don't like you doing this alone. Not if she's half as formidable as you say she is."

She smiled up at him. "I think meeting you in person before she's been prepared would be enough to send her into one of her 'spells.' You don't realize how impressive you are."

"That's nonsense, Amanda. I'm just a person."

"And King Kong was just a monkey." She put her hands on his muscled arms and ran her palms across his shoulders and up his neck so she could stroke her fingers through his hair. "No man with such long hair and an earring and only one name has ever set foot in Mother's house. On top of that, you look more like an artist's model than an artist. You're the sexiest man I've ever seen. Mother doesn't admire that in a man."

"She doesn't have to admire me or even like me. I only want to be there to protect you."

"I don't need protecting from my own family. They won't hurt me, for goodness' sake!"

"Maybe not physically, but every time you've come back from visits with them, you've been an emotional basket case. This is a particularly bad time for you to be upset. Not only are we going to have a baby, but we have to finish the canvases for the exhibit. You know you don't do your best work when you're emotionally upset."

"It's only for the weekend," she repeated. "I'll only be there tonight and tomorrow and I'll leave on Sunday. And with me gone that'll give you more uninterrupted time to do your own work. I'm not the only one who isn't ready for the exhibit."

As his lips touched hers, Amanda opened her mouth

to him, sending a clear message of the passion she felt. Although they had been lovers for a long time, he still excited her beyond all reason. She had never been in love before and her love for Dakota was greater than any feeling she had thought herself capable of. When he finally pulled away, she said, "I love you, Dakota. I want everyone to know about you. About us. And in seven months our baby will be born. I have to tell them now. I can't wait until I'm showing or the baby is already here to break the news. No, this weekend is the best possible time."

"What if you can't tell her?"

She turned away and pretended to resume her packing. "Why wouldn't I be able to do that?"

"Maybe for whatever reason you weren't able to tell her on the other visits to Houston this past year. What is it about this woman that intimidates you so? You sure as hell aren't intimidated by anything else."

"You haven't met her. Mother is difficult to explain. When she's in public, she's the image of the perfect lady— soft-spoken, genteel, beautifully dressed. At home she can be a dragon. The worst part is that she's skilled at manipulating people without them ever realizing what's happened. She can do that to me. It's hard for me to be myself around her." She added a dress to her bag of hanging clothes.

"You're taking a dress?" Dakota noticed with some surprise.

"She expects us to dress for dinner. We always do."

"You hate to wear dresses."

"She dislikes pants. My jeans are a constant irritation to her." She tossed a smile at him. "But I wear them anyway."

"At least that's something."

"My brother will be there. I haven't seen Nathan since last year."

"But he lives in Galveston. That's only fifty miles from Houston. Why don't you visit him while you're that close?"

"I'm not sure. Every time I've been in town, Nathan doesn't have time for me. I've never seen his place. I guess his chain of clothing stores keeps him pretty busy."

Dakota's expression made it clear that he disagreed.

"You can't understand my family. There's no reason for you to try."

"I wish your sister wouldn't be there this time."

"Grace wouldn't dream of missing the reunion. It's the only time we'll all be together until next Thanksgiving. Besides, if anything is chiseled in granite in my family, it's that we never miss going to Mother's house on Mother's Day." She paused and reflected that she'd never understood why being with her family was supposed to be such a desirable event. "Grace never does anything to disappoint Mother. Of the three of us, she's the most like Mother, though the only one who looks like Dad. She's Mother's favorite, I think."

"I should be going with you. After all, I have to meet them someday. I'm the father of our child." His deep voice held a note of hurtful resentment.

"I know and you will. But not when I haven't told them anything about you. Mother will be furious with me for living with a man, and more so for getting pregnant."

"We planned to have the baby."

"I know. But can't you see what a shock this will be to her? She's not a young woman. She married late in life and I'm the youngest child. She has heart trouble. I can't spring too much on her at once."

"How can she be that frail and terrorize you at the same time?"

Defensively, she snapped, "Mother doesn't terrorize me." She didn't meet his eyes.

"Amanda!"

"I have to go, Dakota. I don't have a choice. Not on Mother's Day."

She heard him sigh and knew he was finally giving in. "All right. But all you have to do is call me and I'll be on the next flight to Houston. Or you can say hello to everyone, receive your mental abuse, and fly back home tonight."

She smiled at him and tiptoed up to kiss him. "I have to leave now. Will you call a taxi for me?"

"No, I'm going to drive you. That way, if you change your mind, I'll be there to bring you back home."

"I love you."

"I love you, too." He looked as if he wasn't entirely sure he shouldn't get on the plane and go with her in spite of her protests.

In Dallas, Grace Hillard and her husband were also packing to leave for Houston. "Don't take that gray suit, Todd," Grace nagged. "You've put on too much weight and it looks awful on you."

"I haven't gained that much." Todd looked at himself in the mirror and tightened his stomach muscles. "I don't look bad for forty-two."

Grace frowned at him; she hated it when he brought up his age. It reminded her that she had turned forty on her last birthday. "You should go on a diet."

"You could lose a pound or two yourself," he retorted.

"Nonsense. I don't weigh a pound more than I did the day we got married."

He let loose with a derisive laugh. "Right."

Grace automatically felt the waistline of her skirt. She knew it was two sizes larger than she'd ever worn, and even at that, it was a bit tight. Despite her continuous, stringent dieting, she was starting to gain weight just as her father had at about the same age. She dreaded what her mother would say. Elizabeth Wainwright still had a trim figure at seventy-one and saw no reason that Grace shouldn't as well.

Todd selected a tie from the several dozen in his closet and added it to his suitcase.

"Not that tie, surely!"

"What's wrong with it? Your sister gave it to me three Christmases ago."

"She couldn't have been serious about it. I think she was insulting you and you didn't get the joke."

He frowned at her. "Amanda wouldn't do that."

"Forget that tie. Take the expensive navy-and-red one I just got you."

"Your mother probably won't like that one, either, but it will give her something to bitch about besides our personal business. At least she's finally stopped harping on us not having children," Todd complained as he hung the tie back in his closet and looked for the one Grace had bought.

"It's only natural Mother would want one of us to continue the family line. But of course Nathan is the right one to do that, because he can hand down the family name. Besides, I never wanted children. They're too messy and loud. And we could never have had so many nice things if we'd had children running about." She looked around Todd's bedroom with smug satisfaction. "We have a lovely house. I've seen to that. It's a house we can be proud of."

"I suppose."

"I'm going back to my room and make sure I've packed my alligator shoes and bag. You pack the things I've laid out here."

He grunted his assent.

Grace went to her own bedroom and checked the items on her pink-flowered bedspread. Her room was utterly feminine, just as Todd's was thoroughly masculine. Grace wasn't particularly feminine by nature, but she knew Elizabeth would approve of the room if she came for a visit. When she and Todd had people over, she put the women's coats in her room and the men's in Todd's because she wanted the ladies to see what impeccable taste she had.

Standing before her full-length mirror, she turned around to see if her weight gain was as obvious as Todd implied and grimaced. The waistline of the skirt *was* irritatingly tight. They had a long drive all the way to Houston and she would be decidedly uncomfortable, but because the color was so flattering to her blond hair, she chose not to change. Of Elizabeth's children, she was the only blonde. Both Amanda and Nathan had Elizabeth's black hair and blue eyes. Grace had considered getting blue contacts so her green eyes wouldn't look so out of place, but she was afraid Elizabeth would make fun of her.

Grace loved her mother and had sought her approval all her life. Her brother and sister had doted on their father, but Grace had known from childhood that the real power of the family was Elizabeth. Grace had done everything possible to emulate Elizabeth and to learn to wield power as effortlessly as her mother, but it didn't come easily to her.

She sucked in her breath and tightened her stomach. Did she look as if she had gained weight since her last visit to her mother's? She didn't see how she could continue to gain when she ate such a Spartan diet. Of course she had splurges that frequently overcame her willpower, but those didn't count. Everyone had setbacks in dieting. She never had let anyone know she was subject to such weakness, and after denying it for so long, she almost believed that she ate only the most rigidly controlled fare.

Todd came to the doorway. "Are you ready? We have

to go if we're going to miss the noon rush-hour traffic. It's going to take us a good five hours to get there as it is."

She closed her suitcase and snapped it shut. She had chosen their luggage in the same manner she had decorated their rooms—hers in feminine shades of rose and cream, his in a masculine tan and olive.

"I can't afford to get another speeding ticket this month. Our insurance will go up."

"I hate it when you grouse about money. If it goes up, we'll pay it. It's as simple as that." She strode to the door. "Get my luggage, please." She didn't look back to see if he would follow her instructions. He always did.

She waited at the car for him to open her door after he had deposited the luggage in the trunk. "There's no room in cars these days," she complained as Todd tried to shut the trunk and had to open it again to rearrange the suitcases. "They look cheap."

"I can assure you, this one wasn't." He managed to shut the lid on his second try and came around to open her door. "I'll be paying on this car for years."

"Don't be ridiculous. We'll trade it long before that." She slid in and glanced around to be certain the interior was impeccably clean. Elizabeth's vehicles never had a speck of dust on the dashboard nor a leaf on the carpet, and she'd made sure Todd understood she would settle for no less. She was pleased to find he'd complied yet again.

That was only one of Grace's triumphs. She and Todd had married soon after she finished college, and she had pushed and prodded him up the ladder of success from a job as a mere assistant to a construction engineer to the owner of one of the finer construction companies in Dallas. She had insisted he specialize in commercial buildings and as usual her judgment had been right. The house they now lived in was as large and as fine as her mother's.

Grace smiled as she thought about the difference between her standard of living and that of her siblings. Amanda was living in some artist's garret, she supposed. Nathan must not have been able to afford as nice a house, either, because he never asked any of them to visit him. Besides, he had no wife to see to it that his home was, indeed, a fine place. These decisions couldn't be left to men. She and Elizabeth were in complete agreement on that.

"When do you think Amanda will arrive?" Todd asked as they pulled away from the house.

"How should I know? She usually takes the late-morning flight in order to be there before dinner."

"I wish we were flying. It's a damned long drive."

"We're driving because I don't want to be stranded without a car, and rental cars are simply awful. You know I like to spend Saturday shopping."

"I wish you'd hold back on spending this weekend. That new investment hasn't paid off yet and I'm concerned about it."

"Todd, don't be boring. We can certainly afford for me to go shopping with my mother from time to time. It's not like I get to see her every day."

"That's something anyway. We don't have to live in the same town."

Grace snapped her head around and glared at him. "What's that supposed to mean?"

"You and your mother spend money as if it grew on trees and we owned the orchard."

"I knew you were going to be unpleasant on this trip. You always are." She took her satin sleep pillow from the backseat and arranged it behind her head so her hair wouldn't be mussed. "Wake me when we reach Houston." She closed her eyes. There was no doubt that she would be able to fall asleep. Not with her having taken two pills before leaving the house. Driving bored Grace and she hated to be bored.

The melodious tone of the doorbell signaled Elizabeth that the first of her children had arrived. The maid opened the door while Elizabeth remained seated in her living room, waiting in regal calm. When she saw her son, she rose and extended her hands to him. "Nathan. How nice to see you." She had almost no accent though she had been born and raised in Houston. As a young child she had picked up a southern drawl from her classmates, but with the encouragement of her parents she had rid herself of it by the time she entered high school.

"Hello, Mother." Nathan came to her and placed a kiss on the cheek she offered him, then stepped back.

"You're the first to arrive. I expect Grace at any moment, and you know how Amanda is. She'll be here, but predicting when that may be is impossible."

"I'm looking forward to seeing Amanda. I wasn't able to see her on her last visit."

Elizabeth was quite aware of that. She had told Amanda that Nathan was tied up with business and couldn't drive up. She hadn't told Nathan that Amanda was in town until after she was gone. One of the ways Elizabeth maintained control over her children was not to let them see each other too often. Amanda and Nathan had always been closer to each other than either of them had been with Grace. "She was so disappointed. I'm sure you'll have a great deal to talk about."

The maid brought in a tray of coffee and the tiny crescent cookies that Elizabeth ordered from a bakery across town. When the woman was gone, Elizabeth said, "How is business?"

"Quite good. I'm thinking of opening a store in Baytown or Beaumont."

"Don't spread too thin. Your father would never have approved of that. If you expand too quickly, you might hurt your cash flow and could lose all your investment." Elizabeth had never heard Nathaniel say such a thing in his life, but she always couched her financial advice in those terms. Her children had no way of knowing if her husband had been the financial wizard of the family or not.

"I'm being cautious. It's time to expand."

She sipped her coffee. "Are you seeing anyone socially?"

Nathan glanced at her and reached for his own cup and a cookie. "No, there's not time for that."

"I see." Although she kept the tone of her voice regulated, Elizabeth was displeased. Nathan was her only son and he had the responsibility of passing on the family name. If he shirked that duty, he would be ending a branch of the Wainwright family that could trace its ancestors back to sixteenth-century England.

Elizabeth had another reason to want Nathan to find a suitable woman and marry. At thirty-three, he had never married and some of her friends were starting to question why. Privately, so was Elizabeth. Nathan wasn't effeminate, but he did own clothing stores and he had a natural feel for fashion and what his customers would want to buy. Nathaniel wouldn't have been pleased to know this. While her husband wasn't really the macho type, he had understood the importance of fitting into society's mold.

Elizabeth had no intention of allowing her son to be homosexual whether he was that way or not. She was of the opinion that one did what one was expected to do and that included the only son of the family marrying and producing a son to carry on after him. It was time for Nathan to do exactly that.

She waited until he had eaten another bite of the cookie. "Martha Herring's daughter is home for a visit. You remember her."

"Beatrice? Isn't she one who goes to Yale?"

"She graduated last year. She still hasn't married, though I can't think why not. She's a perfectly lovely young lady."

"I'm not interested, Mother." Nathan put the remainder of the cookie on his saucer and regarded her warily.

Elizabeth trilled her silvery laugh. "What a way to look at me. I was only suggesting that you two might go out for dinner sometime."

"Maybe someday," he evaded.

"She won't be in town for long. She's a lawyer and is practicing in Atlanta."

Nathan smiled. "Then there's no reason for me to get to know her better. Georgia is a long way from Texas."

"There are airplanes, darling." Elizabeth disliked her children arguing with her, and Nathan was dangerously close to doing exactly that. "She comes in often to visit her parents."

"Mother, she's only twenty-four. She's younger than Amanda. I'm not interested in meeting her. What would a lawyer and I find to talk about?"

"I was considerably younger than your father and we had a perfect marriage." Her voice cooled as she drew herself up.

Nathan accurately read the signs. "I'll try to call her. I want to visit with you a while first."

Elizabeth relaxed a bit. She would win. "Of course, darling. You know I love to talk with you."

The doorbell sounded again and the maid showed Grace and Todd to the room. Elizabeth rose to greet them. Her ice-blue eyes swept over Grace. She had gained weight and was trying to hide it by wearing a dress that was much too small. Todd looked rumpled as if he had slept in his suit. "How nice to see you. Did you have a good drive?"

"It was quite relaxing," Grace said. The maid was already arriving with more coffee and cookies. She reached for one.

Elizabeth caught her eye and gave her the silent look that she had always used to quell her children's unfortunate impulses. Grace withdrew her hand and settled for the black coffee.

Todd was immune to her signals and he picked up three cookies at once and popped a whole one into his mouth. Elizabeth let a tiny frown pucker her forehead. Todd had been a terrible choice for Grace. At the time he had seemed a nice enough fellow and he was from a fine family who lived in the prestigious neighborhood beside Rice University. Elizabeth's house was located in the far more elite River Oaks section, but she had been willing to bend her standards when she learned both Todd's parents were doctors. Todd, unfortunately, had taken after some remote ancestor, and only Grace's influence had boosted him into a position of professional prestige.

"I don't suppose Amanda is here," Grace asked, her eyes still on the forbidden cookies.

"Not yet. She'll probably be here by dinnertime. I told her not to be late."

"You know how Amanda is," Grace said disparagingly. "She never does what one expects."

"That's what I like about her," Nathan said with a grin. "There's nothing boring about Amanda."

"Are you saying that I'm boring?" Grace demanded. "Or that Mother is?"

"No, only that I like Amanda's spontaneity." Nathan glared at his older sister, but only long enough for her to see his displeasure. "I'm looking forward to talking to her."

"I'm sure we all are," Elizabeth said. "Todd, what are you involved in these days?"

Todd shifted in the chair. "I've invested in a new mall. Instead of only building it, I'll own a share of it once it's completed. Right now the board is looking for businesses to commit to leasing space in it. Until we're assured of at least thirty percent occupancy, we can't go forward with the building."

"That's so ridiculous," Grace said. "Once the mall is built, businesses will be pushing each other out of the way to rent space. That's the way it always is."

"Not as many are willing to be the first to jump in and commit," Todd said. "We have to interest some of the large chain stores first."

"I'm telling you, that's not the way to do it," Grace insisted. "I think it would be darling to have a small-shop mall. All the chain stores look alike and that's so boring. I would love to have a place to go where every shop had an individual look. Wouldn't you, Mother?"

"I think that would be a novel idea."

"There, you see? Mother agrees with me."

"But, Grace, the small stores can't afford to pay the rent at the mall to support itself. That's why you see the larger chain stores in all the malls. They rent a large volume of space and are more likely not to move out after a few months. The small stores change frequently. They can't all stay in business. The large stores draw in the customers and the small ones profit by it."

"You don't know anything about women shoppers," Grace told him. "If you did, you'd know how silly that statement is."

Todd looked at Nathan. "Tell her I'm right."

"He's right," Nathan said.

"You're just saying that because men stick together." Grace gave her husband a look of disgust.

Nathan shrugged.

Elizabeth smiled at Todd. "I don't think it would hurt to try it Grace's way. I agree with her. All the clothing in those chain stores look alike and I don't think most women want to dress like everyone else. You could have all specialty shops. One could sell only tropical clothing, another East Indian items. I think it would be terribly chic."

"Tropical clothing in Dallas? We have ice and snow every winter. The shop could only stay open in the summer months."

"I knew you'd find something wrong with it," Grace said. "Now stop being rude to Mother and unload the car."

Todd sighed and looked as if he was swallowing his angry retort but he left to do as she said.

Before he was out of the room, Grace said, "You see what I have to put up with, Mother?

"Well, I found a lovely new shop in the Village," Elizabeth consoled her. "We'll spend several hours there tomorrow and you'll be in better spirits."

Grace smiled and sipped her coffee.

At Intercontinental Airport, Amanda shifted her suitcase and purse to her other arm so she could sign her name on the rental car agreement. The airport was busy because of people coming and going for Mother's Day, as well as the usual Friday rush.

She took the car keys and thanked the woman behind the desk as she shouldered her belongings and stepped into the crowd making its way out of the terminal.

The airport had always been crowded but Amanda was almost overwhelmed at the number of people jostling her and jogging past to catch planes at the last minute or to retrieve luggage. She had never liked crowds and Dakota shared her feeling. They lived in a rented loft but in time wanted to find a house in the country. One that wasn't in view of a road or neighbors and that was miles from crowds.

Amanda located her rental car and piled her things in the backseat. Her flight from Los Angeles had been late taking off and that had put her behind schedule. Since the Houston freeways were certain to be filled with bumper-to-bumper traffic at this hour, she knew she was going to be late for dinner. She sighed dismally. She was barely in town and already she was making mistakes that would annoy her mother.

She drove the car out into the traffic and hoped for the best.

Chapter Two

"It's about time you got here," Grace complained as soon as Amanda stepped through the front door. "We've held dinner for you."

"I'm sorry." Amanda dropped her purse and luggage on the floor of the entry hall and went to tell her mother she had arrived.

"Amanda. At last." Elizabeth stood and presented her cool cheek to her youngest child. "There's no time to change now. Dinner is ready."

"I'm sorry, Mother. My flight was late leaving L.A. and the traffic between here and the airport was awful."

Elizabeth didn't respond to the apology. Instead, she turned her head away and said to the others, "Dinner is waiting. Let's go in to eat."

"Hello, Nathan," Amanda said in a softer voice as she moved to his side. "I'm glad to finally see you. What have you been—"

"Come along," Elizabeth encouraged, cutting her off. "There'll be plenty of time to talk around the table."

An outsider would have thought her mother's words were merely an invitation, but Amanda knew different—it was one of her mother's imperious directives. Even as she was recalling her resolve to respond to her mother's commands as an adult and not be manipulated, she found herself doing as she'd been told and feeling like a chastised child. She hadn't been in the house five minutes and she had already apologized twice and been subtlely reprimanded by her mother.

"You're looking good," Todd said as he moved closer to her. "L.A. must agree with you."

"Thank you," Amanda said, stepping away from him as quickly as she could without being obvious. The way he always made a point of standing too close to her and looking at her as if there was something too personal between them made her loathe her sister's husband all the more and wish she didn't have to hide it.

The unexpected death of her father when she was fifteen had left Amanda defenseless against her overbearing mother. For over a year she lived every night as if it were her last, slipping away from her house under the cover of darkness and into the arms of men who welcomed her reckless behavior.

She lost her virginity to Jason Tabor, the high school football star all the other sophmore girls merely drooled over. Jason believed her lie that she was a college coed and bragged that he only went to bed with older women because he was too good to waste on the inexperienced. Fooling him about her age had been easy. Because Amanda had developed early, she was often judged to be only a few years younger than Grace, even though a decade separated them. She soon learned that older men could be as easily deceived as the schoolboys and her trysts with the truly more experienced proved to be far more pleasurable.

One was a good-looking twenty-seven-year-old who had sought her out and seemed to enjoy sex with her to a greater degree than any of her other lovers. It wasn't long, though, before she learned that his special delight was because he was dating Grace at the same time and had known they were sisters from the beginning. Amanda was not only repulsed by his perversity but stricken with guilt. She loved Grace and would never have done such a thing to her on purpose.

Although the shock brought her to her senses and ended her promiscuity, her attempt to break off her relationship with Todd didn't work because he threatened to tell Grace and her mother of their affair if she didn't comply with his demands for sexual favors. It was only a few months later that Grace announced her engagement to Todd. Amanda tried to discourage Grace but had to be so careful about what she said and how she said it that Grace was not influenced. Although Todd's sexual interest in her diminished as soon as she'd found him out, it didn't end, even after he and Grace were married.

Amanda had been sickened by what she was forced to do to earn his silence and for a long time didn't date anyone at all. Only when she had moved to California— more to get away from Todd than to attend college there— had she let herself care for anyone.

Todd was there at every family gathering with his smirking smile and his scarcely masked innuendoes. Amanda had long since matured to the point of knowing she didn't have to give in to his blackmail, but she still suffered from the knowledge of what had transpired between them. Todd had never told and she knew now he probably never would, but he never stopped trying to get her alone.

She went to her place at the table and sat down. The

table was covered by a starched white linen cloth with creases so sharp they looked lethal. When she unfolded her napkin and put it in her lap, the fabric opened with a starchy protest. The china was pure white with a narrow gold rim. The glasses were etched crystal whose pattern complemented that of the sterling silver flatware. Elizabeth used her best things for every family occasion. As a child Amanda had lived in terror that she would break the delicate stemmed glasses or spill gravy on that pristine cloth.

Evelyn, the woman who had worked for the Wainwright family longer than Amanda had been alive, began serving the meal in steaming bowls that soon filled the center of the table. Amanda met her eye and they exchanged a small smile unnoticed by the others. Evelyn had often helped Amanda escape from her mother's anger by hiding her in the broom closet or spiriting her out the kitchen door. She was as much a part of the house as the lemon-oiled furniture or the quietly ticking grandfather clock. Amanda was upset to notice Evelyn was aging. Someday soon she would retire and Amanda's visits would be even less bearable.

Amanda was seated directly across from Todd, so every time she lifted her eyes from her plate she had to look at him. On some occasions he even dared touch his foot against her leg under the table. Amanda wrapped her ankles around the legs of her chair to keep them out of his reach.

"Dating anyone interesting?" Nathan asked from her side.

"As a matter of fact, I am." She couldn't believe how easily the topic had presented itself. "His name is—"

"Nathan, if anyone should be dating, it's you," Grace interrupted. "Here you are, thirty-three years old and you've never been married. Are you seeing anyone?" Grace made it more of a challenge than a question.

Elizabeth cleared her throat warningly and shot a dark look at Grace. "We needn't have unpleasant conversation at the dinner table."

"I'm sorry, Mother. I only wondered if Nathan is seeing anyone special," Grace protested.

"Well, *I* am," Amanda tried again. "I've met this wonderful man named Dakota and—"

"What sort of name is that?" Elizabeth asked with raised eyebrows. "It sounds more like a state or a western movie. Evelyn, bring more rolls. Todd took the last one."

Todd glanced around defensively.

"Todd, you're going to weigh five hundred pounds if you don't stop eating everything in sight," Grace admonished. "He's already outgrown his gray suit," she explained to her mother. "And it's the expensive one I bought for him only last Christmas. I can't do anything with him." She brought a forkful of plain lettuce to her lips.

"You've gained, too," Elizabeth pointed out, "so surely it's not fair to point out Todd's weight."

Grace flushed an unbecoming pink. "I never eat fattening things. Look. I have only lettuce without dressing, some fruit, and diet toast on my plate. This is all I ever eat. I can't possibly have gained weight. I wear the same dress size I always have." She delivered the lie without flinching.

Elizabeth only smiled but it was in a way that clearly branded Grace as a liar.

"I don't!" Grace said defensively.

"Grace, dear, if you're going to raise your voice, perhaps you had better finish the meal in the kitchen."

Grace stared at her, then grabbed her plate and left the room.

Amanda watched all this under the pretense of cutting her roast. She was seeing them the way they would appear to Dakota and it wasn't a pretty sight. Grace was insuffer-

able, but she was forty years old and a married woman.
She was far beyond the stage in life where she should be
sent from the table in disgrace.

Todd used the diversion to reach under the table and
touch his stocking foot to Amanda's leg. She kicked out
without changing her expression and felt her shoe make
solid contact with his ankle. Todd grimaced and turned
his attention back to his plate.

Amanda didn't want Dakota to meet her family. When
she was with them, she was frozen in childhood, and this
would seem freakish to him. It seemed foolish to her, too,
but she didn't see a way of changing it.

One thing was certain. This wasn't the time to tell them
about Dakota and the baby they were expecting.

After dinner Amanda slipped out of the house and went
to the playhouse that still stood in a corner of the backyard.
No one had played in it for years, but the gardener kept
it in good repair so it looked as if she had left it only weeks
before. It had often been her refuge. For all Elizabeth's
icy calm, when she was angered, she could be terrifying
to a small child.

"I thought I might find you out here."

She jerked her head around in the direction of the voice
and was pleased to find it was Nathan who had spoken.
"I'm glad it's you and not Todd," she affirmed aloud.

"The last I saw of him, Grace was herding him into the
sitting room to entertain Mother."

"Why do we continue to come back here?" she asked
him. "Every Mother's Day, Thanksgiving, Christmas, on
birthdays. Why do we still do it when it's always so uncomfortable?"

"I come because it's easier than explaining why I don't
want to. Grace is here because she intends to actually

become Mother some day and because she wants to be certain she's in the will if Mother ever dies.''

"If?"

He smiled. "I don't really believe that she ever will. Do you?"

She shook her head. "I can't imagine her growing older and one day just ceasing to exist. The idea of Mother in a nursing home is ludicrous."

"She never would be. She would hire people to care for her here. Evelyn, most likely."

Amanda glanced back at the kitchen end of the house. "Evelyn's starting to show her age. Have you noticed it? I forget she's almost as old as Mother."

Amanda turned back to face him when he admitted he hadn't noticed and changed the subject abruptly. "I have a gallery tour coming up."

"You do? A tour, not just a solitary exhibit?"

She nodded her head and smiled. "My publicity agent arranged it and I'll be exhibiting all across the country."

"A one-man show?"

"No. There's another artist who will be traveling with me." She proceeded cautiously. Although she was closer to Nathan than to anyone in her family, she wasn't entirely sure she could trust him, either. "His name is Dakota. I tried to tell everyone about him at dinner."

"What's his last name?"

"He doesn't use one. Just Dakota."

"I think I've heard about him. It's an unusual name."

"He's an unusual man. Maybe we could visit you while we're in Houston and you could meet him."

Nathan's smile became stiff. "I think I hear Mother calling. We'd better go back inside."

"I didn't hear anything."

"It's almost dark anyway."

Amanda followed him back toward the house. He obviously didn't want her to visit him and she was hurt. Maybe Nathan wouldn't be receptive to hearing more about Dakota, either. She sighed in frustration. Perhaps she would find them all more receptive the next day.

Inside, Grace was watching them from the window. She hated Amanda and had for years, though she tried to hide it. Amanda had been their father's favorite as well as Nathan's. Even Todd had once had an interest in her, though Grace was positive nothing could ever have come of it. Amanda had been only fifteen at the time, and Todd had been practically engaged to Grace. All the same, Grace was jealous. Amanda seemed to have everything and to be throwing her life away in her ridiculous attempt to be an artist.

No one in their right mind was a professional artist, in Grace's opinion. If a woman was determined to work, she could be a lawyer or a doctor or have some high-powered office job. Artists belonged to the culture of hippies and flower children that had gone out of style decades ago. Grace was convinced that if their father had seen how Amanda's goal in life was to smear paint on canvas, he would have chosen herself as his favorite. As it was, Grace was certain she had never been the favorite of anyone.

She turned away from the window as she saw Amanda and Nathan approaching. Her mother was talking to Todd about an event she had seen on the news the evening before and Todd was pretending to have an opinion on the subject. Grace doubted he had seen the news piece or that he had understood it if he had. Todd wasn't a bright man. If she had realized it, she wouldn't have married him. But her father had died at the time and she was eager to be in a house of her own and Todd had seemed to be the perfect man to rise to the pinnacle of achievement Grace expected in a husband. All his success was to her credit and she never let him forget it.

When Amanda and Nathan came into the room, Todd followed Amanda with his eyes. Grace watched him angrily. He stared at her younger sister as if she were the last brownie on the plate. Todd felt her glaring at him and turned his eyes back to Elizabeth.

Had her mother noticed? Grace wasn't sure. If she had, Elizabeth was certain to take Grace to task for not keeping her husband under better control, while all the time Amanda was to blame.

Amanda hadn't gained any weight and she looked even younger than her thirty years. Although Grace would never admit it, she envied her sister for her figure and dark blue eyes. Her hair was another matter—a serious flaw in Grace's opinion. It wasn't so much the color, though she didn't care for dark hair on a woman, but the style. Todd had said Amanda's long, straight hair made her look exotic, but Grace disagreed, arguing that it was an unfortunate look on a mature woman. Privately, she objected because it made every man's head turn when she entered a room. Although Grace had been dying her hair for years to hide the gray and to lighten its natural color to a youthful blond, Amanda didn't have a gray hair or a single wrinkle. Grace had had both when she was thirty.

Todd covertly watched Amanda fold her leg beneath her and sit on the earth-toned couch. She moved like a goddess and looked like one, too. His body responded when he remembered how she had felt when he had made love with her years before. She had been even younger then, of course, and incredibly lustful. Todd grew hot remembering. Amanda was so passionate, he had assumed that her older sister would prove to be passionate as well once they were married. He had been wrong.

When Amanda had found out he was seeing Grace at the same time, she assumed he was having sex with Grace, too. He'd let her believe it because he couldn't admit that he had turned to Grace's younger sister for relief from the sexual frustration Grace created by teasing him to the threshold of intercourse, then denying him access to her until they were married. He had also never admitted that he had coerced sex from her afterward as a bluff and that knowing she no longer came to him willingly robbed him of the pleasure their encounters once had been.

At first he'd feared Amanda would tell her mother and the authorities would put him in prison for statutory rape, or at the least, he'd lose his chance to marry into the Wainwright fortune. Once he and Grace were wed, he was even more concerned.

Every time he forced Amanda into bed with him, he worried that he was pushing her too far. When she graduated from high school and announced she was enrolling at UCLA and would be moving to California, he breathed a private sigh of relief. Even though his periodic demands for sex had grown farther apart with the passage of time, he knew she had chosen a West Coast school to escape from him, and he was comforted by that. His blackmail scheme had worked that far, and from then on all he would have to do to keep her in line was to make her think he was always on the verge of renewing his coersion.

What he hadn't expected was that it would backfire. Being away from Amanda for long periods of time coupled with increasingly bland sexual relations with Grace rekindled Todd's fantasies about Amanda. One day Todd finally admitted to himself that he had never stopped wanting Amanda, or at least the Amanda he had first known. And she was more beautiful now. Her young angles and softness had matured into luscious curves and a beauty that hinted of mystery and passion beyond his wildest dreams. Her eyes were a curious dark blue. In a subdued light they sometimes turned jet black, then the light or her mood would change and they would be the color of the evening sky. Todd wanted Amanda desperately, and in his fantasies, she wanted him, too, but he was unable to act on that desire because he was married to her sister.

What would it have been like if he had married her instead of Grace? Todd had thought about that question for years. He was positive it would have been better than anything he had ever known with Grace. Amanda would have given herself to him then, day or night, to do with as he pleased. But he could not have married her, not at fifteen.

Over time he tried to content himself by thinking that as Amanda matured, she would return to wanting him as much as he wanted her. After all, she had never married. He could be the reason. As far as he knew, she had rarely dated anyone after they had been lovers. She could have been saving herself for him. For years now, such thoughts had kept Todd on razor's edge every time he was near her.

Grace. There was a thorn in his side. In addition to her other faults, she spent money as if it had no end. Although he tried to tell her they were facing hard times, she refused to listen. Matters were even worse than he had told her.

Todd had invested more heavily in the mall than he had admitted. He was, in fact, the principal investor. The mall was to be built in a prime location and would be larger than any of his previous projects. Todd believed in it. So much so, he had mortgaged the house and put every penny of his assets in the venture. Unfortunately, other investors were more cautious. So far, none of the large chain stores were interested because they already had outlets in the general area of the proposed site.

Todd hadn't expected that. He had talked to everyone who would listen and, while most agreed that the idea was feasible, none of them were willing to sink money in it. Todd didn't have the resources to hold out indefinitely while the others thought about it. He had to get the mall built and earning money before his creditors became insistent. The thought of what could happen wasn't pleasant. He could lose everything he had worked so hard to get.

Grace's reaction to financial ruin would be catastrophic. No, he had to get more backers and he had to get them fast. He had hoped Elizabeth would be one of them, but so far he hadn't been able to get her alone to present the proposal to her. He was determined to do it before they left on Sunday.

Amanda was refusing to look his way. This made Todd all the more aware of her. It was as if electricity bound him to her. The thick sweep of her hair seemed to beg him to wrap his hand in it and to force himself on her. That was a large part of his fantasies about Amanda—that she would want him to force her to give herself to him. Just thinking about it made him hot.

He tried to turn his attention back to Elizabeth and the news event she was determined to discuss. Todd hadn't watched the news in days and couldn't have been less interested in what was going on in a part of the world he would never visit and to people he would never meet.

But Amanda—now that was a different matter. He almost groaned from knowing she was so near, yet so inaccessible to him.

Chapter Three

Amanda couldn't sleep. Instead of her room being familiar from her childhood, it, along with several other rooms in the house, had recently been redecorated and no longer held memories for her. Even the color, a pale pink, was nothing Amanda would have chosen.

Rather than toss and turn, she decided to go downstairs and read for a while, hoping that would help her quiet her thoughts. As she made her way down the hall, checking to be sure the sash of her robe was tied securely, she noticed lights shining from beneath both Grace's door and Elizabeth's. Apparently they were having trouble sleeping as well. She lightened her step and crept as quietly as she could down the carpeted stairs.

As she had hoped, there was enough light coming in through the windows from the landscape lighting for her to move about without turning on any lamps. She was looking forward to curling up with a book in her father's study and being alone amid the things her father had surrounded himself with. It had been his haven; even as a young girl she had known that. And for reasons her mother had kept to herself, this room had been left undisturbed while every other square inch of the place had been redecorated—not once, but several times since his death. She'd long ago gotten over her anger at her father for dying when he did and held dear to her all the pleasant memories, including the times the two of them had shared in the study with him reading to her or telling her stories that had been passed down to him from his father.

It suddenly occurred to her that a nice cup of hot tea would help relax her even more, so she headed for the kitchen. If she was careful, she could heat a cup of water in a pot on the stove and have her tea without disturbing anyone.

Only after she pushed the kitchen door open did she notice the light in the breakfast area was on. Todd was sitting at the table opposite a half-empty bottle of bourbon. Her first inclination was to turn and leave, but he looked straight at her. She stopped in her tracks, her nostalgic mood shattered by his presence.

"Well, well. Look who's here. Come in and have a seat," he said, an obvious slur in his voice. "I'll get you a glass so you can have a drink with me." He turned away from her as he rose.

Amanda had a strong urge to leave. For years she'd avoided being alone with Todd; it was safer that way. But wasn't that running away? Wasn't that just what she was determined to stop this trip? This time she had resolved to face her fear of her overbearing mother and tell her about Dakota and the child she was carrying. She had all but promised Dakota she would do so, but what he didn't know was that she had also resolved she would no longer allow Todd to intimidate her. She had never told Dakota about her affair with Todd and her concern that each time the family got together her brother-in-law might start blackmailing her again. She hated hiding anything from Dakota, but the shame she still felt every time the sordid memories of that time crossed her mind was too strong. Although Dakota always had been understanding and she was certain he loved her, it was incomprehensible to her that he could know about that darkest period of her life and not think less of her. It made no sense, but then nothing about that time made any sense.

Undoubtedly her mother was going to be upset when she told her about Dakota and their baby. Might even disinherit her. With Grace having turned on her years before because she had tried to talk Grace out of marrying Todd, things between her and her sister couldn't be much worse for her knowing what happened so long ago. The risk that anyone would tell Dakota was remote, because she was convinced everyone in her family except for Nathan would shun her and Dakota. She had to stop worrying about what Todd might do or say and begin this transformation now by joining him in the kitchen, alone, and with him half drunk. Taking a deep breath to bolster her courage, she went to the table and sat down.

When he turned back around, he looked as if he was surprised that she had taken him up on his offer. Without speaking, he joined her at the table, poured her a generous drink and pushed the glass toward her.

"Do you do this often?" she asked. "Drink alone, I mean."

"Only when I can't sleep. Most nights, in other words."

As she read the label on the bourbon bottle, she said, "I assume you got this from Mother's liquor cabinet. She usually saves this brand for special occasions."

"If you're asking if I got her permission, the answer is no. Besides, she can afford to buy more." He raised the glass to his lips. "I gather you couldn't sleep, either."

"I seldom can in a strange bed. What's your excuse?"

"I can't sleep with Grace." He chuckled softly, apparently finding that statement humorous. "When enough time has passed for her to fall to sleep, I'll go up." He made bleary eye contact with her. "We have separate rooms at home. We haven't slept together in years."

"That's none of my business."

"I thought you might be interested."

Amanda let a sip of the fiery liquid glide down her throat.

"Grace and I aren't happy together," he confided in a conspiratorial voice.

"How long have you been sitting down here drinking?" she asked in an attempt to change the subject to something less intimate. This was proving to be as difficult as she guessed it would.

"Not long enough. I've been thinking about divorcing Grace. Things have been really rocky between us for quite a while now. Did you know that?"

Amanda shook her head. "She doesn't confide in me. You know that." She hoped he wasn't serious about the divorce, not for Grace's sake but for her own. She had assumed his desire to stay married to Grace might have been a major reason he had not made any demands on her, thinking she might call his hand. Without Grace in the picture, he might renew his blackmail by threatening to tell Dakota. The prospect was terrifying and her heart rate increased as her body dumped adrenaline into her system.

"I haven't said anything to her yet. I just wanted you to know."

She averted her eyes. "It has nothing at all to do with me." Realizing she was revealing her vulnerability, she decided to take a more aggressive posture. "If you're expecting me to choose sides, you'd better not hold your breath. Surely by now you know how Mother will react. I don't want to be anywhere near her when she finds out."

"Don't get all excited. I have no intention of telling anyone else yet." He poured himself another drink. "My business is doing great, by the way. I'm making money hand over fist. I don't need Grace. You know how she's always going on about my successes being all due to her. That's bullshit." He leaned closer. "She's not woman enough for me, if you know what I mean."

Amanda couldn't hide the disgust she was feeling. "I don't want to hear about it." It had been a mistake for her to come into the kitchen and a total waste of time and energy; he was too drunk to remember any of this by morning.

"Okay. I'll stop talking about her." He cleared his throat. "Did you know I'm known in Dallas as a high roller. I like to give expensive presents. I even gave a lady friend of mine a mink coat."

"Amanda had heard enough. She stood and pushed her chair up to the table. "Remember to turn out the light when you go upstairs."

"Don't go yet. I want your opinion on something."

Amanda hesitated. "I don't see how I could offer you any suggestions on anything. I seldom see you and Grace and I don't know anything about your business."

"This is about something else."

With a sigh Amanda sat back down. "Okay, but make it fast."

"There's this woman I'm interested in." He gave her a long, meaningful look. "She's beautiful. Probably the most beautiful woman I've ever seen."

Amanda waited.

"I want to know how I can get her to see that I want her and have for a long time. I'm having trouble getting her attention. Any ideas what I should do?" He licked his lips and took another swallow of bourbon. His eyes never left hers.

Reasonably sure he wasn't going to remember any of this, she figured this would be a good time to practice telling him things she'd been wanting to say for a long time. But just in case she was wrong, she decided to temper it a little. "If you're talking about having an affair, the first thing you should do is divorce my sister," she replied. "I'm not going to tell you to have an affair on the side. Grace and I may not get along, but I believe in fidelity. You've got no business looking at another woman as long as you're married." She bit back the desire to tell him that he had no business doing any of the things he had done to her, either.

"But you think I'd have a chance with this woman if I divorce Grace?" He reached for the bottle and knocked it off the table. As he scrambled to retrieve it, he tipped his chair off balance and it fell with a crash.

She waited for him to get the chair upright and sit down again before speaking. "If you want someone else, why would you want to stay married to Grace anyway? It's obvious that you two haven't been in love for years, assuming that you ever were. I don't recommend staying together when your house is a war zone."

Upstairs, Elizabeth was startled by a noise from the area of the kitchen that was directly beneath her bedroom. She was lying in her bed, propped up by mounds of satin pillows. A magazine lay discarded on the bed beside her. She rarely read books. Decorating magazines were far more to her taste, but tonight even *Architectural Digest* didn't hold her interest. Earlier, she had heard a sound in the hall and now a noise from downstairs. Curious as to who it was and what the night owl might be doing, she got out of bed and reached for the filmy robe that matched her negligee.

Although she hadn't slept with anyone in the room since Amanda was born, she liked to look good at all times.

She opened her door a crack and listened before peering out. No one was in sight. She stepped out into the hall. A quick glance told her that Amanda's bedroom door was open. What could she be doing downstairs at such an hour, especially with all the lights off?

Feeling justified that it was her house and she had a right to know everything that happened there, Elizabeth crept down the stairs. Not wanting to announce her presence prematurely, she left the lights off and made her way to the kitchen through the relative darkness. Knowing the house as well as she did, she had no trouble steering clear of the furniture. At the kitchen door she paused and listened. Voices could be heard, one male and the other female. It sounded like Grace and Todd to her, but why would they come downstairs to talk since they slept in the same bedroom? Amanda's door had been open, and she could have come down to talk to Nathan, but Elizabeth couldn't think why those two would seek out a private conversation in the middle of the night.

She eased the door open enough for her to see in but not be seen.

To her surprise, it was Amanda and Todd who were sitting at the kitchen table drinking together. Elizabeth drew in her breath. Amanda was barefoot and dressed in a robe, which indicated she was probably wearing little or nothing beneath it. Todd was in his shirtsleeves and socks. The scene was entirely too intimate to be allowed to continue.

As quietly as she had come, Elizabeth retraced her footsteps and went upstairs. Discreetly she knocked at Grace's door.

Grace opened it. "Mother? What's wrong? Are you ill?"

Elizabeth affected a shallow breathing pattern. "Yes, I

am. My heart, you know. I left my glycerin tablets in the kitchen cabinet. Would you be a dear and run down to get them? I would go myself but when my heart is acting up like this, I'm afraid to do anything as strenuous as going down the stairs."

"Of course," Grace exclaimed in concern. "You come in and lie down until I can get them."

"No, no, dear. I don't like to impose and when I have these spells, I have difficulty getting up and moving around. I'll just go back to my room and wait for you." She gave Grace a wavering smile and put her hand on the wall as if she needed the support.

"Here. Let me help you." Grace put her arm around Elizabeth and helped her back to her bed.

Elizabeth hated to be touched, but she allowed it because it made her appear more like an invalid. When she reached her bed, she let Grace help her lie down and she closed her eyes as if from weakness. "Hurry, Grace," she whispered. She didn't want the conversation in the kitchen to end before Grace could discover her husband and sister there alone.

Grace rushed from the room. Elizabeth's eyes flew open and she positioned the pillow more comfortably under her head.

Grace all but ran across the living and dining rooms. She had seen many of her mother's spells but this one seemed worse than usual. The kitchen door was shut, which she found odd since she had left it open after coming down for a glass of milk and a large slice of chocolate cake before going to bed. She put her ear to the panel and listened.

"I've always wanted you," Todd said.

"If you're going to start that, I'm going back upstairs." It was Amanda's voice.

"We get so little time alone together," Todd protested.

"Don't go yet. Grace always goes to bed this early. You and I could meet down here tomorrow night as well."

Grace shoved open the door and strode in with bristling vengeance. "So this is what you're up to!"

Todd leaped to his feet. Amanda turned to look at her sister but didn't seem particularly upset to find they had been caught in a "tryst."

"We were just talking, Grace!" Todd blustered, then tossed down the last of his drink. "I was down here and Amanda just happened to come down, too. We weren't doing anything but talking." Todd starting backing toward the door. "Grace, I swear, we weren't doing anything."

"I heard what you said about meeting! I know there's something going on between you!"

Todd gave Amanda a desperate look, turned, and left the kitchen.

Grace turned on her sister. "Well? How long has this been going on?" she demanded.

"Nothing is going on," Amanda answered in a tired voice. "I couldn't sleep so I came down. Todd was here and I sat for a while and talked to him."

"You're trying to take him away from me, aren't you?"

Amanda's temper flared. "I wouldn't have Todd as a gift, even if you gilded him and turned him into a lamp! I can't stand the man. Frankly, I don't know why you didn't leave him years ago."

"My marriage is none of your business!"

"That's exactly what I just told Todd!"

"I've seen the way you parade in front of him, giving him those looks and tossing your hair around."

"If there's something wrong in your marriage, it has nothing to do with me," Amanda retorted.

"You're in for a big surprise if you think Todd will leave me for you! Why, you're nothing but a hippie! I wonder what Mother would say if I tell her what I discovered in here!"

"Go ahead and tell her," Amanda challenged. "I have nothing to hide. Todd was trying to come on to me, not the other way around. If you were listening at the door, you'd know that."

"I'm going to tell Mother about this . . ." Suddenly Grace remembered why she had come to the kitchen in the first place. She went to the cabinet by the sink and found the bottle of heart pills. "Our mother is lying there sick," Grace chastised, "and you go try and seduce my husband!"

"Mother is sick? What's wrong with her?"

"It's her heart again, Amanda. She has a bad heart. Remember? We almost lost her last winter. She was upset because you said you wouldn't be here for Christmas and she had such a bad spell she almost died."

"I remember. I canceled my plans and flew down. She seemed fine by the time I got here. She got her way and she was well by the time I got to the house."

Grace gasped. "It would kill Mother to know you accused her of lying about her health."

Amanda sighed. "I'm not accusing her of anything. I only said it was a coincidence that she recovered so quickly."

"One of these days we're going to lose her, Amanda, and when that day comes, I just hope you can live with yourself!"

"Take the pills to her and leave my conscience and me alone."

Grace stomped to the door. "You keep away from my husband, too!"

When Amanda was alone in the kitchen, she sat back down at the table. Todd wouldn't return to bother her.

Grace would see to that. She would keep him on a short leash for the rest of the weekend.

She rubbed her eyes and tried to relax her tense muscles. She had been home less than six hours and already she was embedded in a slough of emotional turmoil.

She would leave in the morning, she decided. Mother's Day or not, she didn't deserve treatment like this. She didn't believe Elizabeth was really sick, though she might possibly have a minor heart condition that would warrant her doctor prescribing the glycerine pills.

But what if she was wrong? Elizabeth was seventy-one and had been in frail health off and on for years. Or at least that's what she claimed. Amanda had left Dakota on their first Christmas in their loft apartment to rush to Houston only to find Elizabeth looking as healthy as ever. That was when she began wondering if Elizabeth's heart problems were a fabrication to coerce her children into doing what she wanted. But what if they weren't?

Amanda straightened the kitchen, turned out the light and went upstairs. When she tapped softly on Elizabeth's door, Grace answered it, blocking her entrance.

"Mother heard everything we said in the kitchen," she hissed, "and it's given her a turn for the worse. Just go to bed and let me take care of her."

Amanda looked past Grace to where Elizabeth lay propped on her pillows. Her eyes were shut and she looked older in the pale lamplight. Maybe she was ill after all. "Should I call the doctor or take her to the emergency room?"

"She doesn't want to go. I've already asked. Now go away and let her get some rest." Grace shut the door in Amanda's face.

Elizabeth had heard the angry words and Grace had shut the door loudly enough to wake her if she really had been asleep. Elizabeth didn't move so much as an eyelash.

Grace had interrupted whatever had been going on in the kitchen and that was the important part.

Grace came back and sat beside the bed. In a whisper she said, "I sent her away, Mother. You can rest easy now. I'll take care of everything."

It was all Elizabeth could do not to scoff. Grace couldn't even handle her own husband. As she lay there, she wondered if there might really be something between Amanda and Todd. For years she had seen the way he stared at her. Amanda had never seemed to like him but given tonight's events she could be wrong about that. Elizabeth didn't like being wrong and she detested thinking her children were capable of putting something over on her.

Elizabeth believed it was her duty as their mother to keep her children on the paths she had mapped out for them. Her only failure was Amanda. That one insisted on marching to her own drummer no matter what Elizabeth resorted to in order to bring her in line. Amanda had even tried to get out of coming home for Christmas. That was almost as intolerable as not showing up for Mother's Day. Elizabeth had brought her to heel, but it had dulled the occasion for her. The fact that Grace and Nathan had appeared on schedule didn't matter. They always did as they were told.

Nathan always returned to his house on Christmas Eve after they opened gifts, but he could be counted on to reappear for Christmas dinner. That was acceptable to Elizabeth. He was there for the important events and she didn't necessarily want him around the other times.

Grace, of course, was always there when she was supposed to be, even if she or Todd were ill. Elizabeth liked that kind of loyalty. Eventually she would train Amanda to be just as obedient. It was her right as the head of the family.

* * *

Amanda was packing when Nathan came to her door.

"What are you doing?" he asked.

"I'm going home." She threw a sweater into her suitcase, not taking the time to fold it.

He came in and shut the door so they could talk in privacy. "You can't leave yet. Mother's Day isn't until tomorrow."

"I never should have come in the first place." She sat on the bed and buried her face in her hands. "Why do we put ourselves through this? We're adults. Why do we let Mother and Grace run all over us?"

"We're all the family we have. Mother is in poor health. She needs us around her from time to time."

"How is she doing today?"

"She's not out of bed yet."

Amanda looked at her watch. "She never sleeps this late."

"Grace said she had a bad night. I understand you and Grace had an argument and it brought on a mild attack in Mother."

"Is that what Grace told you? I don't know, Nathan. I really don't. Sometimes I wonder if Mother isn't the strongest one of us. At others . . ." She let her voice trail off.

"What were you and Grace arguing over?"

"Are you ready for this? It was over Todd." Amanda grimaced. "He's such a jerk! He actually told me that he wants to have an affair and asked my advice! Can you believe that?"

"I can believe anything of Todd."

"Grace overheard us talking and had a tantrum right down there in the kitchen. Apparently Mother heard every word, though that's not likely, even if her room is over the kitchen. Grace accused me of trying to seduce Todd!"

Nathan laughed. "That's ridiculous."

"I know that, but Grace believes every word of it." She picked up a pair of shoes on the floor beside her bed and tossed them into the suitcase. "I'm not going to stay here and be insulted."

"Why give Grace the satisfaction of letting her chase you away?" Nathan pointed out. "You're already here and we haven't had a chance to talk in a long time."

Amanda relented slightly. "I do want to visit with you."

"You know, we could get together on our own. We don't have to meet only here. I could fly out to L.A. I have a buying trip coming up."

Amanda thought about how much Nathan didn't know about her. "Maybe. Or I could fly down to see you instead. That would be better, really, since I'll be in town for that exhibit I was telling you about."

"I'm not sure that's a good idea."

"Why don't you ever want me to come visit you?" she demanded. "What's going on in your life that you don't want me to know about? Just tell me, Nathan."

"What about you? You didn't exactly jump at the chance of me coming to see you, either."

Amanda made a dismissing motion with her hand. "Forget it. I don't want to argue with you, too."

"I don't want that, either." Nathan looked away. "There's a lot I want to tell you, but it never seems to be the right time."

Amanda covered his hand with hers. "I know exactly what you mean. There's a lot I want to tell you, too. Wouldn't it be funny if it was the same thing?"

He laughed. "I don't think that's likely."

"No," she said. "Neither do I, come to think of it. Well, you go first."

Nathan opened his mouth to speak but was interrupted by a knock on the door.

Elizabeth stepped into the doorway before either could respond. "Why on earth are the two of you closed up in here? I should think you're rather old for telling secrets."

"We weren't telling secrets," Nathan said before Amanda could answer. "We were only talking."

"With the door shut?" Elizabeth came into the room and looked from one to the other. "Whatever for?" Her eyes dropped to the suitcase. "Amanda, are you unpacking? I told Evelyn to do that for you. I'll speak to her."

"Evelyn did unpack. I was repacking."

"You're leaving?" Elizabeth's tone remained pleasant but her eyes narrowed and became cold.

"No. I thought I might, but Nathan talked me out of it."

"Why would you leave before tomorrow?"

"Grace ... Last night ... I didn't want to upset you further."

"Don't be silly, darling. Your squabble with Grace did upset me, but you must know I'd be far more upset if you left a whole day early." She turned and went to the door. "Breakfast will be served soon. You know not to be late." She left the room, leaving the door open.

Nathan looked at Amanda and shrugged. "Looks like she's fully recovered. I guess we'll have to continue our talk later. This doesn't seem to be the time."

Amanda agreed. She didn't want to blurt out her news of Dakota and her pregnancy only to be interrupted in midstream by a call to breakfast.

Nathan left and she slowly started putting her clothes away again. Leaving now would be worse than not having come at all and as Nathan had pointed out, Amanda didn't want to give Grace the satisfaction of thinking she had driven her away.

* * *

Down the hall Grace was lambasting Todd for what had happened the night before in the kitchen. "You've mortified me in my own mother's house," she snapped at him as she yanked a brush through her hair.

"This didn't have anything to do with your mother."

"I'm warning you, Todd. If you and Amanda don't stop seeing each other, I'm going to divorce you!"

Their eyes met in the mirror. He looked more thoughtful than fearful.

"Think what that means," Grace sneered. "Texas is a community property state. I'd get half of everything. And by the time my lawyer gets through with you, I'd probably have your half as well!"

Todd turned away and Grace's lips turned up in a cruel smile. "You hadn't thought of that, had you? You thought you could have my sister and I would never do anything to stop you, didn't you?"

"There's nothing between Amanda and me," "Todd insisted. "I told you that."

"Do you take me for a complete fool? You were down there in the middle of the night, barefoot and her in just a robe. Can you imagine what Mother would have said if she saw you two. Thank heaven she couldn't go downstairs and see what I saw! It could have put her in her grave!"

"Let it rest, Grace. I told you nothing happened. I'm sure Amanda told you the same thing. Just drop it."

Grace spun around on her vanity stool and glared at him. "Don't you dare tell me what to do! I won't have it!" Her voice rose to a shriek.

The door to their room opened suddenly and Elizabeth stood framed in the doorway. She didn't say a word, but her cold eyes fastened first on Grace, then on Todd.

Grace's anger curdled inside. "I'm sorry, Mother. I didn't mean to raise my voice in your house."

"Sorry," Todd mumbled.

Elizabeth stood there for another long moment, her eyes sizing them up and finding them lacking. With a last warning stare at Grace, she went out, closing the door behind her.

Grace wilted. Her heart was beating fast and she felt as chastised as if Elizabeth had screamed at her. "See what you did!" she hissed at Todd.

She glanced at the closed door to be sure Elizabeth wasn't still there and turned back to her image in the mirror.

Chapter Four

No one was speaking to anyone at breakfast that morning. Amanda was glad when the meal was over and she could escape from the table. Dakota had been right. She had made a mistake coming here. For the first time in her pregnancy, she had morning sickness and stayed in her room until after lunch.

By the time she came down, the house was empty. Grace and Elizabeth had gone shopping and Grace had insisted on taking Todd with them rather than leaving him alone in the house with Amanda. She assumed Nathan had gone to one of his Houston stores as he frequently did on a Saturday.

Amanda went into the kitchen and sat at the table. Evelyn was washing up the lunch dishes and she turned to smile at her.

"It's about time you came in here to see me," she chided good-naturedly. "The weekend is half over. I thought maybe you decided you had outgrown me."

"I would never do that." Amanda took an apple from the wooden bowl and bit into it. "I'm glad everyone else has gone."

"It's nice and peaceful when the house is nearly empty like this. I can get a lot done without people underfoot."

"Is there anything I can do to help you?"

Evelyn put a pie pan lined with a crust in front of her. "You can peel the rest of those apples for a pie. I haven't had time to do them yet and I need to put it in to cook."

Amanda got a knife and started peeling the apples, making the red skin curl in an unbroken sliver. "I still remember how to do this. You taught me when I was a little girl."

"Lord, do I remember. You were in this kitchen more often than I was." Evelyn laughed and the sound was soft and comforting.

"It was a good place to hide."

"You're pretty old to need hiding now," Evelyn observed. "But I get the feeling that you've got something going on that nobody else knows about."

Amanda smiled. "You've always been able to see through me. As a matter of fact, I do have a couple of secrets. I had intended to reveal them, but no one seems to want to hear what I have to say."

"Well, I do. Shoot." Evelyn sat opposite her and waited.

"I've fallen in love." The admission made her grin and duck her head.

Evelyn rapped the table triumphantly. "I knew it! You can always tell when a woman is in love. You're glowing. Who is he? Is he smart enough to love you back?"

She nodded. "His name is Dakota. He doesn't use a last name. He's an artist, too." She told the housekeeper all about their upcoming show. Can you imagine me being that successful?"

"I always knew you would be. Where did you meet him and how come he doesn't have a last name?"

"I met him at one of his exhibits. We have friends in common. Evelyn, it was love at first sight, just like in the movies! I've never known anyone like him. He's wonderful in every way." She sighed happily. "He's tall and handsome and he's the sexiest man I've ever seen in my life. He's half Indian, so his hair and eyes are black. He wears it down to his shoulders."

"No! That long?"

Amanda nodded mischievously. "And he has an earring!"

"Lord have mercy! Your mother is going to have a fit for sure!" Evelyn laughed as if the prospect was enjoyable. "When do we get to meet him?"

"I don't know. He wanted to come this time, but I wasn't sure what sort of reception he would get, it being Mother's Day and all."

"This time? How long have you had this young man?"

"We've been living together almost a year."

Evelyn stared at her. "And you never told anybody about him?"

"All my friends know him. Dakota is so different, I wasn't sure what my family would say."

"Are you going to marry him?"

A slight frown crossed Amanda's forehead. "I don't know. He hasn't asked me."

"Why not? You've been living together for a year. Can't he make up his mind? Why don't you propose to him?"

"I've thought about that. But our relationship is based on freedom and trust. When we first got together, we agreed that marriage wouldn't be part of the package. It would be just us, loving each other and living together. We felt that we didn't need a paper to legitimize our love."

"Well, I guess if you're both happy that way, it's not for me to talk you out of it," Evelyn said slowly.

"There's more to it. I'm going to have a baby. His baby.' Amanda studied Evelyn's face for any signs of censure.

"A baby!" Evelyn smiled until all her wrinkles met. "A baby! Imagine that! When is it due? No time soon, from the looks of you."

"No, I only found out recently."

"What about this Dakota fellow? Is he balking at becoming a daddy?"

Amanda laughed. "Far from it. The baby was planned. He wants to carry me around on a pillow. I think he's going to have this child spoiled before it leaves the hospital."

"He must be a good person then. What's the problem?"

"I can't tell my mother or the others. Every time I try, I get cold feet. I'm afraid to tell them."

"Well, you don't have much choice. They're bound to notice and ask questions when you show up with a baby in your arms."

"I know. Dakota doesn't understand how they are. I can't just blurt out this news."

"That may be the only way to do it."

"That's one reason this nationwide exhibit is so important. It could boost us to real fame and provide us with security for the baby. Dakota is already more well known than I am. Our agent even has us scheduled for some TV and radio shows."

"You'll do just fine. I know you will. I've always liked your pictures." Evelyn thought for a while. "This baby— it will have more than one name, won't it?"

Amanda laughed. "Yes."

"That's good. You can't fill out a form without a last name." She was clearly worrying about Dakota not having one.

"Okay. I'll tell you. But you have to promise you'll never tell anyone."

"I promise."

"It's Thompson. Dakota Thompson."

"That's it? Why wouldn't he use a nice, normal name like that?"

"Because it *is* normal. You'd have to meet him to understand."

"I suppose. Keep peeling those apples before they go dark."

Amanda went back to her chore. "I feel a lot better for having told you. I just had to tell someone."

"You'd better take my advice and tell your mother as well. If she happens to find out by accident, I'm not sure the broom closet will still hide you."

Amanda sighed. "You're right. I'll try to tell her."

When they returned from shopping, Todd went into the den, shut the door and dialed the number of his investment broker, Fred Willis.

"Things are coming together on this end," Willis reported. "I don't have any of the chain stores signed up yet, but it's just a matter of time. Sears is considering one end of the mall and Saks Fifth Avenue, the other."

Todd relaxed for the first time in days. "If those two come into it, we won't have any problems."

"You're telling me. I think you might be wise to increase your investment."

"Put more money in? Why?"

"Like you say, the mall can't fail if it has outlets for both Sears and Saks. That will draw shoppers from all economic levels. If you were to buy up more of the stock while it's cheap, you could be sitting on a gold mine a year from now."

"You said no one has officially signed on."

"No, but like I said it's only a matter of time now. In a

month or two, this will be the hottest investment in the Dallas area.''

Todd thought carefully for a moment. Willis was right. "I suppose I could put my business up. That's going to be chancy, though."

"Chancy! We're not talking about taking the money to Las Vegas! This is as close to a sure thing as I've ever seen. The chances of it falling through are a million to one."

"But there is that one chance."

"Nothing is one hundred percent certain."

Todd drew in a deep breath. "I want you to call around and get me the best money available on my construction firm."

I just happen to know a banker with a pocket full of money just waiting to be loaned out on an investment like this.''

"Okay, Willis. Go for it." Todd hung up and sat staring at the phone for several minutes. He had a strong urge to call Willis back and tell him he had changed his mind, but he knew the man was right. If two chain stores of that magnitude were interested, others would be pushing and shoving for an opportunity to join them. His mall and his fortune could be within his grasp.

Todd knew the biggest gamblers were the biggest winners. He turned his back on the phone and went back to join the rest of the family.

The conversation was strained that evening. Elizabeth smoothly orchestrated things, asking first one of her children, then another to give an opinion or recount an event. She was skilled at keeping a conversation going under the most adverse conditions.

"Mr. Nathan?" Evelyn interrupted them by saying. "There's a call for you. Someone named Cody."

Nathan looked startled. "Cody? I'll take it in the den."

The others watched him leave. Grace spoke for all of them. "Who is Cody?"

"I have no idea," Elizabeth admitted. "I suppose it's one of his friends." She kept her voice calm but she was tensing inside. Cody was a name that could indicate either a male or a female. Since she was almost positive that Nathan was gay, she was pretty sure this Cody must be his boyfriend. The thought made her livid.

Grace didn't let it die. "Amanda, has Nathan ever mentioned this person to you?"

"No. He hasn't."

"Whomever it is, I'm sure Nathan will tell us about it when he returns," Elizabeth said.

Nathan was gone for a long time. And when he came into the room, he was still smiling.

"Who was that?" Grace demanded.

"A friend." Nathan sat down and tried to pick up the conversation from earlier. "I think the Oilers are going to walk away with next season."

"What sort of friend?" Grace pursued. "You and Todd can talk sports anytime."

"A good friend."

"If he doesn't want to talk about Cody, he doesn't have to," Amanda said in her brother's defense. "We are all entitled to our secrets." She had again tried to tell her family about Dakota at dinner and had again lacked the courage to insist that they listen. She was still castigating herself for her lack of assertiveness.

"What do you think about the Cowboys?" Nathan asked Todd.

"Who cares? You know I don't give a damn about sports." Todd was into his second drink and becoming more belligerent.

"I'm sure Nathan has nothing to hide from us when it comes to his friends," Elizabeth said. "Do you, Nathan?"

"No."

"Then tell us about Cody." Elizabeth waited like a cat at a mousehole.

"I'd rather not."

"Why not?" Her voice wasn't quite so modulated and calm now.

Nathan faced her without flinching. "Mother, I'm a grown man. I have many friends you don't know, and many more people who are acquaintances. I don't have to explain them to you."

Elizabeth's face became dead white. "How dare you speak to me in such an impertinent way!" Her fingers knotted on the arms of her chair and her long fingernails made a scraping noise on the fabric. "Apologize at once!"

For a moment Amanda didn't think Nathan would reply. Then he said in a tone as cold as Elizabeth's, "I apologize, Mother."

Her eyes bored into his but he didn't look away.

"If you're sure you want to hear about Cody, I'll be glad to tell you." He waited in silence.

Amanda could see Elizabeth's inner battle. On one hand, she was dying of curiosity. On the other, she didn't want to give Nathan the power of deciding whether or not she should know.

"I'm not interested. No one is important enough to cause you to be so rude to me in my own house."

He smiled without humor and turned to Amanda. "You mentioned an art show earlier. Tell me about it."

She was caught completely off guard. For a moment she couldn't say a word as Elizabeth's blue eyes pierced her. "I'm going to have an exhibit," she said lamely. "A nationwide one with TV and radio spots." Amanda felt as if she were reporting some event the others felt was too dull to be discussed. She felt her cheeks turning pink. "It's not a solo show. I'm exhibiting with another artist. A man."

"When you have a show of your very own, let me know," Elizabeth said dismissively, then turned to Grace and began discussing the purchases they had made that afternoon.

Amanda stared at them, then jumped up from her chair and left the room. She went up the stairs two at a time and ran to the room she had used as a studio when she was a girl. Only when she was inside with the others shut out did she let the tears come.

They didn't care about her! They never wanted to hear anything she had to say. She crossed her arms protectively over her middle and went to the window seat. She wasn't going to treat her child this way! She would raise this baby with understanding and love and lots of attention.

Even Nathan had turned against her. He had set her up, in her opinion. Why would he do that to her? She had thought he, at least, cared something about her.

The room was illumined by a security light outside the window that threw shadows of silver and charcoal on the walls. Against one wall were the easels she hadn't wanted to take with her when she moved to California. There was a sturdy table large enough to hold the canvases when she was stretching them onto the wooden frames. The rest of the large room was bare. She had spent many hours here, painting and sketching and trying to will herself to be somewhere, anywhere, else.

She had risked almost as much by running from the room downstairs as Nathan had in his refusal to explain his relationship with that Cody person. Maybe, Amanda thought unhappily, he had been offering her a chance of her own to join him in rebellion. If that was it, she had failed miserably.

Amanda didn't really care who Cody might be. Elizabeth had hinted enough times that Nathan was gay and Amanda wouldn't be surprised to learn that Cody was a special male friend. Amanda's world of art and the people drawn to that world had expanded her mind and she had no prejudices in that area. But for Nathan's sake in the family, she hoped the mysterious Cody was female.

Personally, she thought Cody was married to another man and that Nathan was having an affair with her—no more and no less. If Nathan was caught in a love triangle, she hoped it would work out for his best.

Amanda suddenly missed Dakota so much she actually ached for him. Coming here without him had been a mistake. If she hadn't been so stubborn, she would have realized it would be. His presence would have been a shock to Elizabeth and a surprise to the others, but they would have gotten over it.

For a minute she toyed with the idea of marching back downstairs and announcing to them all that she was living with a man and pregnant with his child. The fantasy was so unlike anything she had ever done before, she couldn't even imagine what would happen next. But if her mother really did have a bad heart, making such an announcement in such a dramatic way could prove catastrophic.

Amanda sighed and leaned her forehead against the cool glass of the window. She couldn't tell them for the simple reason that she was afraid of them, even of Nathan. She didn't really know these people even if they were her family. Their conversations never touched upon emotions or pursuits that weren't sanctioned by Elizabeth. Amanda realized with a jolt that she probably knew less about her own brother and sister than she did about the man who was hosting her exhibit in Albuquerque. It was a sobering thought.

They were a house of strangers, touching circles from time to time and drifting away to their own worlds. She didn't even know where Nathan lived other than his house was located somewhere in Galveston.

She got up and went to her room. In less than twenty-four hours she would be home with Dakota. The thought was like a balm to her emotions. There was only half of another day to get through and she would be done with this visit. And only half of another day in which to tell her family about the man she loved and his child that she carried. Why did this have to be so hard? Why did she even care about their reactions? Her mother was a shrew, and Grace had patterned herself after the woman. Only Nathan was friendly, but at times he, too, fell victim to her mother's will.

Had they always been that way? Trying hard to remember how things had been during her childhood, she recalled that her mother had not been so stern and cold and unyielding before her own mother died. Something had changed within her then and by the time Amanda's father died several years later, her mother had become what she was today. And even though Grace had become bitchy trying to copy Elizabeth, she was still Amanda's sister. When she could see past her mother and sister's negative attitudes toward her, she knew she loved them and felt they must still love her. Unfortunately, that was happening less often these days. Was Dakota right that she shouldn't put herself through all this grief?

With her thoughts turning to Dakota and the love she shared with him, she knew she owed it to him to tell her family about him and their baby. But just the thought of facing them and seeing their reactions sent a shudder through her.

By phone. She almost spoke the thought aloud. Why had she never considered calling her mother and the others from L.A. to tell them about Dakota and the baby? She knew why; they would consider it cowardly of her and her vulnerability would show. She needed to be strong around them, but that was so hard. If her expectations of their response proved true, however, it would make little difference whether she showed any weakness.

Mother's Day dinner was held at noon by tradition in the Wainwright house. The only difference between this meal and the usual Sunday dinner was the centerpiece of red roses. Every year Amanda, Nathan, and Grace and Todd bought it for Elizabeth and every year she looked pleased and mildly surprised.

Amanda wasn't hungry. Her suitcases were packed and ready to be taken out to the car as soon as the meal was over. When she ate a bite of the stuffed eggplant, her stomach rebelled and she took deep breaths to quell the nausea.

"What's the matter?" Grace asked suspiciously. "Don't you like the eggplant? It's a recipe that I sent Mother."

"I'm just not very hungry."

"You need to eat," Elizabeth said with an oblique glance at Grace's middle. "You're much too thin, Amanda."

Grace blushed and put down her fork.

Amanda didn't look up. She had always been thin, as was Nathan, but she didn't consider herself to be too thin.

"I've found a wonderful hairdresser." Elizabeth continued to address Amanda. "His name is George and he does wonders with problem hair. I was wondering if you'd like for me to make you an appointment during your next visit."

That got Amanda's attention. Automatically she touched her long hair. "I like my hair just the way it is."

"I'm sure you do, but no one is wearing it long these days, and it looks so . . . Indian."

"Thank you. I like that look," she surprised herself by saying. "I have no intention of cutting it."

"For heaven's sake, Amanda, act your age," Grace snapped. "You'd be much prettier if you fixed yourself up."

"I think she's pretty now," Nathan said.

Amanda hadn't expected anyone to come to her defense. This was new. She looked at Nathan uncertainly to be sure he wasn't teasing her.

"Don't be so hard on her, Grace," Elizabeth purred. "Amanda will grow up someday. She's only thirty."

That did it. Amanda jumped to her feet. "I'm not coming back to any more of these reunions! I start dreading them weeks ahead of time and it takes me weeks to recover from them once I'm home. You all shred each other! No one ever says anything loving or even kind! Do any of you know anything at all about me? About my life? No!"

She shoved her chair away. Tears were rising to her eyes and making her voice crack. "I have a life! A damned interesting life! I'm a talented artist and I'm about to embark on a nationwide exhibit. Do any of you have any idea at all how remarkable that is? Do you?"

She glared at them. They were all staring at her in amazement. Even Elizabeth had lost her equilibrium. Amanda forged ahead. "Can any of you name a single contemporary artist? I'll bet anything that you can't. Well, my name is going to be one that people know! My name and Dakota's! And I'm going to do it with long straight hair and jeans and without a single picture of a landscape or a still life. I'm going to do it my way!"

With tears streaming down her face, she glared at them all. Slowly Nathan began to grin. He winked at her. His kindness, even though it was silent, was more than she could take. She turned and stalked from the room.

Halfway up the stairs, she heard them all start to talk at once. Nathan sounded amused; everyone else was furious.

She slammed the door to her bedroom and leaned against it. "Oh, God," she muttered. "Why did I do that?"

She picked up her luggage and purse and left the room. No one tried to stop her and she didn't go near the dining room. Instead, she went out the front door and slammed it behind her.

She dumped everything on the ground in front of her rental car and put the key in the lock. At the sound of the front door opening and then closing, she looked back to see Nathan coming toward her. She yanked the car door open and tossed her luggage inside.

"That was quite a scene," he said with a grin. "You managed to leave them all speechless. I would have said it couldn't be done."

Amanda didn't answer him.

"Did you mean what you said about not coming back?"

"Yes."

"Will you come to see me?"

"No."

"Why not?"

She glared at him. "Because I don't even know where you live! You've lived in Galveston for four years and I don't have your goddamn address! Every time I suggest visiting you, you change the subject as if you thought I would taint your world! I don't need you any more than I need the others!" She tried to throw her purse in the car, but hung it on the car door and ripped it loose angrily. "Let me tell you this, Nathan. I don't care if you're gay or if you're sleeping with every married woman on the planet! All I've ever wanted from you is affection."

By now she was crying openly. She shoved at her tears with the palm of her hand. "I'm the one who has never fit in here. I'm glad of it now. I wouldn't want to fit in with those people in there! Grace has been a bitch for years now and isn't likely to change. Todd can't keep his hands off me. Did you know that? When I was fifteen he was forcing me to have sex with him! Did any of you ever notice? Did anyone care enough to wonder why I detest him so much?"

"Todd did what?" Nathan exclaimed.

"Just forget it. I needed you then, but I don't need you now. Just leave me alone and don't expect me to come back here!"

She threw herself in the car and jabbed at the ignition with the key.

Nathan leaned over to ask, "Who's Dakota?"

"The same as your Cody!" she shouted as she churned the engine to life. She left the curb so fast Nathan jumped back.

He stood in the yard watching her peel away. He had always liked Amanda best of his two sisters, but she had a point. They didn't know each other. None of them did. He dreaded these visits as much as she did.

After a while he went into the house.

Grace glared at him when he came into the den. "I hope you gave her a piece of your mind! The nerve of her ruining Mother's Day like this!"

"I talked some sense into her," Nathan said with a smile he knew they wouldn't understand. "I think you might say we reached a common ground of communication."

"I'm glad to hear it," Elizabeth said in clipped tones. "She certainly stepped over the boundaries this time!"

Nathan looked at Todd. "We talked about a number of things." He saw his brother-in-law squirm and knew Amanda hadn't been exaggerating. Todd was guilty as hell. How could it be Nathan hadn't known? Was the family so twisted that she hadn't been able to come to him for protection? And why hadn't he noticed? Nathan felt sick inside.

Elizabeth surprised them all by saying, "She has spunk. You have to admire that. Not that I can allow her to behave that way in my house, but the girl has a lot of spirit. She reminds me of myself in some ways."

Grace looked appalled.

Nathan laughed and said, "I'm leaving, too. I want to beat the rush-hour traffic on I-45."

"Need help carrying anything to your car?" Todd asked without moving to get up.

"Not from you." With those final words Nathan left them wondering what he could have meant by that. He was eager to go home.

Chapter Five

Amanda was exhausted by the time her plane landed in Los Angeles. She let herself be bumped by her fellow passengers as she went down the covered walkway into the terminal. Her eyes felt swollen from crying and she was emotionally spent.

She heard her name and looked around. A new spark of energy began to glow in her. She saw Dakota wave to her. Relief washed over her and she hurried into his arms. "You're here," she sighed when she was safely in his embrace.

"I had no intention of letting you take a cab at this time of night." He steered her to the rack where her luggage would eventually appear. "How was your trip?"

"It was terrible!" She put her arm around his lean waist. He held her close to his side. "I was a fool to have gone in the first place."

"Do you want to tell me about it?"

"Not here. I have to be home before I can talk about

it." Amanda had a horror of crying in public and she knew she couldn't talk about the weekend without tears.

"I've been working steadily since you've been gone."

"Have you taken time to eat and sleep?" It wasn't a thoughtless question. When Dakota became engrossed in his art, he could forget such mundane things as his bodily needs.

"I slept whenever my hands went numb," he said with a grin. "I wanted to get what I was feeling on canvas while the emotion was still fresh."

"I can't wait to see it." She thought of the canvas she had been working on. It was a study of serenity and joy couched in mystical symbolism. "I just hope I can finish mine."

"They've done it to you again," he said accusingly. "Amanda, why didn't you just come home right away?"

"It didn't get really bad until today." She felt her breath catch in her throat and she blinked quickly. "There's my suitcase."

Dakota eased forward and retrieved the suitcase and the hanging bag. He lifted them as easily as if they were filled with feathers and Amanda saw two college-aged girls watching him with interest. She was accustomed to it. Dakota stood out in every crowd.

He came back to her without ever noticing the girls and she smiled to herself. Whatever emotions he might stir in others, he was completely faithful to her. She never had a doubt about that. Dakota's only other love was his art.

They went to his car and Amanda settled in the passenger seat, leaning her head back against the headrest. She breathed in the familiar smell of leather mixed faintly with oil. "I hate the way airplanes smell," she said with her eyes closed.

"So do I."

"I can't wait to get home."

Dakota paid the parking fee and smoothly drove onto the freeway. "We'll be home before you know it. Have you been sleeping? You look exhausted."

"I can't sleep there. Mother painted my room pink. It's awful. It was like being in a faded candy cane. I swear, it even *smelled* pink."

He laughed.

"She knows I can't stand pink. That's Grace's color. So what did she paint Grace's room? Green." She sighed. "It was like being a kid again. She did that once before. I went to school one morning and when I came home, my room was pink. I hate pink."

"Spoken like a true artist," he teased.

"It's okay on canvas, in small doses. It's unnatural on the walls of my bedroom."

"I promise I'll never paint our bedroom pink."

She smiled and rolled her head to look at him. "I missed you."

"I missed you, too." He reached out and took her hand. "Are you feeling all right?"

"I had my first bout of morning sickness. I hope it's my last."

"You shouldn't be flying now."

Amanda laughed. "I'm not made of spun glass. It's okay for me to fly. The doctor said so."

"You're hard to take care of," he pointed out. "You're too rebellious."

She sighed. "Tell me about it." She looked out at the darkness interspersed by passing lights. Smog and street-lights blotted out the stars. "I wish we lived in the country. I miss seeing the stars. You can't see them from Mother's house, either. Maybe they aren't still up there."

"They're there. I guarantee it. We'll find a house in the country someday."

"Promises, promises." She tried to make her tone light but she felt tired and depressed.

They reached the parking lot of the loft they rented. It was in a building that had once been a factory. The lower floors had been converted into apartments but the upper story was still one large room. This was the one she and Dakota lived in. No one but artists had wanted so much sunlight and so few walls.

They rode up the elevator and got off at the top floor. For their privacy, Dakota had built a small room. Before, the elevator had arrived in the middle of one wall of their living room. These and the ones surrounding the bathroom were the only permanent walls in the place.

He unlocked the door as she picked up her hanging bag and draped it over her shoulder. As always when she had been gone, she was eager to step back into the world she shared with Dakota.

The door swung open and she went in and breathed deeply of the scents of her familiar domain. Oil paint, linseed oil, and turpentine were the underlying scents, but there was also the rose potpourri in open bowls around the room and the lemon oil she used to polish the furniture. She looked around. She was standing in the living room, but since there were no walls, she could see the bedroom at one end of the loft and the studio at the other.

She dropped the bag on the floor and hurried to the canvas that hung prominently on an easel. Passion moved on the canvas. Dakota had captured the essence of primal love—demanding yet protective and tender. "It's wonderful!" she whispered.

"I missed you. I couldn't be with you, so I put it on canvas."

She put her arms around him. "I love you so much. You've painted our love."

He smiled and held her while he gazed into her eyes. "Tell me what happened."

Amanda sighed and stepped away. "It was awful. Everyone was on edge as always. There was a terrible scene just before I left."

Dakota walked her back to the luggage and picked it up. "I should have been there to protect you."

"I told them all what I think of them."

"Good for you!"

"But I didn't tell them about us or the baby." They reached the bed and she collapsed on top of it. "I'm such a coward."

"No, you're not. And next time, I'm going with you."

"There won't be a next time."

Dakota lay down beside her and put his arm around her. Amanda snuggled closer to him. "I said things Mother will never forgive me for saying. I told her that I hated coming to the family reunions and that I wasn't coming back again, that they were all selfish and uncaring."

"That sounds accurate to me."

"I shouldn't have gone. If I had known I would lose control like that, I wouldn't have placed myself in that position." She paused. On the flight back to L. A., she had decided to tell Dakota about Todd. Early in her relationship with Dakota, she had made it clear to him that she didn't like anything about her brother-in-law. She had stopped short of explaining why, because she didn't want Dakota to think less of her. But now, after having given it considerable thought, she realized not telling him was worse because it showed a lack of trust, and she did trust him.

Feeling the protection of his arms around her gave her strength. "Dakota, you know I detest Todd; I told you I did long ago." She felt his arms lovingly tighten around her, as if he already sensed her need for reassurance.

"Yes. I remember. You said he was a self-centered sonof-abitch."

"But there's more to it than that. Please listen to all I have to say without interrupting because this is hard for me to talk about."

"Of course. I promise. What is it?"

"When I was fifteen, my father died and I went sort of crazy for a while. I was angry and confused and I did some things I am terribly ashamed of." She pulled back just far enough to see his face before going on. "That's when I lost my virginity. But more than that, I was terribly promiscuous . . . with older men." Dakota blinked, but the love never left his eyes. "I'm not even sure how I came to meet Todd, but he was the last. When I found out he was seeing my sister Grace as well as me, I tried to end things with him, but he blackmailed me into continuing—but only for a while. Eventually, he stopped making demands. It all ended long before I met you, I swear." There was fire blazing in Dakota's eyes, but she instinctively knew the anger behind it was not aimed at her but Todd.

After she was silent for a long moment, Dakota spoke. "That bastard! Fifteen? If I could get my hands on him right now, I'd kill him!"

Amanda was shocked by his rage. "Kill him? That was a long time ago."

"I'm sorry, Amanda. I didn't mean that. I just can't stand the thought of someone doing something so horrible to you."

"You're not mad at me, are you?"

"No, no," he assured her as he pulled her back into the warmth of his embrace and kissed her hair. "Kids do stupid things. They don't think things through."

"I love you, Dakota. Thank you for understanding."

"How could I do less?" He caressed her cheek with the back of his fingers in the same loving way he had done so often. "I can see how hard that was for you to tell me, but I'm glad you did." You know I'm not a violent person by nature, Amanda, but damn it, I want to meet him just once so I can punch him out!"

"Thank you for wanting to," she said with a brief smile. "I had hoped he wouldn't be there this year. That's what Mother implied in her last letter. I guess he changed his mind. Or more likely Grace changed it for him. She keeps him on a short leash."

"Not nearly short enough." The fire sparked again in his eyes.

"Grace only sees what she wants to see." Amanda touched Dakota's face lovingly. "Maybe I shouldn't have told you about Todd."

"Yes, you should. We shouldn't have any secrets between us. I'll bet you could prosecute him for molesting you as a child. There are laws, you know. Statutory rape."

She shook her head. "Even if I wanted to, the time limitations have run out. Besides, I don't want the publicity. Not now. Not when we're about to be so much in the news with our art. All that is past."

"No, it's not. You're thirty years old and are only now letting yourself love a man. He scarred you, Amanda, and I'll never forgive him for that."

"I'm glad you're the first man I've ever loved. That way, I had no encumbrances when we met."

"I'd like to break his neck anyway."

She nodded. "So would I." Amanda proceeded to tell Dakota about the late-night conversation with Todd and how Grace thought she was after her husband.

"Why didn't you tell her the truth?" he asked.

"At the time I was still trying to keep the peace. Can you imagine the explosion if I told her what Todd used to do to me? She would see it all as my fault anyway."

"You were fifteen. Todd was a grown man."

"I know, but I came on to him, not the other way around."

"That doesn't matter. You were a child and were going through a traumatic time. He took advantage of you, no matter what precipitated it."

"I want to forget all that. But it keeps following me like a ghost. Maybe it always will. Well, I don't have to see Todd anymore. I'm never going back there." She felt the tears well up inside and she tried to blink them back. As they brimmed over, she said, "I'm not ever going back!"

He held her. "It's okay, honey. I'm right here."

"Why don't they love me?" she sobbed brokenly. "Why don't they care anything at all about me? They don't know me or even wonder what I'm really like. I'm nothing to them!"

Dakota had heard this before. He held her closer. "I love you. We don't need them."

"I know, but I don't see what's wrong with me! There must be something wrong if my entire family dismisses me."

"You aren't like them. You care about people and you're willing to give of yourself. That's what makes you an artist. You give. They're takers."

"You don't know them."

"No, but I've known people like them. I'm glad you don't fit in with them. Being rejected by them is the best thing they could do for you."

"Do you really love me?" she asked as she held him tightly. "Do you honestly love me?"

"You know I do."

She could hear the leashed anger in his voice. When she came back from her mother's house, she felt unsure of herself and that made him angry. She knew the anger wasn't aimed at her. "You're such a good person," she whispered.

"I love you. I'm not ever going to leave you."

She tried to swallow the sobs. "Don't ever send me away, Dakota. I couldn't stand not being with you."

"I'll never send you away."

It was a litany both had recited many times. Amanda always returned from her family visits feeling that their love was too fragile and that someday, for some unpredictable reason, he would cast her aside or reveal that he never loved her in the first place. She hated herself for having to ask him these questions but she couldn't regain her feeling of safety until she had been reassured. "I'm sorry," she whispered. "I know you love me. I do."

"Hush," he said soothingly. "You couldn't get rid of me if you tried. Even if you chased me away, I'd only come back."

She managed a wavering smile. "I'd never chase you away."

He kissed her and gazed into her eyes. "I don't want you to change your mind and go back."

She shook her head. "I don't intend to."

"How about some supper? I have a pizza in the refrigerator."

She laughed and wiped at her tears. "You lived on carry-out food the whole time I was gone, didn't you?"

"Of course. I always do." He sat up and pulled her up to sit beside him. "That's why I can't ever get rid of you. I'd starve."

"Pizza sounds good." She reached for a tissue. "I'm sorry I cried. I didn't want to do this again."

"Amanda, people cry. It's not the end of the world to shed a few tears."

"It feels as if it is. I hate to cry."

He looked at her and brushed the hair back from her face. "They tear you apart. Don't ever go back."

"I've told you I don't intend to."

He was quiet as he studied her face. Then he stood and said, "I'll nuke the pizza. You find the parmesan."

Amanda watched him with love brimming in her heart. She was never going to leave him behind and go back to her mother's house. Never. The tears threatened to start again so she hurriedly got up and started to set the table.

As they ate, Dakota said, "I think while we're in Houston, I should pay a visit to your mother."

"Why would you want to do that?"

"I have some things I'd like to tell her."

"Forget it. That's all over now."

"Amanda, I've heard you resolve not to see them again on more than one occasion."

"I know, but this time I really corked it. After the things I said, Mother won't let me in the house." She thought for a while. "Nathan followed me out to the car and tried to calm me down. I laid into him, too."

"Oh?"

"He just happened to be standing in front of me when I was still exploding. I like Nathan, really. He's not like them. We look the most like Mother, but our personalities are more like Dad's. I told him about Todd."

"You did?" Dakota asked in surprise.

"No details, just that it happened. He was shocked. I wonder what he said to Todd when he went back inside." She reached for another piece of pizza. "Probably nothing."

"I'm going to say plenty to Todd when I meet him. And I will eventually. I'm willing to wait."

Amanda laughed. "You'd tear him in half. Todd is no match for you."

"I want to go to your mother and tell her about us and about the baby."

"Why? You can't possibly care what she thinks."

"I don't. But you do, and whether you ever go back

there or not, it's important to you that she knows about us. I'm going to tell her, make sure she knows that I love you, then I can leave. But not before."

"You'd do that for me?"

"I'd have done it this past weekend if you had let me go with you."

She reached across the table and covered his hand with hers. "We don't need them. We don't need anybody."

"Right," he said with a smile. "And don't you forget it."

She fed him a piece of her pizza and smiled into his eyes.

Nathan drove into his driveway while the sun still hung heavily in the sky. He had built the beautiful house from a design he had drawn himself. It looked out over the beach and the silver water could be seen from every room of the house. Nathan loved the water, even the storms that blew in periodically from the Gulf, and his house was built to withstand all of them.

He got out of the car and went to the side door. As he unlocked it, a pint-size ball of energy plowed into his knees. "Hi, Nate. How's it going?" He picked up his son and hugged him.

"We missed you," Nate said, wriggling happily. "Mom said you might not be home before I had to go to bed tonight."

"I wouldn't miss tucking you in. Where's Mom?"

"In the kitchen."

Nathan deposited the little boy on the floor and went into the kitchen. Cody was stirring chili on the stove and smiled when she saw him. "It's about time you came dragging in here," she teased. "I thought we were going to have to eat without you."

"I got away as soon as I could." He went to her and put his arms around her, pulling her back against his stomach as she cooked. He buried his face in her dark hair and said, "I missed you so much."

"I'm sorry I had to call, but the car wouldn't start and I wasn't sure which garage you wanted me to call."

"We need to trade it in and get one that's more reliable. It's not like we can't afford it."

"I know, but it's a classic. A '57 Chevy," she said as if that explained it. Cody had owned that car since she was a teenager and she loved it, problems and all. "You can't buy a car like that these days."

"No, but you can get one with decent gas mileage and a reliable engine."

"You're just jealous because you don't have a great car like I do." She turned in his arms and kissed him.

"Has Nate been behaving?"

"As much as any two-year-old ever does. He insisted on letting Magic sleep in his room."

"He sure loves that puppy."

Cody turned back to the stove. "Horse, you mean. She's doubling in size every day."

"Golden retrievers are large dogs. She'll be protection for you both when I have to be gone."

"We could go with you," she said. Although she kept her tone light, he knew the subject was one that bothered her.

"I wish it were possible."

Cody turned down the heat under the chili and looked at him. "You can't keep your family from knowing about us forever."

"Darling, we've been over this. I want to tell them, but I can't see a way to do it."

"You could just introduce us. After that, we would talk and all their questions would be answered."

"Right. All I have to do is say, 'Mother, this Cody and my son, Nate. We've been married almost four years but I just haven't introduced you before now.' Yes, I can see how that would generate a conversation."

"My family accepted you," she pointed out.

"Just barely! Your grandmother still thinks the worst of me and probably always will."

Cody smiled. "Probably."

"My mother is less open-minded than your grandmother."

"I've got to meet this woman. I'd have said Granny is the most-closed minded woman in this state."

He embraced her and held her close. Cody put her arms around him. He knew she was hurt that she had never met his family. "I should have introduced you to them when we first fell in love."

"Why didn't you?"

"You know why. Mother and Grace would have thrown a fit."

"Putting it off hasn't changed that. Someday they *have* to know we exist."

"Mother thinks I'm gay."

Cody leaned back to look up at him. "What?" she asked with a laugh.

"I thought you'd enjoy that. Amanda apparently thinks you're a married woman."

"She's right. I am."

"Married to someone else, I mean."

"She sounds like the sanest one of the lot."

"She finally blew a gasket. It was something to see," he said, still marveling over his sister's outburst. "I knew she had a temper, but she's never lost it so completely." He sobered as he said, "She told me Todd molested her when she was a girl."

"Todd did? Your own sister's husband?" Cody was as shocked as if she knew them personally. "Is it true?"

"I didn't ask him, but I believe her." He stepped away and went to the window. He could see Nate in the fenced yard playing with the puppy. "Why didn't I see what was going on? She never told me until today. Damn it, I could have protected her!"

"When did it happen?"

"She didn't give me any details. It was right after Dad died, I guess. She went a little crazy then. I was worried about her, but she wouldn't confide in me. Then she did a complete about face and stopped dating completely. I don't think Mother and Grace noticed, but I did. I should have asked her why she changed so suddenly."

Cody came to him and put her arms around him. "No one could have imagined the real reason. You're not to blame."

"I've never liked Todd. He and Grace make a perfect pair. I don't like her, either."

"That's no way to talk about your sister."

"You wouldn't like her, either. She's a bitch most of the time. Especially to Todd. I wouldn't want to be in his shoes. Thank God you're nothing like Grace."

"If I was, you wouldn't have married me."

"True." He stroked the golden skin of her arm. "Don't you know it kills me a little each time I see them and don't tell them about you?"

Cody didn't answer.

"I hate it that I can't come right out and tell them. But it's gone on for so long. I knew I should have told Mother when we fell in love, but it happened so suddenly and was so wonderful, I guess I didn't believe anything so good could last. Your family was against us being together, too. I wasn't sure they wouldn't talk you into breaking up with me."

"They came around after we eloped. All except Granny."

"I wanted to tell them when Nate was born." He smiled sadly as he looked out at their son. "I was so proud of him, of you, I wanted to tell everyone. But if I had, all that happiness would have been tarnished."

"Are you sure?"

"I'm positive of it. That's why I haven't told. And at times like this, I don't care if they ever know or not." He gazed into her dark eyes and reached out to trace the beloved curves of her face. "They would never see you the way I do."

"You mean they would see a black woman." Cody lifted her chin. "It's what I am. I'm not ashamed of it."

"I'm not, either. You're like a miracle to me. You always have been. But you know what prejudice is like. I don't want to expose you to what they might say. I certainly don't want them to say anything that would hurt Nate."

"He's going to hear it eventually. He doesn't exactly fit in either world." She turned to watch the little boy rolling on the grass while the puppy tried to lick his ears. "That's one of the reason my family didn't want us to marry. They were thinking about our children."

"They were also thinking that I'm white," he said gently. "Prejudice cuts both ways."

"I know." She fell silent.

"Someday I'll tell them."

She didn't answer.

Nathan knew she didn't believe him. "You know I'm proud of you? That I love you?"

She nodded. "I know."

"I don't want them to hurt you."

"I know that, too."

"Maybe I could tell Amanda. She's not like the others."

"That's up to you. One of these days, Nate is going to

start asking questions about your side of the family. We'll
have to tell him something."

"I know. When the time comes, I think we'll know what
to say."

She didn't answer, but he knew she disagreed with him.
He knew Cody's moods as well as he knew the sea beyond
his back yard. He also knew that he should have told his
mother and sisters. At least Amanda.

Next time, he thought. There was always a next time.

Chapter Six

"You've done well," Elizabeth said grudgingly to her lawyer. "It didn't take you as long this time, either."

"Mrs. Wainwright, I have to urge you not to make so many changes in your will."

"No one knows about them," Elizabeth said smugly. "It's our secret."

Clay Bennett leaned forward earnestly. "You've changed your will so many times more than likely it will be contested when the time comes."

"That won't be for many years. I'm in perfect health." She glanced over the legal document again. "I don't have time to run by my safety-deposit box this afternoon. Can you keep my copy until tomorrow? I'll pick it up around three o'clock."

"That means I'll have both copies. I don't think that's a good idea, either."

"Clay, you're a worrywart. So was your father. What difference can it possibly make if I pick up my copy today or tomorrow? I could have just as easily made this appointment for then. It's as safe here as it would be at the bank."

"Lawyers' offices have been known to catch on fire," he began pedantically.

She cut him off. "Nonsense. I'll be back to get it tomorrow afternoon. I have an appointment then and have to get out anyway."

Bennett watched her stand to leave. "Mrs. Wainwright, are you sure you want to leave this will the way it's written? If this is a frivolous decision, I have to counsel you against it."

"The document is completed, signed and notarized. Nothing I do, I can assure you, is ever frivolous." Her icy stare pinned him until he moved uncomfortably. "Now I have to be going. I'll see you tomorrow." She swept out of his office.

Elizabeth didn't nod to his secretary as she passed, though the woman spoke to her by name. She had never liked the girl and saw no reason to say good-bye. On more than one occasion she had told Elizabeth that Clay wasn't in the office when Elizabeth knew perfectly well that he was. Elizabeth hadn't been civil to her since the first time that had happened.

She drove home and parked her car in front of the garage. It could use washing and this would signal her yard man that he should do it. Horace, like Evelyn, had worked for Elizabeth for so many years, he knew as well as she did how to keep the place in perfect order.

Elizabeth glanced critically at the flower bed. She had instructed Horace to plant red begonias in that bed but the leaves looked more the color of the white variety. White flowers against the white of her house would look faded. She made a mental note to question him about this.

She went in the front door as she usually did. The side door was used by Evelyn and the back one was only used when she went into the backyard. Elizabeth rarely went out there because she disliked Houston's sweltering heat in the summer and there was little to see out there in the winter. Houston's spring and autumn were too short to matter. Elizabeth kept up the yard because that was the thing to do when one lived in River Oaks, not because she enjoyed being in it.

Inside, the house was perfectly quiet. She nodded in approval. Evelyn was working somewhere but she didn't make a clatter while she cleaned. Elizabeth would have preferred to have completely invisible and silent workers but Evelyn and Horace were close enough to the mark. Once she had seen a movie on TV that indicated at one time, at any rate, the staff at the White House was instructed to stay out of sight. Elizabeth would have loved that.

She went up to her room and sat on the padded bench in front of her vanity mirror. After only walking upstairs, her heart was racing and she felt out of breath. Looking at her reflection in the mirror, Elizabeth took deep breaths and forced herself to stay calm until her heart was beating normally again.

Tomorrow was her doctor's appointment. She thought it was an amazing coincidence that the bad heart she had claimed to have for years had recently become a reality. In the past two weeks she had frequently experienced palpitations and an uncomfortable pressure in her chest. Most likely her doctor would prescribe a diet that she would follow for a few weeks before returning to her normal habits. This was Elizabeth's usual concession to health limitations.

Years earlier, she had a bout with her heart. That was when her doctor, Frank Hastings, had first given her the glycerin pills. She rarely took one before the last couple of weeks, but they had been marvelous tools to use with her children. She had only to keep the prescription valid and she could get them to do almost anything.

That reminded her of Amanda. The girl had to be reprimanded, but Elizabeth hadn't decided yet how to do it. During the two weeks since Mother's Day, Elizabeth hadn't written or called her daughter and she knew she must be nervously wondering when retribution would strike. That was the best tool to use with Amanda—to keep her worrying about a future punishment that might or might not ever come.

Grace lacked the imagination that would work to keep Amanda on tetherhooks. With Grace the best method was to strike and to strike hard. Nathan was much the same way, though guilt worked excellently as well.

Elizabeth had perfected her methods over the years. Although all her children were grown and had lives of their own, she never doubted for a moment that she still maintained control over all of them.

But sometimes she felt she was losing control over Nathan. As the only son, he was naturally the most assertive, or at least Elizabeth believed it to be so. That was why Amanda's outburst at the dinner table had taken her so by surprise. Nathan had left almost immediately after Amanda and she knew he was upset. Strangely, though, he didn't seem to be angry with Amanda as Elizabeth would prefer. Instead, he seemed to be more angry with Todd, who had done nothing as far as she could tell. That made no sense. Elizabeth prided herself on keeping a tight rein over her children and all that went on in their lives and especially in her house. If Todd had done anything to upset Nathan, Elizabeth would have known.

Was Nathan gay? Elizabeth hated to even consider the possibility but nothing else seemed likely. That could also explain why he would be put out at the only other male in the family. Elizabeth couldn't have explained the logic in that, but it made sense to her.

What was she going to do if Nathan was gay? She had

to prevent anyone from finding out, of course. That was obvious. The Wainwright name had been respected in Houston society for several generations. Now that she was the matriarch of the family, it was her duty to see no mark of shame touched that name.

If Nathan *was* gay that would be difficult, because it was up to him to pass the family name on to the next generation. Elizabeth was certain she could coerce him into marrying. After all, being gay didn't preclude one from fathering a child. Once he had done his duty, he could separate from his wife and do more or less as he pleased, as long as no one knew and as long as the separation didn't end in a divorce. Since he lived in Galveston, the distance would make it easier for her to dispel any rumors as mindless gossip.

Who should he marry? Elizabeth didn't have a favorite to champion. The daughters of most of her friends were too old to give Nathan a son, and that was the primary reason she wanted him to marry. At the same time, all their granddaughters were too young. It was a dilemma she would have to put some thought to.

Since her heart was behaving again, Elizabeth stood and went to the drawer where she kept her calendar of events. She liked to stay busy, though she managed not to do any of the actual work of her various committees and clubs. This afternoon there was to be a tea for a visiting author. Elizabeth particularly liked this sort of thing. She went to her closet to decide what to wear.

The following day Elizabeth dressed as impeccably as ever and went out to her car to drive to the doctor's office. She didn't tell Evelyn where she was going because she never did unless she expected that information to somehow affect the maid's day. This was only a checkup, she told herself, and would amount to nothing. Dr. Hastings might not even change her glycerin pills. She almost expected him to laugh at her fears and send her on her way with a fairly clean bill of health, though that wasn't what she would report to Grace, of course. Elizabeth had Grace in a lather already over the fact that she was seeing the doctor at all.

Elizabeth smiled coolly as she started her car. She had led Grace to believe that her appointment was a direct result of heart trouble brought on by Grace threatening to divorce Todd after that unfortunate incident between him and Amanda. Elizabeth knew she would be able to use this appointment to control Grace for months if she played her cards right.

Dr. Hastings's office was in the Medical Center. It wasn't necessary for Elizabeth to take the freeway to get there. She habitually avoided the freeways whenever possible and had driven on Houston's streets for so many years, she almost could have found the Medical Center blindfolded. As she drove, her mind wandered and she didn't notice the red traffic light until she was passing through the intersection with one of the freeway off-ramps.

There was a deafening squeal of brakes and she looked to her left to see the grille of a speeding truck. Although the hood almost filled her window, above it she saw the horrified face of the man at the wheel. There was a grinding screech of tearing metal and then nothing.

The ambulances arrived on the scene within minutes. A large crowd of onlookers clogged the intersection in spite of the police efforts to clear the lanes. It was hard to tell where Elizabeth's car started and the truck left off except for the respective colors. The truck driver was relatively uninjured but it took the jaws of life to remove Elizabeth from her car.

Dr. Hastings received word of the accident late that

afternoon and hurried over as soon as he had finished seeing his remaining patients. He found the emergency room doctor and said, "How is Elizabeth Wainwright? What's her condition? I'm her physician."

The man pulled Elizabeth's chart and handed it to the other doctor. "It's not good. She was hit broadside and her door buckled like cardboard. She hasn't regained consciousness and frankly, I don't think she's likely to do so."

Hastings read the chart and found his worst fears confirmed. "Damn! She was on her way to my office. She missed her appointment and I wondered what happened. It wasn't like her." He glanced at the younger doctor. "She said she was having heart problems."

"We didn't monitor anything out of the ordinary. Her heart is doing fine, all things considered. The primary injury, as you can see, is to her head."

"I'll go up and take a look at her." He closed her chart and put it under his arm. "She'll be under my care. Has her family been called?"

"No, we've been working our tails off this afternoon. There was a three-car wreck on the southwest loop and we've had a steady stream of gunshots and knifings as well. It's been a mad house around here today."

"Okay. I'll call them." Hastings headed for ICU.

Elizabeth was lying on the bed with tubes and machines sustaining her life. He looked at her for several minutes. He had known Elizabeth most of his life. After the death of her husband, he had even gone out with her a few times. Nothing had come of it for either of them. Elizabeth had room in her world only for herself and the things she deemed important. Hastings hadn't been one of them. Which was just as well, because he had soon discovered she wasn't as kind and thoughtful in private as she seemed to be in public. When they parted socially, she had continued to see him professionally.

He had never thought he would see her lying so helpless or looking so old.

Bruises were forming on her face and left arm. There was a swollen area on her forehead and a shaved place in her hairline just above it. A bandage covered the stitches from the operation. Hastings read the name of the surgeon. Craig Reynolds. A good man. Hastings knew him casually and was familiar with his work. She had been in good hands. The man tended to be pompous and full of himself, but he was a fine surgeon.

Reluctantly, Hastings went to the phone. He had to call her children.

Amanda held the receiver for a moment, then hung up, her eyes glazed with shock.

"Who was that?" Dakota asked. He wiped his paintbrush on a cotton rag as he came to her. "Amanda? Are you all right?"

She shook her head and slowly sat down. "Mother was in an accident. She's in ICU." She looked at him. "There's a chance she might die. That was the doctor. He said I should come home as soon as possible. Evelyn gave him my number," she added numbly. "He's calling Grace now. He's still looking for Nathan."

"What happened? Did he say?"

"No." She was having trouble thinking at all. "It was a car accident. That's all he told me. She was in a car accident."

"I'll get cleaned up and start packing."

Amanda watched him walk back to the canvas he was working on. "I have to go."

"I know that."

"You can't go with me."

He turned and frowned at her. "Don't start that, Amanda. I'm going and that's final."

She stood and went to his canvas. "You can't leave now. This painting is in a crucial stage. You have to finish it while the paint is wet."

"I'm not going to let you go back there alone."

"She can't hurt me," Amanda said softly. "She's not conscious."

Dakota stopped and came to her. "I'm sorry, honey. I know what you must be feeling."

"Do you?" She was filled with an odd numbness. "I don't feel anything. It's as if all my emotions are out there somewhere. When they come back, they may be crushing, but for now, I don't feel anything at all."

"He shouldn't have told you over the phone. There should have been a gentler way of breaking the news to you."

"I don't think there *is* a gentler way of telling something like this. Mother isn't dead." Her voice broke on the word. "She's only injured. She could still recover."

Dakota didn't answer.

"But if Dr. Hastings thought that, there wouldn't be a reason to send for all of us, would there?"

Dakota held her close. She breathed in his aroma of soap and oil paints and tried to memorize it for security. "I have to go and you can't go with me because I don't know how long I'll be gone."

"Amanda . . ."

"Please, Dakota. You know I'm right. This show is too important. There's nothing you can do. I'll stay at the house until there's some change. As soon as I can, I'll come home." She knew she had won when he didn't argue. Again she repeated, "This show is too important to both of us."

"What about your own canvases? You're not ready, either."

"No, but I'm closer to being finished than you are. I may not be gone that long."

"I hate it when you're right about things like this."

"I know. I don't want to be right, either. I'd much rather take you with me. Or not go at all. That's a possibility. I said I wouldn't be back, you know."

"I know. But that was before." He looked into her eyes. "I love you, Amanda. I'm going to love you forever. Can you take that with you and keep it close?"

She nodded and managed to smile. "I'll call you every day."

"You do that. If you need me for anything at all, just tell me and I'll be there on the first flight. The show is important, but it's only a show."

"Bite your tongue," she said with a more genuine smile. "We're going to be household names. Mothers will name their babies after us. You'll see." Before she could lose her courage, she went to pack.

The next morning, Amanda, Nathan, Grace, and Todd met Dr. Hastings in his office. He looked from one to the other. "I assume you've been in to see your mother?"

Grace began to cry. "She looks just awful! There are all those bruises and bandages and tubes! I almost didn't recognize her."

"I know. These next few days are going to be tough on all of you, I'm afraid."

"What is her prognosis?" Amanda forced herself to ask. Like Grace, she had been shocked to see her mother as a helpless old woman.

Dr. Hastings looked down at his hands clasped on the desktop. "It's not good, I'm afraid. The longer she goes

without regaining consciousness, the worse it is for her.
There are several tests we can run to determine the extent
of her brain damage.''

"Brain damage!" Grace wailed.

"That's why she had the operation," Todd said impatiently. "Why else wouldn't she be conscious?"

Amanda frowned at him. Grace was acting as if the accident had ended her own life but Amanda still thought her
sister was due more compassion than Todd was showing
her. "She can still come out of it. Right, Dr. Hastings?"

"It's possible," he hedged. "I don't personally think
that's going to happen, but there's still a chance. I only
want you to be prepared for the worst."

"Don't say that!" Grace cried. She buried her face in
her hands and sobbed brokenly. "She said she had been
having heart problems."

"No one told me," Amanda said.

"Certainly not after the way you left that day," Grace
said, turning on her. Her tears had smeared her mascara
and she looked like a ravaged clown. "We didn't owe you
any information after upsetting Mother that day."

"I didn't know, either," Nathan said. He had been silent
through all this. "I would have called you."

"She told me," Grace said with a sniff. "I was her favorite. She wanted me to know."

"You talk as if she's already dead," Todd said. "Just
calm down."

Grace looked as if she would like to hit him. Amanda
wouldn't mind hitting him herself.

"She had an appointment with me for yesterday afternoon," Dr. Hastings said. "She was on her way when she
had the accident. If it's any consolation, it happened so
fast I doubt she knew what hit her."

"Thank you," Amanda said. She knew the doctor meant
his words to be a comfort.

"We want you to run all the tests," Nathan said. "We have to find out exactly where we stand."

"I assumed you would say that. I've already made the arrangements to start testing as soon as you sign the consent form. It only needs one signature. You're the son, so I assume you want to sign them." He pushed several papers toward Nathan.

Grace pulled them in front of her. "I'm the eldest. I'll sign." She scrawled her name in the appropriate places.

"As a friend of the family as well as Elizabeth's physician, I have to tell you not to hold out too much hope. I'm sorry, but I can't in good conscience advise you differently."

Amanda nodded. She still felt that bone-chilling numbness.

Dr. Hastings looked at Grace, who was close to hysterical. "I'm going to prescribe a sedative for you, Grace. Todd, see that she takes one twice a day. She can have three if she needs it." He scribbled words on a prescription form and handed it to Todd.

"Thanks, Doc."

"I have to go back to the hospital," Grace said as she got shakily to her feet. "Todd, you go get that prescription filled and bring it to me. Nathan, I'll ride with you and Amanda."

"All right." Nathan stood and shook hands with Dr. Hastings. "We know you're doing your best."

Amanda nodded, not trusting herself to speak.

The ride to the hospital was thankfully short. Grace cried all the way. Amanda handed her a tissue and the mirror from her purse. Grace pushed them both away. She entered the hospital wearing her smeared mascara like a war medal. Amanda was painfully aware of the glances and outright stares from the people they passed. Grace was pretending not to see anyone as she cried her way to the ICU unit.

At the first opportunity, Grace and Nathan went in to see Elizabeth. Amanda was willing to wait until the next visiting time. Only two at a time, once an hour, for five minutes. She could wait.

She went to the window and gazed down at the busy traffic whizzing by the series of hospitals and clinics. Always changing, the city never really changed. She had looked out these same windows the day her father died. Even the waiting-room furniture was the same, as far as she could tell. The walls were the same color, the adjacent buildings the same, even the same people could be passing, for all the difference there was in that day and this one.

Was her mother going to die?

Amanda had just turned fifteen that other day. Her father had dropped from a heart attack while walking from the dining room to the den. The ICU units were so sterile and similar, Elizabeth might be lying in the same cubicle, in the same bed. The thought made Amanda's stomach tighten.

She had loved her father. He had been almost opposite to Elizabeth in every way except that he, too, had found it difficult to show emotion. Although she loved him and had believed he loved her, Amanda had never been completely sure he had. And he had died before she could ask him.

Elizabeth had been very much in evidence that day. She had looked younger then and was even more forceful in her manners. She had alienated all the nurses of every shift during the day and a half Nathaniel had been in the hospital, lashing out at everybody. Amanda had been thoroughly embarrassed and had spent as much of the difficult time as far from her mother as possible. Amanda had never seen her act that way except at home.

When Nathaniel died, Elizabeth had thrown her body over his as if to prevent the doctor from removing it. Not that they would have with the family present, Amanda knew now, but at the time she had thought the hearse must be waiting at the curb and the gravediggers at work. She had feared death after that day. That had been one reason she had rebelled into the rash of reckless behavior that had resulted in her liaison with Todd.

She glanced at Todd as he came into the waiting room, a drugstore bag in his hand. "Grace and Nathan are with Mother," she informed him.

He came to her. "How are you holding up?"

"I'm all right," she lied. "I was just thinking about the day Dad died. It was the first time I realized that Mother didn't control the universe."

"Yeah, that happened here, didn't it? I was dating Grace at the time."

Amanda frowned at him. "I know." She turned back to the window.

"What do you think? Will she pull through?"

"I have no idea. You heard Dr. Hastings say he'll start the tests as soon as possible."

Todd looked at his watch. "I ought to make a phone call. Can I leave Grace's medicine with you?"

"Sure." She took the bag and continued looking down at the traffic. In the back of her mind a guilty thought was forming. If Elizabeth died, her tyranny would end.

Amanda clenched her hand into a fist. She was horrible for thinking such a thing. Her mother lay in the next room near death and Amanda was thinking how this would bring peace in her life? Angry tears gathered in her eyes but she refused to let them fall. The thought hadn't meant anything, she told herself superstitiously. A thought couldn't kill.

She was still chastising herself when Todd returned from making his phone call.

"Are they still in there?" he asked needlessly.

She nodded.

He looked back at his watch. "I thought they would be out by now." He sat in the nearest chair and it gave a plastic sigh as the cushion settled. "I wonder how long it will be before we know anything for certain," Todd said, determined to make conversation.

"I guess it depends on when the tests are run and the results read."

"Makes sense. I have this big deal going in Dallas, see? I can't be away too long."

Amanda looked at him in disbelief.

"It's true. It could be a real sweet deal. It could put us on easy street for good."

"You sound like a cheap detective novel," she said and turned back to the traffic.

Todd was quiet for a while. She wished he would go away. Loneliness was preferable to being with Todd.

"It's a good thing you don't have any commitments," he said, breaking the silence. "You don't have a real job that would keep you from coming here for as long as you like."

"I have a career. I'm an artist," she said pointedly. "I'm trying to get my canvases together for a show."

"Yeah, well, nobody is grading your paper, if you know what I mean. Nobody is watching to see if you're working or not. It's different if you have a regular job. Now you take me. I own my own company and it's one of the top construction companies in the Dallas area, but I can't take off indefinitely. Even the boss has to be on the job."

"You could always fly back to Dallas. I'm sure we could get along just fine without you."

Todd chuckled. "That's not the way Grace sees it. She wants me here for as long as she's here."

"I don't know a way to rush Mother on this one," Amanda snapped. "I guess you'll just have to wait it out."

She turned and left the waiting room to take refuge in the women's room where she could be free of Todd's irritating presence.

Todd watched her go. She was wearing those tight jeans that drove him crazy. And that straight black hair hanging below her waist. He thought what she would look like if all that hair was covering only her skin and had to shift position in the chair. He was looking forward to being in the same house with Amanda for a few days. He could afford to be gone from Dallas that long, he figured.

There might even be times he and Amanda would be alone.

Todd licked his lips. He wanted her so much she was becoming an obsession with him. She liked him. He could tell. She was fighting it, but she wanted him. That was why she had gone to the rest room. He tried to imagine what she was doing in there and when she didn't return in the next several minutes, his imagination soared.

Grace was standing beside him before he knew she was in the room. "Where's my medicine?" she demanded.

He took the bag off the windowsill where Amanda had left it. "Here it is. Remember, the doctor said to take only two a day."

"He said I could have three if I need them," she reminded him, then turned away from him and went to find a water fountain.

Nathan was sitting wrapped in his thoughts on the chair nearest the nurse's station. Todd had no interest in talking to him and he was frankly glad Grace was gone. With luck she wouldn't find a fountain anywhere near and have to go all the way to the cafeteria for water to take the pills. Todd preferred being as far from Grace as possible.

He settled back in his chair and watched the door to the women's room and let his thoughts sink again into a mire of erotic possibilities.

Chapter Seven

Amanda sat with her brother, sister, and Todd in one of the hospital's small conference rooms. Dr. Hastings took a pen from his coat pocket and thumbed through the papers on the table between them.

"What do the tests indicate?" Grace asked impatiently. "That's why you called us to meet you here, isn't it?"

"Yes, of course." He returned the pen to his pocket and looked at each of them. "I'm afraid it's not good. I had hoped the tests would prove me wrong but instead they have reinforced my original prognosis. The injuries to your mother's brain have been very extensive."

"What does that mean?" Amanda asked.

Hastings spoke with reluctance. "One thing I don't like to do is destroy hope. There are such things as miracles. When you've been in the business as long as I have, you see them from time to time. But they aren't something you can count on. From the results of these tests, I don't expect Elizabeth to regain consciousness."

"Then you have to run some more tests," Grace said quickly.

Nathan ignored her. "And if she does regain consciousness?"

"She will never be herself again. Of that I'm positive. For now, Elizabeth is exhibiting some sporadic brain activity, so I can tell you she isn't brain dead. That's the closest thing to good news the tests revealed."

"Thank God," Grace sighed dramatically.

"She's lost a significant portion of her brain and the injury is irreversible. If she wakes from the coma she's in, she probably won't ever recognize any of you again."

"There's rehabilitation," Grace protested. "She could be taught to recognize us, to talk or whatever."

Hastings shook his head. "Not with the sort of damage she sustained. No, rehabilitation is completely out of the question."

"We'll pray," Grace said stubbornly. "We'll pray for her to get well."

Amanda and the others stared at her. They all knew Grace hadn't been inside a church since her wedding.

"Did your mother leave any instructions as to taking her off life support if that ever became an issue?"

"Take her off the machines?" Todd spoke up. "Wouldn't she die if we did that?"

"Of course she would," Grace snapped at him. "That's completely out of the question." She glared at the doctor.

Hastings nodded in answer to Todd's question. "Of course, before I would recommend such an action, I would have to be certain that she was brain dead, which isn't the case at this time."

"Then why bring it up?" Grace demanded.

"You have to be considering the possibility," Hastings explained. "I recommend that you all discuss what you want to do. I certainly won't force you to make a decision like that. I must tell you, however, that keeping her on life support is terribly expensive."

"We can afford it," Grace said angrily.

"I don't know if Mother ever considered that this might happen," Nathan said doubtfully. "Did she ever say anything to you, Amanda?"

"Never. Mother thought she would live forever." She felt a chill to think she would have to be part of the crucial decision. "Grace? Did she tell you how she felt about it?"

Grace broke down into hysterical sobs. "I won't listen to talk like this! Todd, get me out of here!"

Todd shifted his weight in his chair. "Doc, are you sure we need to talk about this? How expensive are you talking?"

"It could run around two thousand a day."

"Two thousand dollars?" Todd exclaimed.

"Or more," Hastings added. "I'm sorry. I wish it were different."

Grace glared at her husband. "It doesn't matter how much it costs to keep Mother alive. She's has tons of money and she must have insurance as well. We all know that. Even if she wasn't wealthy, I am, and I refuse to let her die!"

"I understand your feelings on this issue," Hastings said. "No one wants to have to make a decision like this. But insurance only pays a certain amount and no bank account can last forever. There comes a time when reality has to be faced."

"I'm leaving!" Grace stood and grabbed Todd's arm to pull him to his feet. "Come on, Todd!"

He reluctantly followed her from the room.

"I apologize for our sister," Amanda said to Dr. Hastings. "She obviously is very upset about Mother."

"I understand. I would be remiss in my duty, however, if I hadn't prepared you for what I believe to be inevitable."

Nathan stood and shook his hand. His face was drawn

as if he was having to fight hard to keep his own emotions in check. "Thank you. I know this wasn't easy for you, either."

"No, it wasn't." The doctor smiled sadly at Nathan and Amanda. "Your parents and I go back a long way."

"I think we ought to get a second opinion," Nathan said. "It's nothing personal, but on a matter of this magnitude, we need all the information we can get."

"I agree. I'll give you several names of men whose judgment I respect. If you like, I'll call them for you."

"No, I think I need to do that." Nathan touched Amanda's elbow to lead her out of the room.

She murmured good-bye to Hastings and walked in silence to the coffee shop.

"What do you think?" Nathan asked as he sipped his coffee.

"I don't know what to think. Grace is going to milk this for all it's worth." She grimaced. "I shouldn't have said that. I know she's hurting. We all are."

Nathan nodded. "It's funny, the way I feel about Mother. We were never close. Nothing I did ever pleased her, but I can't imagine a future without her."

Amanda met his eyes. "I feel the same. Except that she cares more for you than she does for me. I'm the black sheep of the family. That's why I'm reluctant to give an opinion of what we should do."

"We all feel that way for one reason or another. Grace is probably her favorite, but their relationship is rocky to say the least."

"Nathan," Amanda forced herself to say, "do you think my outburst on Mother's Day was somehow the cause of this?"

"Of course not. Mother's Day was weeks ago."

"I know, but Grace said that Mother had been having heart problems since that day. If that's true, she might

.ave run the red light because she was having a heart
.ttack."

"Nothing like that showed up on the tests Dr. Hastings
.an. He would have mentioned that."

"Maybe he didn't check her heart all that closely since
.he primary injury was to her head. I could be the reason
.he's near death."

"Don't do that to yourself," he said firmly. "It could
.lso be my fault. She called me at work last week and
.hewed me out again for not going out with Beatrice Her-
.ing."

"Why don't you? Go out with Beatrice, I mean. She's
pretty and seems friendly."

"She also lives in Atlanta, Georgia. Even if she lived here
.n Houston, I wouldn't go out with a woman my mother
picked for me."

Amanda studied his face. "Do you date anyone?"

"My love life isn't the question here. What are we going
to do about Mother?

"The bigger question is what are we going to do with
Grace?"

"I know." He sighed. "She goes into hysterics every time
she has an audience. Maybe the tears are real. I don't
know."

"They seem pretty artificial to me. You and I both know
Grace has always been able to cry at the slightest provoca-
tion."

"You're as different from each other as two people can
be." He turned the coffee cup on the table, cradling it in
his palms. "Do you realize this is one of the few times
we've talked, you and I, since we grew up?"

"It seems odd," she said with a small smile. "I guess we
need more practice."

He doggedly went back to the matter at hand. "I can't
be the one to decide about Mother and life support. Not

with the ambivalent feelings I have toward her. I might make the wrong decision and have to live with it for the rest of my life."

"I feel exactly the same way. Especially since the argument on Mother's Day."

"Grace won't decide."

"Eventually I guess we'll all have to face it. The decision will have to be unanimous."

He nodded. "In the meantime, I guess you and Grace should stay in town."

"What about you?"

"Galveston isn't that far away. I'll stay here as much as I can, but I'll divide my time between here and my home."

"No way," Amanda said insistently. "If I have to stay in the same house with Grace and Todd, you do, too. Your business can get along without you for a while."

He gave her a searching look. "Is Todd still giving you trouble?"

Amanda looked away. "He's trying to. I think I can handle him."

"I'll stay in town as much as possible. Years ago, I didn't know you needed protection, but I can be there for you now."

Amanda was touched by his caring words. "Thank you, Nathan. I didn't expect you to say that."

"Come on. We had better go to the house. Grace will be expecting us."

"I suppose." She was reluctant to go back to that house. So many bad memories were attached to it.

"I don't care what that doctor said, Mother isn't going to die," Grace said for the tenth time since returning home. "I was so embarrassed that you just sat there and listened to all that drivel!"

"What could I say?" Todd demanded. "Hastings is the doctor. I don't know what your mother's condition is. I couldn't contradict him."

"Of course you could. You could have come to my aid. refuse to take Mother off life support."

"Grace, be reasonable. Two thousand dollars a day, or more, he said! No one can afford that forever."

She turned on him. "We're talking about my mother's life. You're standing in her house, surrounded by her things and talking about letting her die!—or *worse.*"

Todd shook his head. "You hear only what you want to hear. I don't know why I bother trying. I only said that he huge expenses could eat up your inheritance. And Hastings didn't even include his fee and that of the other doctors or the operation."

"My inheritance! How can you think of money at a time like this? My mother's life is at stake!"

"Not if she becomes brain dead. If that happens, she's already gone and the machines will only be keeping her body alive."

"She's not brain dead! Dr. Hastings was very clear about that! We're going to get other opinions, as many as it takes to find some doctor who can bring Mother back to life!" She went to Elizabeth's chair and sat down. "The house feels so odd without her in it."

"It feels the same to me."

Grace frowned. "You have no heart, Todd. Go away and leave me in peace."

Todd was glad to escape. As he passed the entry hall, Amanda and Nathan came in. "I was wondering where you two were."

"We stayed at the hospital a while longer," Nathan said. "Dr. Hastings is going to give us the names of some specialists."

"Grace will be glad to hear that. I tried to tell her that

no one can afford to pay for expensive treatment indefinitely but she won't listen to me." Todd said with a nod continuing on his way to the kitchen.

Grace had heard the conversation and came out of the den. "So you finally got home."

Amanda turned to her. "I think it's important for us to know how Mother felt about living wills. She may have one for all we know. I'm going to ask her lawyer. Do you remember his name?"

"It's Clay Bennett," Grace said as if any good daughter would already know this. "I'm sure Mother has no such thing as a living will."

"Probably not, but it's worth asking. I'll call and make an appointment with him."

"Go ahead and ask, but don't expect me to go along with it," Grace said. "Even if Mother signed such a thing, she had no way of knowing it would be like this. For all we know, she could know everything that's going on and just not be able to communicate with us. No, I'm not going to agree to removing her from life support."

"Then what's the point of my asking?" Amanda countered.

"Do it for me," Nathan encouraged.

Grace looked from one to the other. "Well, you two have certainly become chummy. What's going on here?"

"Nothing, Grace. Sometimes family tragedies pull families back together," he replied.

"Nonsense. You two are scheming against me. You aren't going to take her off life support! Do you hear me?"

"Grace, listen to what you're saying," Amanda reasoned. "Nathan and I don't want to make that decision, either. But it may become necessary."

"Have you considered what people would think if they knew we did that?" Grace demanded.

"No," Amanda said honestly. "It never crossed my mind.

What do I care what people think? But I don't believe
Mother's friends would want her suffering prolonged. That
wouldn't be humane."

"See? See? You believe she can still think and feel, too, or
you wouldn't refer to it as her suffering!" Grace exclaimed
triumphantly.

Amanda shook her head. "I'm going up to rest. I'll be
down in time to help with dinner. It's Evelyn's day off."

She took the phone into her room, closing the door on
the cord the way she had as a teenager, and dialed her
home phone number. When Dakota answered, Amanda
lay back on the bed. "Hi, honey. I just got back from the
hospital."

"Are the results back on the tests?" his familiar voice
said.

Amanda wished she could touch him. "Yes, but it's not
good. She's not brain dead, but Dr. Hastings thinks it's only
a matter of time. Grace is throwing her usual tantrums."

"Do you want me to fly down there?"

"No, not yet."

"It's that bad? I expected a firm no."

She smiled into the receiver. "I'm okay. Nathan is going
to stay here at the house, too. I think we're becoming
closer. At least we've talked. That's more than I can say
about Grace."

"I'm glad you won't be alone with them. I particularly
don't want you alone with Todd."

"Don't worry. I can take care of myself." She tried to
sound more confident than she really was.

"All right, but I'm here if you need me."

"Okay. I love you."

"I love you, too."

She missed Dakota more than ever.

She returned the phone to its table in the hall and went
back to close herself in her room. Why hadn't he ever

mentioned marriage? As protective as he was of her wouldn't that be a natural progression in their relationship? Especially now that she was pregnant?

She ran her hands over her flat stomach. Their baby was safe and secure. It made her smile to think she had a tiny person who was half Dakota inside her. They were going to be wonderful parents. This child and the future ones would be raised with love and gentleness.

"I promise," she whispered to her unborn baby.

"No, Miss Wainwright, your mother never drew up a living will."

"She did her legal work with you, didn't she?" Amanda asked.

"Yes, but I'm not at liberty to discuss that with you." He smiled to soften his words.

"I would never ask you to tell me something like that." Amanda was a bit shocked that he would even suggest it and she wondered if Grace had called him with that question. No, she told herself, Grace was too adamant that Elizabeth was going to live. "Dr. Hastings has told us that Mother probably won't recover. We wanted to know if she had any feelings about maintaining life support."

"I'm certain she must have. She has very definite ideas about everything. She never discussed them with me, however. It's possible, of course, that she drew up a living will on her own. It's not necessary to have a lawyer do that. You can merely fill out a form and have it witnessed."

"What would she have done with it?"

"I have no idea. Are you able to look in her safe-deposit box?"

Amanda shook her head. "Grace called the bank. None of us can get into the box because we aren't on the list. There was no reason we should be."

"I thought that was probably the case." He waited patiently to see if she had any other questions.

Amanda picked up her purse. "I guess I should be going. There are so many decisions that need to be made and none of us has a clue what Mother would want us to do."

"I truly wish I could be of help."

Amanda thanked the lawyer as she left his office.

The air outside was already hot, though it was only May. She had almost forgotten how early summer came to Houston. Large white clouds were mounding in preparation for the usual afternoon thundershower.

Amanda went to her rental car and drove back to the house.

Grace was waiting for her. "Well? What did Mr. Bennett say?"

"Mother never talked to him about a living will or her wishes if she was ever put on life support."

"Why on earth couldn't he have simply told us that over the phone and saved you a trip downtown?"

"He's probably after money," Todd said from the chair by the den window. "That's the only reason to have her drive down there."

Grace frowned at Todd. "You always believe the worst in people. That's so irritating."

Todd went back to reading his newspaper and Grace turned back to Amanda. "I've called in a specialist, a Dr. Edward Santon. He's going to review Mother's tests and get back to us. I told him to run whatever extra tests he thinks are necessary. Dr. Hastings is fine as far as he goes, but he's not a neurologist and is probably wrong about Mother's condition. I expect an entirely different prognosis from Dr. Santon."

"I hope you're right," Amanda said without conviction.

Grace watched her leave the room, then went to sit back in Elizabeth's chair and picked up a magazine. She had already read the magazine, but since it was almost certainl the one Elizabeth had laid aside before driving to th accident, she wanted to read it again. It was like a lin between her mother and herself.

Grace genuinely missed Elizabeth. While their relation ship was far from smooth, she loved her mother more than she loved anyone. She regretted having married Todd and would have preferred staying in her mother's house. If she had been around her more often Grace could have learned to be more like Elizabeth and in that way earned her love

She touched the pages of the magazine where she thought Elizabeth had been likely to touch them. She could imagine Elizabeth's hands under her own. If Eliza beth were actually there, Grace never would have dared to touch her because her mother hated to be touched for any reason. But touching the place where her fingers had held the magazine was perfectly permissible.

Tears came to Grace's eyes and this time they were real.

"I've run some extra tests," Dr. Santon said as he seated himself behind his expensive oak-and-leather desk. He was a young man but his smile was fatherly. "It's not quite as dark a picture as you've been told."

"I knew it!" Grace exclaimed. "She's going to be all right!"

Dr. Santon held up his hand to slow her down. "Now don't get your hopes too high. I didn't say that."

"What *did* you mean?" Nathan asked.

"She may not have lost as much brain function as Dr. Hastings thought. The damage is extensive—I'm not implying that it isn't—but the new tests show some definite brain activity."

Amanda leaned forward. "Are you saying she could recover?"

"Not completely, I'm afraid." He made a gesture of resigning to fate. "But on the other hand, the brain is a tricky mechanism. It can do things that seem impossible at times." He indicated several pictures framed on the far wall. "Those are photos of my miracles, as I call them."

Amanda went to look at them closer. Smiling men, women, and several children looked back at her from the frames. "These are your patients?"

"Former patients," he corrected. "All of them were expected to die or be so damaged that they would never lead normal lives. Every one of them beat the odds."

"There aren't many of them," Amanda said.

Dr. Santon obviously had a different opinion. "On the contrary, there are more than medical science could have predicted. What I'm trying to say is that your mother could recover enough of her functions to eventually leave the hospital."

"That would be wonderful!" Grace gushed.

Nathan looked at Dr. Santon. "I don't understand why your prognosis is so different from Dr. Hastings's."

"He's a specialist," Grace said reprovingly. "A neurologist. Dr. Hastings is only a general practitioner."

Dr. Santon gave her a beatific smile. "I'm not saying my colleague is wrong. Only that your mother does have a chance."

"What should we do?" Grace asked, sitting on the edge of her chair as if she were prepared to jump up.

"We have to give it more time." Dr. Santon stood and brought a plastic model of a human brain to the desk. "Your mother is injured here on the left side." He indicated the curve of the cerebrum. "There is a great deal of bruising. The operation relieved some of the pressure, but we may have to go back in at a later date and do it again."

"Another operation?" Todd asked. "While she's still in a coma?"

"I guarantee we won't let her feel any pain," Dr. Santon said with impeccable bedside manner.

"Is that advisable with a condition as precarious as hers?" Nathan asked.

"We have to do whatever is necessary," Grace snapped at him. To the doctor she said, "We'll do anything. Price is no object."

"Grace!" Todd objected.

"I trust you," Grace continued. "If anyone can bring Mother back to us, I believe you can."

Dr. Santon smiled more broadly. "I believe I can, too."

Amanda's eyes met Nathan's and she saw that her brother had no more faith in the doctor than she did.

Chapter Eight

Dakota held the phone with the same hand in which he held his extra paintbrushes. "What do you mean you're going to have to stay indefinitely?"

"I don't trust the new doctor," Amanda explained. "His answers seemed too pat. His name wasn't on the list Dr. Hastings gave us. Grace found him on her own."

"I don't understand why that means you have to stay there." He added a slash of yellow to the canvas and narrowed his eyes to study the painting. It was one of the New Age paintings for which he was so well known. He was trying to capture the feminine spirit of the universe and it was proving elusive. Amanda's phone call wasn't helping. He smoothed the yellow into a contour that suggested a woman's face. The earth and moon fit into the design so that it seemed she was in the act of thinking them into existence. He finally relaxed, then realized what Amanda had just said. "You want me to send your painting materials?"

"I wouldn't do this if I didn't think it was necessary. I have a studio here. Mother let me turn one of the unused bedrooms into a studio when I was in school and it's still the way I left it."

"You won't be able to work there," he said bluntly.

"Of course I can. A studio is a studio. This one isn't so bad. It has good light, even if the room isn't as large as ours." She laughed. "Not many are."

He put his brush in the jar of turpentine and wiped it on a cotton rag to clean it. "You're making a big mistake. Come home. If your mother gets worse, you can be there in a matter of hours."

"Hours are a long time," she argued. "It's not that I want to do this, you know."

"No one is forcing you," he pointed out. "Come home."

"What if she wakes up and asks for me and I'm all the way out there on the West Coast? It could be the last time I have a chance to talk to her. Can't you see that?"

Dakota put down his brush and frowned. "It's not going to happen, Amanda. I'm not saying she won't ever come out of the coma, but if she does, nothing will have changed. She's not going to suddenly become the mother you wish she was. She's still not going to accept you."

There was a long silence on the other end.

"Amanda?" Dakota realized too late he had been too frank. "Honey, I'm sorry. You caught me at a bad time." Sometimes when he was working hard he was short on tact.

"You're having a bad time?" she exclaimed over the phone. *"You're* having a bad time? I'm here in the same house with Grace and Todd while my mother is dying in the hospital and I caught you at a bad time?"

"Amanda, I didn't mean . . ." The sound of her slamming down the receiver stopped his words. "Shit!" he growled, then glared at the canvas. It wasn't right and he couldn't seem to fix it. He threw down his brushes into the tray and started cleaning his hands. There was one thing he could fix.

If Amanda wouldn't come to him, he was going to her.

Amanda stayed angry for hours. She and Dakota had argued before, but never long distance. This time she couldn't go to him and put her arms around him and coax him into a better mood or to allow him to coax her.

She dialed the number and waited. After what seemed to be an eternity, the answering machine came on. He wasn't even there!

All Amanda's demons flew into her mind. He had been in an accident or a burglar had broken in and murdered him, all because she had hung up on him in anger. Or he had left her for another woman because she had been too shrewish. Or he had never loved her in the first place because she wasn't worthy.

Amanda tried to calm her thoughts. She knew he loved her and that he wouldn't go running off to another woman simply because they had an argument. As arguments went, it hadn't even been that big. More likely that he was in the other end of the apartment or in the bathroom. He could have stepped out to go grocery shopping. There was, some reasonable explanation why he wasn't there to answer the phone.

Several minutes later, she called again with the same result. That ruled out the bathroom as well as the other end of the apartment theory. Shopping. He must have gone shopping. Or he was so angry with her he wouldn't answer because he knew she was calling.

Again the panic rose. Again Amanda battled it back down. All her insecurities were overwhelming her. Why did she think she was worthy of any man loving her? Of putting up with her quick temper? It didn't matter that in reality Amanda's temper wasn't particularly quick or that she normally felt she was worthy of anyone. All her mother's remonstrances normally came back to her: she wasn't perfect, she didn't conform to much of anything, and she would never be able to hold a man because she refused to learn how to manipulate one into doing as she wanted.

Amanda's breathing was shallow and she was trembling as if she had been running. Her skin felt cold and damp. She hadn't had a panic attack in a long time but she was having a giant one now.

Although she wanted to hide in her room and wait for the end of the world, she forced herself to go to the den to be with Nathan.

She was relieved to find him alone. When he saw her, he smiled. "What's up? Did Grace say something to upset you?"

She closed the door and sat on the chair nearest him. "No, I haven't seen Grace."

"Are you okay?" he asked, looking at her more closely.

"It's just a panic attack. I'll be all right in a few minutes. I have them from time to time."

"I've had them myself," he told her. "Just breathe deep and remind yourself that you're safe."

"Am I?"

He went to the small refrigerator beneath the wet bar and brought her a canned drink. "Here. Something carbonated may help. And yes, you're safe." He waited until she drank several swallows of soda, then said, "Are you better now?"

She nodded, feeling foolish. "I shouldn't have come running in here like the boogeyman was after me. Sorry."

"There's no need to apologize. It's nice to know you have moments of doubt like the rest of us."

Amanda stared at him. "What are you talking about? I'm full of doubts."

"You'd never know. Of the three of us, you're the one who has always struck me as having it all together. Well, except for Mother's Day," he amended teasingly.

She smiled. "Yeah, except for then. Nathan, I'm probably the least together one in the family. I don't know where you got that idea."

"You never seem to need help. Not with anything."

Amanda thought about that. "That's because you don't really know me. Sometimes I feel as if I'm coming apart at the seams. That my world is like a balloon that's about to go fluttering around the room and fizzle out. It's not easy being an artist."

"No? I thought it would be."

"Well, it is if you don't care whether you have any money or whether there will ever be any in the future. I don't have the security of a pay check, no company insurance, no retirement plan. I love to paint, but I'll have to do it for the rest of my life unless we really make it big." She smiled wryly. "I say we're going to, but there's always the chance that we'll give a showing and no one will come."

"Who is we? Does Dakota have anything to do with it?"

She drew in a deep breath and let it out. She did feel better now and someone in her family was finally asking her about her life. "Yes. Dakota is a very big part of my life."

"Do you want to tell me about him?"

"Right now, he's angry with me. That's what brought on the panic attack. I never feel entirely safe. We've never argued over the phone before, and when I tried to call him back, he didn't answer."

"Maybe you need to give him time to cool down."

She shook her head. "He doesn't have a cool-down sort of temper."

"Is he also an artist?"

"You'd love his work. He's wonderful! His canvases sing! Wait until you see what we're doing for the exhibit. It's fresh and wonderful." She laughed. "I sound like a school-girl with a crush. I can't explain Dakota. You'll just have to meet him."

"Why hasn't he ever come with you?"

"You'll understand that when you meet him, too. Mother would have gone into orbit. And now that we're actually having a conversation about our lives, who is Cody?"

For a moment Nathan seemed to pull back, though he never actually moved. He opened his mouth to answer when the den door flew open.

"Why are you two locked up in here?" Grace asked suspiciously. "You know Mother never wanted us to have private conversations behind closed doors."

"There's nothing wrong with wanting privacy from time to time," Nathan said. He didn't look pleased to see his older sister.

She sat on the couch. "So? What are you talking about?"

"My upcoming art exhibits," Amanda risked saying.

"Oh. I thought it was something interesting. Nathan, I want to go see Mother and Todd won't take me. Will you drive me to the hospital?"

"Why don't you drive yourself? You know the way," he replied.

"I don't want to go alone. Seeing her like that upsets me so much I'm afraid I'll have an accident, too."

"Are you saying that you feel unsure of yourself, too?" Amanda asked in surprise.

"Don't be ridiculous. I only want a ride to the hospital. Nathan, are you coming or not?"

"Okay. But we aren't going to stay long. I'm going to

run down to Galveston tonight and I don't **want** to get there too late."

Amanda got to her feet. She wasn't going to be left alone in the house with Todd. "I'll come, too."

"In those jeans?" Grace asked disparagingly. "Well, come on. I don't want to wait for you to change."

Nathan and Amanda exchanged a glance before following her. At least, Amanda thought, it was a start.

Early the next morning the doorbell rang and Amanda went to answer it. When the door swung open, Dakota stood there on the porch. Without a word, he pulled her to him, kissed her, and held her as if he would never let her go.

"You're here!" she said needlessly, her words muffled against his chest. "I'm so glad!"

"I'm sorry I upset you."

She laughed. "You flew halfway across the country to tell me that?"

"That and the fact that I'm staying here for as long as you do. You'll go crazy in Houston and I have to protect my painting partner."

She stared up at him. "I tried to call and apologize."

"I left right after we talked." He nodded toward a pile of boxes tied with string. "I brought all the things I thought we would need. I'm assuming you have easels in your studio here. I couldn't get one on the plane."

"Yes." She suddenly realized they were still standing on the porch. "Come in."

Dakota bent to pick up the assortment of boxes and stepped into the house. His size dwarfed the entryway. She couldn't stop staring at him. "You're really here!"

Grace came into the room. When she saw Dakota, her smile vanished. "May we help you?" she asked warily.

Amanda laughed. "It's okay, Grace. This is Dakota."

Grace didn't come forward to greet him. "Who?"

Todd and Nathan heard the voices and came to investi
gate. Todd's reaction to Dakota was exactly like Grace's
Amanda repeated, "This is Dakota. Dakota, this is Grace
Todd, and my brother Nathan."

Dakota leaned forward to shake Nathan's hand. Todd
and Grace didn't offer theirs. He drew back, his dark eyes
speculative.

Amanda smiled up at him. His long dark hair was pulled
back in a colorful woven band and he wore the lightning
bolt earring made for him by one of their friends. His T
shirt fit him like a second skin and his muscles rippled as
he shifted the heavy box from one arm to the other. He
looked as if he had come straight from the western plains

"Who exactly are you?" Grace asked frigidly, horrified
at his appearance.

"Dakota is my . . . friend." Amanda found she was losing
her nerve even with Dakota at her side. Although Grace
didn't resemble Elizabeth, their ways were so similar, old
habits were being triggered in Amanda. "We paint
together."

Dakota looked at her with wry amusement. In his deep,
resonant voice he added, "We also live together."

"Live together!" Grace gasped. "Amanda, is this true?"

Amanda's eyes met Dakota's and she nodded with a
smile. "Yes. We live together and we're in love. And we
also paint together." She looked at Nathan.

He stopped staring and grinned. "I think I understand
now why you didn't come with Amanda before. Come in
and sit down. Let me help you with those boxes."

"They're heavy. Maybe I should carry them to the
studio."

"It's upstairs. I'll show you the way," Amanda said.

"No, no," Nathan said, his eyes sparkling with laughter.

"You stay here and let me show him. Come on, Dakota."
He led the way upstairs before Amanda could stop him.

Amanda turned back to Grace and Todd. With a shrug
she said, "Now you know what I've been doing in L.A."

"You live with him?" Grace exclaimed. "He's . . . What
is he—Indian?"

"Half of him is. His mother is Choctaw."

Todd seemed not to have grasped that part of the conversation. "You paint together?" he asked.

"We have a joint exhibition coming up. That's why he
brought all those boxes. They're our painting supplies.
We'll work here in the studio."

"You can't paint here!" Grace exploded.

"Of course I can. I painted here for years."

"Not with that . . . Indian!"

"Are you having some problem with Dakota's ancestry?
A lot of people are part Indian."

"Not in this house! He looks so . . . savage. He can't
possibly be an artist." She shook her head firmly.

"No? He is. In fact, he's the best artist I've ever known."
Amanda looked up the stairs after the two men, though
they were already out of sight. "I didn't expect him to fly
down from L.A."

"He can just fly back again," Grace said firmly.

"He's staying." Amanda crossed her arms across her
chest and dared Grace to argue.

Todd came to the bottom of the stairs and looked up.
His manner was that of someone who had come in during
the middle of a movie and didn't quite understand the
plot.

"Why aren't you saying anything?" Amanda asked him
suspiciously.

He shook his head. "Grace, do you want me to drive
you to the hospital?"

"I've been trying to get you out of the house for the

past hour. Yes, that's exactly what I want." Grace gav
Amanda another frown and went to get her purse.

Amanda found herself alone with Todd. To her amaze
ment, he said, "Will you meet me later in the kitchen? W
could pick up where we left off."

She turned and ran up the stairs. He would dare sa
such a thing to her with Dakota in the house? She wa
furious, but she didn't want Dakota to know. At least no
the minute he got there.

They were in the studio. Nathan sat on the window sea
watching Dakota unpack the box of rolled canvases an
disassembled stretcher frames. Dakota smiled when he sav
her. "This is a good studio."

"See? I told you."

"Grace is taking all this better than I would hav
thought." Nathan said, grinning at Dakota. "I'm glad
you're here. You may just be what this family needs."

"Need me or not, I'm here." Dakota straightened. "
love your sister. We've been living together for a year. She
was afraid to tell any of you."

"We all have our secrets, it seems," Nathan said.

"What does that mean?" Amanda asked as she went t
stand by Dakota.

"I'll explain another time. I imagine the two of you have
things to talk about. I'll go watch Grace pick on Todd."
Still grinning, he left.

"I like your brother," Dakota said. "He's not at all wha
I expected him to be. But Grace and Todd are."

"Good. I wouldn't want you to be disappointed." She
pretended to frown at him. "I ought to throw that pain
box at you. Do you have any idea how worried I've been
I pictured you in hospitals and morgues and with loose
women and all sorts of things."

He laughed. "Loose women?"

"You know what I mean." She swatted at his arm. "You worried me!"

"You hung up on me. You've never done that before. I decided it was time to see for myself what was going on here."

"I'll bet you just got lonesome for my home cooking and sparkling conversation."

"Maybe the conversation." He pulled her to him and kissed her in a way that made her head spin. "God, I've missed you. I don't ever want to be away from you again."

She nodded, too overcome by emotion to speak. She held him tightly.

"Where do we sleep? Not all of this is paint and canvas."

She led him to her bedroom and stepped aside to let him view it.

"Damn!" he gasped. "It's so *pink.*"

"Would I lie? Can you taste the peppermint in the air? Every morning I expect to wake up and find a gaggle of ballerinas in here."

"They come in gaggles? Like geese?"

"Maybe it's a pride of ballerinas or a herd. You'll see. The entire effect hasn't soaked in yet."

"Just tell me it doesn't glow in the dark." He went to the ruffled lace curtains and fingered them warily.

She laughed. "You look so out of place in this room."

"Thank goodness."

More seriously she said, "I really am glad you came. And I really did think you had left me."

He looked at her. "I'm never going to leave you. What does it take to convince you?"

"I guess coming here to brave my family with me. That's one good way to convince me."

"I would have been here every visit for the past year," he reminded her. "It wasn't my idea to stay behind."

"Sometimes I guess I don't know what's good for me." She went into his embrace again.

"I like Evelyn," Dakota said as they undressed that night. "I like Nathan, too."

"Evelyn is like the mother I never had. And I've gotten to know Nathan better on this trip. He has a secret, too. He always evades telling me about this Cody person."

Dakota grinned. "Maybe because it's none of your business."

"It's more than that. And there was that remark he made in the studio about us both having secrets. I'm really curious."

"We could wait until he goes to Galveston and follow him," Dakota suggested with a smile. He pulled his shirt off and tossed it onto a chair.

"All those years I lived in this room, I wondered if anything exciting would ever happen to me," Amanda said as she watched him. "All those speculations would have been answered if I could have seen you in here the way you are now."

He unfastened his jeans and came to her. "I'm glad you have a double bed. I was afraid it would be a twin." He bent and placed a string of kisses along her neck.

Amanda felt her pulses leap but she evaded him. "I'm going to go brush my teeth. I'll be back in a minute."

"You can brush them later." He pulled her back and laced his fingers through her hair.

Amanda wanted him. She kissed him quickly and went to the dresser.

"A nightgown?" He said in surprise as he saw what she had pulled out, "I didn't know you owned one."

She didn't meet his eyes. "I always sleep in a gown when I'm here. This room doesn't lend itself to nudity."

"We could retrain it." He tried again to take her in his arms.

Amanda put her hand firmly against his chest. "Not tonight, Dakota. Not here."

He pulled back but didn't release her. "What do you mean, not here? We're alone. This is your bedroom. Surely Grace doesn't do a bed check every night."

"I feel inhibited here."

"That would be something new," he said with a laugh. Then, "Are you serious? You don't want to make love with me in this house?"

"I can't." She frowned at him and tried to step away.

"They know I'm in here with you. Grace and Todd are going to be together in their room eventually. I'll bet Nathan and his Cody go into a bedroom from time to time."

"Don't let Grace hear you say that. She's convinced Cody is a man."

"I'm not concerned about Grace's hang-ups. Did you hear her ask if I knew how to tan hides?"

"Yes, and I also heard you say our wigwam is made of canvas, not hides. You shouldn't encourage her."

"I'm trying to encourage *you*," he said. "Amanda, they know we live together."

"But what would Mother say?" Her eyes widened. "Did I really say that?"

"I'm afraid so. Both of us couldn't have imagined it." He had dropped his arms to his side and was regarding her as if she was a stranger.

"I'm sorry, Dakota. This house just affects me strangely." She stepped closer to him and put her arms around him. "I love you. I want you."

He put his arms around her gingerly. "Are you going to sleep in that gown?"

She smiled. "No."

"If anyone comes in, I'll toss them back out."

"I always sleep with the door locked here."

He was quiet for a minute. "Okay. I'll lock it for you." He went to the door and twisted the lever, then tested it by pulling on it a few times. "All secure." He went to the windows and felt for the hardware. "All locked tight. Nobody can get in." He turned off the lights. Moonlight filled the room. "Now if I can just find you, everything will be great."

She pulled off her blouse and tossed it aside. "I'll bet you can if you try."

He laughed softly. "I've always had good night vision."

"I'm counting on that." She pulled back the covers and waited for him.

When Dakota lay beside her, she noticed he had removed his jeans somewhere between the light switch and the bed. "Now I know why we have a king-size bed," he said. "My feet are hanging over the end."

She laughed softly. "I guess we'll just have to sleep all tangled up so neither of us falls off the bed."

He laughed, too. "If we have to, we have to. That's one thing about us Indians, we're stoic. I'll have to point that out to Grace tomorrow."

"You're also full of baloney." She nestled in his arms and kissed him with all the longing in her soul.

Chapter Nine

"You're going back to the hospital? Not painting?" Dakota asked as he pulled canvas taut over a stretcher and tacked it in place.

"I have to. I've only been there once today." Amanda frowned. "I don't like having to explain where I'm going and why. You don't ask me to explain at home."

"At home, you usually stay put and paint. To go to the hospital, you have to wash off the paint, change clothes, be gone for at least an hour, come back, and change back into your painting clothes before you can start work again. I just thought one visit a day was enough."

"Grace can't be expected to be there all the time. Nathan has to check on his Houston stores or drive to Galveston frequently. I have to hold up my end."

"Grace isn't there all that often. She just tells you she is. You're up here painting and don't know if she's in the house or not. A few times when you thought she was still gone, I've seen her car pull in thirty minutes before. And sometimes she's carrying packages as if she's been shopping and not to the hospital.''

"You're spying on Grace?''

"I don't care if Grace is here, at the hospital, or on the moon. The point is, she has you spending most of the time at the hospital.''

Amanda drew herself up. "I've never found it necessary to count who spends the most time with Mother.''

"But that's just it. You can only be with her five minutes every hour. The rest is spent in the waiting room or in traffic. Even when you're in her room, she doesn't know you're there.''

"We don't know that.''

He put the canvas aside and came to her. "Honey, let's not argue. If you want to go, you should go. But don't do it because Grace says you have to.''

"I don't!'' Amanda turned away from him. She hated going to the hospital and seeing Elizabeth lying there looking like a stranger.

He put his hands on her shoulders to turn her back to him but she shrugged them off. He didn't reach out to her again. "You haven't done much work since I've been here. You haven't finished one canvas.''

She whirled to face him. "Will you stop nagging me about finishing those paintings? I was an artist before I ever met you and I know how to work!''

He frowned back at her. "I don't nag you. Apparently someone has to remind you how important this upcoming show is. If the paintings in this series aren't finished, we'll be wasting what could be our only chance to make it big.''

"Then paint more of yours!''

"They're supposed to be equal!'' He glared at her, then said with an effort, "I don't want to fight with you.''

"Then quit making me angry!''

Dakota went back to the canvas he was stretching. "Okay.

Have it your own way. Go to the hospital and sit there for hours. I'll do extra paintings and maybe no one will notice.'' His voice was bordering on sarcasm.

"Why are you doing this to me!"

"Because someone has to talk sense into you. The world goes on, Amanda. Your mother could be like this for years! Are you going to stay here forever neglecting a promising career to sit beside a woman who doesn't know if you're there or not? Damn it, when she was conscious, she treated you like dirt and you're going to throw away your career for her?''

Amanda stared at him. Her anger was so great she couldn't speak. Worst of all, she knew he was right. Without saying a word to him, she turned and left the room. She had the satisfaction of hearing the canvas clatter to the floor, which meant her silence had scored a point.

She drove to the hospital, her anger building. Traffic was terrible and it took her almost an hour to reach the medical center and find a place to park.

She arrived in the ICU waiting room just as that hour's visitation time was over. Seething, she dropped into a chair to wait until she could see her mother.

Dakota was right. She was wasting her time in the hospital. The only reason she had come back after her morning visit was because Grace had complained that she had to shoulder the burden all alone. What was the point of coming here at all? The chances of Elizabeth waking up during those short five minutes was minuscule. She was in town and could arrive at the hospital quickly if one of the nurses or the doctor called. After four weeks of waiting and watching and seeing no change whatsoever in Elizabeth, she doubted that her mother would ever regain consciousness in spite of Dr. Santon's optimistic words.

Grace was supposed to be at the hospital but she wasn't in the waiting room. It was possible they had passed on the streets or the halls, but that wasn't likely. She remembered what Dakota had said about Grace sometimes arriving with shopping bags when she had ostensibly been at the hospital. It wouldn't be unlike Grace to take advantage of her.

Amanda rested her head back against the wall. What really hurt was the fact that her mother hadn't loved her before and that if she regained consciousness, she probably wouldn't love her now, either.

She sighed miserably. Why *didn't* her mother love her? She couldn't think of anything she had ever done that was of great enough magnitude to destroy a mother's love. Amanda hadn't been a model child. She certainly had been more rebellious than Grace or Nathan. But she hadn't been really bad. She knew other parents who loved their children even when those children were the scourge of the neighborhood and probably destined to see the inside of a prison. So how did she deserve Elizabeth's censure?

There was no answer to the question. She knew because she had asked it all her life. And since it was true, why was she wasting her time in the waiting room when she could be in the studio working on canvases that could establish her name throughout America and possibly even abroad?

That one had no answer, either. She waited with growing impatience for the nurse to tell her she could go back for the prescribed five-minute visit.

When at last the nurse came, Amanda went to the now-familiar cubicle and stared down at her mother. Elizabeth didn't look at all like herself. The bruises had faded and the swelling was gone on her forehead, the stitches had healed, but she still looked unfamiliar. Her black hair was clumped together and greasy-looking against the pillow. Without her weekly beauty shop-appointments, it was slowly reverting to its natural gray. The skin on her face, neck, and arms was slack and pallid. This couldn't be her immaculate, domineering mother.

She sat in the chair beside the bed and touched Elizabeth's hand. The fingers lay flaccid on the sheet. Amanda noted that Elizabeth's fingernails were no longer the perfectly smooth ovals they had once been. She would have to remember to bring nail clippers on her next visit.

Amanda sat there without speaking, though Grace had firmly instructed her that she wanted Elizabeth to hear their voices nonstop during the visits. There was nothing to say to this stranger. Elizabeth's eyelids fluttered as they did occasionally. These flutterings always gave Grace hope, but Dr. Hastings had explained to Amanda they were normal muscular twitches and not an indication of anything else.

After a while the nurse came into the cubicle. "Time's up," she said.

Amanda sat there a few more seconds. As she rose, she asked, "Has there been any change?"

The nurse shook her head.

"Thank you."

Instead of returning to the waiting room, Amanda went back to her car and drove to the house.

Grace sought out Dr. Santon and cornered him for a conference while no one else in her family was around.

"How is Mother doing today?" she asked in tones that implied she was the only one in the family capable of truly understanding.

"She may be improving slightly," he said with the smile that told her he, too, thought she was singularly capable of comprehending his words.

"I knew it! I'm so glad Dr. Hastings didn't convince us

to take her off life support. We could have killed her!''
Grace's green eyes grew round at the dire prospect.

"Frank Hastings is a good doctor,'' Santon said slowly
as if he didn't really mean his words but felt compelled to
voice them. "He's just getting on in years.''

"I know. I've told Mother countless times to find a
younger physician. Someone who is up on the latest tech-
niques.''

"There is something to be said for age and experience,''
Santon said doubtfully, "but I'm more familiar with the
newest innovations in medicine. Why, I trained on equipment that hadn't been thought of when Dr. Hastings was
in medical school.''

"What improvement do you see in Mother? Have her
brain waves become more constant?''

"No, in fact, they seems to have dropped slightly. That's
not to say she won't gain consciousness. As I've told you,
coma cases can fool everyone by suddenly opening their
eyes and coming back to the world. That's how I think of
it. When they are in a coma, they seem to be hanging
between this world and the next. I feel it's my duty to bring
them back.''

"Tell me. What changes have you seen?''

"Her skin tone seems to be better and so is her color.
She's not as ashen as she was a day or two ago.''

"That's it? There's nothing else?''

"We have to take it inch by inch,'' he assured her.
"There's no hurrying these things. I still hope that eventually we may be able to remove her from life support.''

"When she regains her mental abilities, you mean.''

"Well, we can't hold out much hope there, I'm afraid.
As you know, her damage is extensive. But she may live.''

Grace frowned. "Are you saying she may live, but as a
vegetable? That she won't regain her ability to function?''

"That's pretty much it, I'm afraid. But as long as there's

ife, there's hope. And there are three of you to share the
work involved in caring for her."

"But none of us live in the same town. I've assumed that
when she recovers, she'll be able to live alone as she has
for years."

"No, no," Santon said hastily. "I never said that she
would improve to that extent. No, her brain damage is
such that she will never be completely independent again.
She will have to be cared for."

"You mean she'll improve to the point of being able to
fly to visit first one of us, then another?"

"No, she will have to remain at one place. She would
need an ambulance for transport." He smiled at her. "As
the eldest, I assume you will want to care for her in your
home. I only meant the others will be able to help financially."

"I can assure you that Mother is quite able to pay for
her own expenses. She's quite wealthy." Grace's mind was
reeling. She had thought all along that Elizabeth would
return to more or less her former self.

"She's very fortunate. Medical costs can be astronomical.
I think it's a shame, but I'm caught in the system like
everyone else."

"Yes." Grace wondered for the first time just what Santon was charging them. She hadn't opened the bills
because they were addressed to Elizabeth and she assumed
that her mother would take care of them once she was out
of the hospital. Grace wasn't certain how much money
Elizabeth had in savings and investments, but she was certain that even great wealth could be used up. "How long
do you estimate until she is able to leave ICU?"

"I have no way of determining that." He smiled at her.
"She's a lucky lady to have such a loving daughter as
yourself. You might want to contact her attorney and look

into having her declared incompetent so you can take over her finances."

"Declare Mother incompetent?" The very idea was frightening. If Elizabeth did somehow manage to recover and found that Grace had done such a thing, she would be livid. "Perhaps it would be more appropriate if Nathan took care of that."

"Whoever does it will have control of her estate and responsibility for paying her medical bills and whatever other expenses she has."

Grace nodded as if she already knew this. She didn't like the idea of Nathan having control of everything and it was out of the question that Amanda should do it. That gypsy she was living with would probably spend every cent of the Wainwright fortune. No, Grace was the most logical person to take control. "You've given me a lot to think about, Dr. Santon."

He reached out and patted her arm. "Let me know if I can be of further service."

She nodded absently. If she took control of Elizabeth's fortune, did that mean Elizabeth would have to live at Grace's house? Couldn't nurses be hired to watch after her at her own home here in Houston? But there was no way to know if she was being cared for if Grace was in Dallas. She had a great deal to think about indeed.

That night Grace waited until Amanda and Dakota had gone up to bed and Nathan had left for Galveston, then she went into the den to search for Elizabeth's will.

She went through the desk and even pulled the drawers completely out to be certain the document hadn't dropped behind them. She wasn't too surprised when she didn't find it. Elizabeth had always kept her important papers in the wall safe. The problem was that Grace had never known the combination.

She went to the picture that hinged against the wall

and opened it to reveal the safe. Although she tried a combination of the numbers in their birthdays, anniversaries, their phone numbers and zip codes, nothing made the safe open. Grace hadn't expected it to be that easy but it had been worth a try.

Halfheartedly she went to the bookshelf and looked through several of the books Elizabeth might have written the combination in. She had no luck until she noticed one that had belonged to her father, but that hadn't been moved to the less accessible shelves as the others had been. Inside was a series of numbers. Grace went back to the safe and spun the dial. It opened soundlessly.

Inside was a stack of documents and other official papers. The deed to the house, other deeds to property dating back to Grace's childhood years, several coins her father had considered valuable enough to safeguard. And Elizabeth's will.

Grace took it to a chair and turned on the lamp to read it better. The notarized date was recent and Clay Bennett's name was signed at the bottom. Elizabeth had drawn up the will after the family Christmas visit.

Nervously Grace started to read. In a few short sentences her heart began to hammer. She was the sole beneficiary. Amanda and Nathan were mentioned, but they were left nothing at all. Grace would inherit it all.

She let her hands drop into her lap and she stared off into space. She would inherit a fortune.

A sound from the kitchen drew her attention and she hurriedly went back to the safe and returned the will to its proper place. She didn't want the others to know its contents for fear they would leave and go back to their own lives.

No, it was better to let them go on believing they might inherit the Wainwright fortune. Amanda and Nathan were useful in their visits to the hospital. If Grace was there alone, the family's absence would be noted because she found it too boring to spend so many hours in the waiting room. It never occurred to Grace that her brother and sister might not be as financially motivated as she was.

Grace turned to find Todd had come into the room, a sandwich in his hand. She gave him a cool look. "Don't get crumbs all over everything," she warned him, then left the den and went upstairs.

There was so much for her to think about. For one thing, since she would inherit everything, it would be logical for her to move to Houston. In her opinion, the family home was much nicer than the one she had in Dallas. River Oaks was the grandest addition in Houston and the Wainwright house one of the largest on the carefully tended streets. It had the patina of old money, and Todd, no matter how hard he tried, would never be anything but nouveau riche. He could stay in Dallas and she could live in Houston without the unfortunate business of obtaining a divorce.

Grace could step into Elizabeth's shoes without so much as a flurry on the surface of society. She would belong to the same clubs and support the same charities and it would be as if Elizabeth had never left.

It took only moments before reality crept in. That would be a glorious picture if it weren't for the specter of Elizabeth lying in her room, fed by tubes and lulled by the almost inaudible sound of the machines. Grace would seem to be a saint for giving up her own life in Dallas to live in the house and care for Elizabeth, but wouldn't there be talk if she was gone from the house too often? Her sacrifice could be a double-edged sword.

There was another possibility that was even more fearful. What if this wasn't the last will Elizabeth had made? Elizabeth frequently changed her will and had made very certain Grace knew about it. She had used it as a means to assure that Grace was present for every family occasion. It was possible that Amanda and Nathan also knew about Elizabeth's whim. There could be another, more recent one that named someone else as the sole beneficiary.

Grace slowly climbed the stairs to her room and went down the hall. As she passed Amanda's door, she heard voices in conversation and she hurried by. She wanted to know as little as possible about Amanda and her lover.

She went into her room and closed the door. As she undressed for bed, she wondered if she would be capable of stepping into Elizabeth's shoes. Elizabeth seemed to have a talent for managing the family business as well as for cultivating the right people. Her friends bore the names of Houston's most socially prominent families. Would they accept Grace?

She had known most of them all her life. Not only had she gone places with Elizabeth as a teenager, she had accompanied her on many occasions as a woman. When she and Todd drove down from Dallas—Grace hated to fly so they never did—she went with Elizabeth to whatever functions were on the calendar for the length of their visit. In this way, she had continued acquaintances with the elite of Houston society and politics. At the time, she had done it to win Elizabeth's approval and to have names to drop at her Dallas functions. Now she was glad she had done so. It would make it so much easier to take over Elizabeth's place.

A tiny, niggling thought had been in the back of her mind ever since her conversation with Dr. Santon.

It would be much better for everyone if her mother died.

Grace couldn't have said the words out loud. They were almost a blasphemy. Elizabeth, even in a coma and near death, still maintained control over Grace's thoughts. But her death would simplify so many things.

There would be no need for expensive nurses and equipment. The house would belong entirely to Grace and no one would wonder at her not spending more time at her mother's bedside. Elizabeth dead would be better than Elizabeth living as a vegetable. She looked nothing like her former self. If her friends insisted on visiting, wouldn't they think less of Grace for letting Elizabeth look the way she did now? Grace could have a beautician in to dye her hair and care for her nails, but that wouldn't change the way her mouth drooped open or the imbecilic expression on her face.

Grace told herself that Elizabeth would hate for anyone to see her looking the way she now did. It might even be said that Grace wasn't keeping her mother in the best possible way and that could be catastrophic socially.

Then there was the awesome responsibility of being the matriarch of the family. Elizabeth's house was the hub of the family and the children were expected to visit at the prescribed times: Thanksgiving, Christmas, Elizabeth's birthday, and Mother's Day, as well as other times during the year that Elizabeth had deemed proper. Grace wasn't at all sure she could exert this kind of influence over Amanda or Nathan, or even that she wanted to. It would suit her just fine if she never saw either of them again. But that would look distinctly odd to Elizabeth's friends. Families were supposed to visit together.

Grace put cream on her face and carefully massaged it in with the upward strokes that were supposed to erase wrinkles. She could learn to do all that had to be done. Elizabeth had been drilling it into her head all her life. She knew the right people and she could find some excuse if Amanda and Nathan refused to honor the family traditions. She didn't worry about Todd at all. He always did as she told him to do. He would probably be glad to live in Dallas and have her stay in Houston.

Grace frowned, then noticed the wrinkles that movement caused and smoothed her face at once. Todd, alone in Dallas, might do anything. She couldn't depend on him not to have blatant affairs and thus damage her standing in that city. She would have to somehow divide her time between the two cities. That would almost certainly mean having either to fly from Dallas to Houston or to drive herself. Neither prospect was appealing to her. Perhaps Todd could hire a CEO to overlook his business there and he could start another construction company in Houston. He would balk, but Grace knew she always won the arguments. He would give in eventually. He always did.

Todd was pulling the picture away from the den wall. He had known a wall safe must be behind it, because Grace had installed an almost identical one in their home in Dallas. It was locked, of course, but he had watched her from the doorway long enough to know the combination was in the large brown book with the gilt lettering on the spine. In no time he had the safe open.

Elizabeth's will lay on top of the stack of papers. Todd, like Grace, took it to the lamp to read it. He frequently glanced over his shoulder. It wouldn't do for Grace to know what he was doing.

Quickly he ascertained that Grace was the sole beneficiary. A vast relief flooded through him. He didn't know the amount of the Wainwright fortune, but it was common knowledge that Elizabeth was extremely wealthy. That meant he wouldn't be destitute even if his desperate investment didn't pay off. He would still be solvent and Grace need never know. *If* it didn't pay off. There was still a chance that the investors would come through in time. If that happened, he would be wealthy in his own right and Grace couldn't throw that at him during their arguments. She might even have some respect for him.

He knew Grace would never divorce him in spite of her angry words from time to time. Elizabeth had always refused to acknowledge divorce among people of quality, and even if she died, Todd was certain her opinion would keep Grace married to him. He would have the use of the Wainwright money for the rest of his life. If his business scheme paid off, Grace would be even less apt to leave him. He didn't like being married to Grace, but there were definite advantages to being married to an heiress. For one thing, it impressed potential investors and banks.

The only fly in the ointment was Elizabeth's current condition. If she stayed in ICU too long, she could use up a sizable portion of her money. Todd wasn't sure how much her medical treatment was costing but he knew it must amount to a small fortune already. He had seen Elizabeth and was positive she would never recover, though Grace was convinced of it. That meant she would continue to need medical aid indefinitely. The hospital and doctors could, in effect, get everything.

Todd wondered how he could convince Grace to take Elizabeth off life support and decided it was too risky. Better to have the fortune slightly diminished than to find himself divorced and penniless, especially now that Texas had introduced alimony into the legal system. It would be just his luck to be bankrupt and have a judge order him to pay support to Grace, who already would have everything she could possibly want.

Todd decided it would be best to bide his time and see what happened with Elizabeth in the next few days.

Grace standing by the fence, motioned for Horace to come to her. "I want you to take up those begonias in front of the house. Red is such a common color. I want pink ones."

"Yes, ma'am, but Mrs. Wainwright told me to be sure and plant red. She was very particular about that." Horace stared at her as if he didn't know which order to follow.

"My mother is gravely ill and can't possibly care if the flowers are red or pink. If I'm going to live here, I want the flower beds done to suit me."

"Yes, ma'am," he said doubtfully. "It's pretty hot to plant anything now. Those red begonias are already established. Maybe it would be better to wait until next spring and plant the pink ones then."

"I want pink, Horace," Grace said sharply. "If you want to keep your job, you'll replant them today."

"Yes, ma'am." He kept his face and voice expressionless.

Grace nodded in determination. She knew the only way to control servants was to keep the upper hand. Horace had been with her mother for many years, but he was starting to age and Houston was full of young gardeners Horace knew it, too.

She drove to the office of an interior decorator Elizabeth had used and went into the air-conditioned building. The place was exclusive and only saw clients by appointment. Grace loved it.

"Yes, Mrs. Hillard." The decorator smiled as she came toward Grace. "I was expecting you. Dana, hold my calls, please," she said to her assistant. The younger woman smiled and nodded. Nicole Dupree showed Grace to a comfortable chair in front of a table draped in fabrics. "I've pulled the samples of the last things your mother ordered so we can see what we're working with."

Grace fingered the material Elizabeth had chosen for the curtains in her bedroom. "I want to change my room. I don't like green and I can't think why Mother put it in there. I much prefer pink."

"Like this, you mean?" Nicole indicated the colors that

were in Amanda's bedroom. "These are lovely and the two rooms would match."

"No, I don't want my room to look like Amanda's. I would prefer something in a rosier tone." She tried to look as if she did this every day, though in reality she found the decorator slightly intimidating. "And I prefer silver for this room, not gold."

Nicole laughed briefly. "I should think you would with pinks. Gold and pink are rather garish."

"Exactly." Grace was glad Nicole couldn't know her own house was predominately pink and that all the accessories were gold. Until just now she had thought that made the house look more elegant.

Nicole brought a folder of cloth samples to the table. "These are lovely, aren't they? And I recently happened upon a rare find—antique cherubs fashioned on curtain brackets. They were in a London estate and I was fortunate to see them on my last buying trip. They are sterling, of course, so they have that lovely patina of old silver."

"They sound marvelous!"

"You have, let's see, four windows in that room," Nicole said as she consulted the Wainwright folder. "You're in luck! I have enough of them to do the windows. You'll need two to a window, of course." She made quick notations in lilac-colored ink on her pad. "Let me show you some damask I happened upon in Italy."

For the next hour Grace pored over samples of fabric, paint chips, and curtain styles. When she disliked something, she was careful to check if Nicole was leaning toward the same opinion. If she was, Grace refused the sample. Nicole was equally vehement in her own choices. They sparred back and forth until Nicole convinced Grace of her original choices.

Finally Grace rose and extended her hand to Nicole.

"It's been a pleasure consulting with you. How soon can you get started?"

Nicole looked at her leather appointment book. "I could work you in next Tuesday. I'll need to see the room to be certain of those drapery measurements. When we decided to change the style so drastically, it threw off the old ones."

"Certainly. I'll be home on Tuesday." Grace nodded to the assistant as she left. The heat of Houston in June swallowed her and she felt moist and sticky before she could get in her car and start the air conditioner. She felt good about the day's work. She had always hated all that green in the room. Soon everyone would be accustomed to her using the house as her own and it would make the transition easier.

Grace was convinced she could maintain control of the Wainwright empire.

Chapter Ten

"I can't get it right," Amanda said in frustration. "Look at this!" She stepped back from the canvas to let Dakota see the painting.

He stood behind her for a while, studying the canvas. "Something is off," he agreed.

"I was too ambitious on this one. I should have left the New Age ones to you."

"No, I like what you've done. There's just something that's off. Let me think a minute." He pointed to the lower right-hand corner. "My eye keeps coming back to this area."

"Mine, too. I've reworked that corner half a dozen times." She sat down tiredly in the wooden chair. "I've painted feathers a thousand times. What's throwing me off?"

"I think it's the emotion. The feathers look as if they could float off the canvas, but they have no heart."

Amanda rested her elbow on the back of the chair and regarded the painting from another angle. "Maybe."

Dakota came to her and rubbed her shoulders gently. "You're working too hard on it. Start another one and come back to this later."

"I'm running out of time." She felt as if her nerves were abraded. "Grace and I had an argument this morning."

"Over what?"

"You. She thinks you should conform more."

He laughed and went back to his own painting. "What should I conform to?"

"She wasn't specific. Everything, I suppose. You know how she is." She looked over at him. "Have you noticed anything odd about her lately?"

"Everything about Grace is odd to me."

"She seems to be taking over the house. She had Horace dig up the begonias in the yard and put in pink ones. Evelyn says Grace has started giving her a week's menu and a list of chores. Evelyn has been taking care of this house forever and now Grace is going to start giving her orders? I'm afraid Evelyn will want to leave."

"I'd leave too if Grace started giving me orders."

She finally managed a smile. "I can imagine the fireworks there would be if she tried."

"At least Todd has been staying out of our way. I'm still waiting to catch him saying something out of line to you so I can confront him."

"I like it better this way." She paused as she considered the painting. "It really is unusual, isn't it? He's started staying in his room or leaving with Grace whenever we're likely to be around."

"I'd say he's finally showing good judgment. Men like Todd are cowards. He won't do anything while I'm here and I plan to be here as long as you."

"I wonder how long that will be. We can't stay here

much longer. We all have other commitments. Or at least Nathan and you and I do. Todd seems able to take off work for as long as he likes. Doesn't that seem odd to you?"

"I never thought about it."

"All he ever talks about is his business and how much in demand he is. If he had so many projects, wouldn't he have to be in Dallas minding the shop?"

"Got me. I don't know anything about the construction business." His voice had a distracted quality the way it always did when he was trying to concentrate on two things at once.

She got up and went to stand behind him. Dakota was painting what at first appeared to be a cliff in the moonlight over a peaceful sea. Only after a moment did the canvas also reveal subtle faces and forms that suggested life in the rocks, clouds and waves. The living earth was a favorite theme of his.

"You do that so effortlessly," she said a bit jealously.

"So do you, usually."

"Not lately." She propped her foot on a stool and leaned her elbow on her thigh as she watched him. "Lately it's like pulling teeth to get the paints mixed, let alone on to the canvas."

"Honey, you've got to stop letting your family drive you crazy."

"Oh, is that it? Okay. I'll stop."

He grinned back at her. "I know it's not easy, but that's your problem, you know."

"I know. I just don't know how to tune them out." She was silent for a minute. "Grace is up to something. I've seen her walking around the house, looking at the rooms as if she's considering buying the place. And she's started using Mother's expressions and way of speaking."

"Are you getting a mild case of paranoia?" he teased. "Hand me that cobalt tube."

Amanda took the blue paint from her tray and tossed it to him. "My jeans are getting tight."

He looked at her with interest. "Oh?"

She smiled. "You look so pleased with yourself—as if you invented babies."

"You may have to buy some new clothes before our tour. We can't have the baby squashed if your old ones are too tight."

"Don't worry. Babies don't squash that easily. Evelyn asked me if it will have two names."

"We're still negotiating that one," he said with pretended seriousness.

"No, we're not. We just haven't decided if it will have your last name or mine. Since you're Dakota, maybe we should name the baby North if it's a boy and South if it's a girl."

"I was hoping for Washington or Oregon," he said with a grin.

"Georgia or Carolina if it's a girl."

Amanda turned her head as the door to the studio suddenly opened and Grace stepped in. Like Dakota, Amanda didn't like uninvited people in the studio and she stepped forward to keep her sister from coming further into the room.

"I must have a word with you," Grace said. "I assume you aren't able to smell it yourselves, but the oil paint and turpentine odor is becoming quite unbearable. I'd appreciate it if you would either turn off your air-conditioner vents so it doesn't circulate throughout the house or stop painting for a while."

Amanda stared at her. "We can't stop painting!"

"The vents, then." Grace pointed to the lever beside

the grate. "I'm sure your friend can reach them, or you can climb on a chair."

"We aren't going to shut off the air vents. This room would be as hot as an oven. It's June, Grace."

"I'm aware of that. But the smell is terrible."

For a moment Amanda could hear Elizabeth behind Grace's words and she automatically started to apologize. "Wait a minute," she said. "You can't smell the oil paint in the other rooms. Mother put in a separate system in this room for that very reason."

"I can smell it and it's overwhelming." Grace frowned from Amanda to Dakota, who was ignoring her. "It's also embarrassing for you two to be holed up here together all the time." Even Dakota reacted to that statement.

"Grace, you're talking nonsense. We're up here working. Even if we weren't, we *live* together," Amanda reminded her.

"I can't do anything about that, but while you're in Mother's house, you must behave appropriately. So I'm moving his things into the guest room." She wouldn't even say Dakota's name if she could help it. "Evelyn is taking care of that."

Amanda pushed past her and went to their bedroom.

Evelyn was standing in the middle of the room as if she wasn't sure where to start. "Grace told me to move Mr. Dakota's things, but I'm not sure I ought to."

"Grace had no business telling you to do any such thing." Amanda stood firmly in front of the dresser and crossed her arms as Grace came into the room. "Grace, you're pushing me too far."

"Someone has to be in control around here. Mother could be sick for a long time. Some changes have to be made." She looked over her shoulder to be sure Dakota hadn't followed her. "I think it's time he left. Don't you?"

"No, I don't. Dakota is staying for as long as I do. Why are you talking like that?"

"Like what?"

"As if you're doing a poor imitation of Mother."

Grace ignored the barb. "I have a decorator coming next Tuesday and I don't want her to see him."

"Excuse me?" Amanda said in disbelief. "A decorator?"

"I'm redoing my bedroom. I hate green. I've chosen nice shades of rose and ivory."

"You can't hire a decorator to paint a room in Mother's house! If she finds out . . ." Amanda stopped. It was highly unlikely that Elizabeth would ever know. "You shouldn't be doing this. We won't all be here much longer and the house isn't yours to alter. What does it matter what color the room is when you'll be back in Dallas soon?"

"I may not be back in Dallas for quite a while." She smiled as if she knew a secret she wasn't going to share.

"I detest pink, but I'm not repainting," Amanda pointed out. "It's a waste of money to hire a decorator for something like this. If you really hate green, buy some paint and have Todd put it on the wall."

Grace wrinkled her nose. "That's fine for you, Amanda, but some of us have more taste."

"I have to get back to work. Evelyn, don't move Dakota's things. He's staying right where he is."

Evelyn gave her a relieved look and escaped from Grace's glare.

"I can't have you undermining me like this to the servants."

"You can't refer to Evelyn as a servant. Where are your manners? Evelyn practically raised us!"

"*You*, perhaps. Mother raised me."

Amanda pushed past her. "Go away, Grace. You're enough to drive a saint to drink."

"I notice the liquor cabinet is running low, speaking of drink. Dakota should buy his own."

"In the first place, Dakota isn't the one drinking, it's Todd. In the second, he has as much right to be here as your husband."

"I wasn't aware that you had married," Grace said with an acid smile.

The barb struck home. Amanda bit back her retort. She had better things to do than argue with Grace. She went back to the studio and slammed the door shut.

"Where am I sleeping tonight?" Dakota asked, knowing full well who won the argument.

"With me!" She picked up her paintbrush and attacked the corner again.

Of all the subjects Grace could have chosen, she had managed to pick the one that hit her on a raw nerve. Dakota still hadn't asked Amanda to marry him. Each day it became more of a burning issue with her. She was carrying his child. They were in love. So why hadn't he mentioned marriage? Dakota was as determined to be free as she was, but why did that preclude marriage? Amanda felt entirely free in their relationship. She didn't want to see other men any more than he wanted to be with other women. It was a lifestyle they had chosen freely. She was beginning to think he might never ask her to marry him.

In the pretext of putting raw sienna on her palette, she looked at him. He was fully engrossed in his work. When he had that look in his eyes she could talk to him for minutes on end and he wouldn't remember a thing she said. She envied him his ability to concentrate to such an extent—especially now, when she couldn't seem to concentrate at all.

* * *

Grace left Amanda's bedroom and went down to the den in a huff. Todd was there reading the newspaper. "I can't stand that man," she burst out.

"Who?"

"Dakota, of course. I even hate his name! It sounds like something out of a western movie."

"What's he done now?" Todd went back to the paper.

"I asked him to move into the guest room and Amanda threw a tantrum. It's disgusting, her living openly with him under this roof. What would Mother think!"

"Living with him?" he asked vaguely.

"And she had the nerve to take me to task over hiring a decorator to redo our room."

"A decorator?"

"For heaven's sake, Todd! Don't repeat everything I say." She dropped into the leather chair and glared around the room. Her eyes lingered on the painting that hid the wall safe.

"I have to go to Dallas for a few days. I was waiting for you to come downstairs to tell you. I talked to Fred Willis a few minutes ago and he says I need to be there for some meetings."

"He can handle matters, surely. It's what you hired him to do." Grace had more on her mind than Todd's business dealings. "You can't possibly go off to Dallas when I need you here with me."

"There's nothing I can do to help around here. The doctors are doing all that's necessary with your mother. I have to convince some investors that the mall is important to them and Fred feels they won't listen to him as well as they will to me. There's a meeting set for tomorrow afternoon."

"It's out of the question." Her brows knit over her nose. "I've got to get that man out of this house. Todd, you go tell him to leave."

"Who?"

She lost her temper entirely. "Will you put down that stupid newspaper and listen to me? Go tell that man he can't live here anymore!"

Todd shook his head. "I can't do that." His voice had that vague note to it that she had noticed lately. "I have to go to Dallas."

Grace got to her feet and said angrily, "I'm going shopping. We'll discuss you going to Dallas when I return." She stalked from the room.

Todd watched her go, before turning back to the paper. He wasn't reading it. Actually he hadn't even been reading it when she came into the room. Every time he tried, his eyes refused to focus and his mind kept skittering off on other subjects. He wanted Dakota to leave as much as Grace did, but for other reasons. With Dakota in the house and living in Amanda's room, it was increasingly hard to ignore the fact that they were lovers.

For Amanda to have a lover other than Todd was unbearable. So his brain refused to think about it.

Amanda was in his mind almost constantly. He was no longer building the mall just for himself. Todd had twisted it in his mind that the success of the mall would convince Amanda to come back to him. Not that he could have her as his wife. Not just yet.

He remembered all too well how she had felt and tasted when she was little more than a girl. Todd had always liked young girls. In his mind, Amanda at fifteen had been an adult. Amanda hadn't changed all that much. Her curves were more rounded, her hair longer, but her face and voice were the same. She was a perpetual child-woman.

When he saw her with Dakota, especially when they didn't know he was watching, jealousy ate him alive. Dakota was free to kiss her or hold her hand whenever he pleased and Amanda seemed to like it. Amanda was *his* and such demonstrations were impossible for Todd to watch. So he had worked it out in his mind that she didn't really want Dakota. She was only using him to make Todd jealous. It was a lover's game she was playing. Now that Todd understood that, he was able to see them together and not want to kill Dakota. He even fantasized that Amanda hated for Dakota to touch her and that she was only allowing it because of the jealousy it roused in Todd.

He could allow her to play her game for a while longer. First he had to put through the deal with the mall and find a way to rid himself of Grace, at the same time getting half her inheritance. Todd wasn't sure of the legal aspects, but he knew there must be a way. Money could buy anything.

Nathan smiled when Cody answered the phone. "Hi, darling. It's me."

"Hi, me. I was hoping you'd come home tonight."

"I expected to, but Grace is in a snit. She and Amanda had an argument this afternoon and I've been trying to calm Grace down."

"Why don't you let them settle it themselves?"

"It's not how we do it." He loosened his tie and pulled it off. "I went by the Galleria store today. That new manager is working out pretty well."

"The one you had doubts about? I'm glad to hear it. Did that shipment of suits come in?"

"They were delivered this afternoon." He unbuttoned his collar. "How did Nate do today?"

"Fine. A new family moved in the Bateman house and they have a boy about his age. I'm hoping they'll be friends. I met his mother and she's nice."

"Good. That house has been vacant for a long time." Talking to Cody about mundane affairs was like a soothing balm to Nathan's nerves. "I sure hated to leave you this morning." He glanced at the door to make sure he couldn't be overheard in the kitchen. "You're beautiful in the morning."

Cody laughed in a way that told him she was pleased. "Flattery always works with me. How much longer do you think you'll have to divide your time between there and here?"

"I don't have any idea. Mother is no better. Dr. Hastings thinks that she'll never gain consciousness, and even on the remote chance she does, she'll be little more than a vegetable. You know what decision that leaves us to make."

"I'm sorry. I wish I could help you. I could come up there and be with you."

"That wouldn't be a good idea, especially since Grace is on a rampage. I was able to convince her that Dakota isn't illegally trespassing by being in the house, but that was as far as she's willing to go."

"Trespassing? He's there with Amanda, isn't he? How is that trespassing?"

"That's exactly what I told her, but she's convinced that Dakota is somehow using Amanda to gain something. She lost me on that line of reasoning. Todd is acting strange, too."

"From what you've told me, your whole family is pretty strange."

At times it's as if Todd doesn't remember who Dakota is or that he's here with Amanda. It's enough to make your spine crawl. I must be imagining it." He changed the subject abruptly to ask, "Is Nate asleep?"

"Yes, he gave it up about half an hour ago."

"I was hoping I'd get back to the house in time to call him earlier. Give him a hug and a kiss for me. Okay?"

"Sure thing. Will you be home tomorrow?"

"For a while, anyway. It depends on whether Grace and

Todd both go off the deep end at once. I plan to be there at least for dinner, if that's all right."

She laughed. "Of course it's all right. It's your house."

"I miss you something awful," he said softly.

"I miss you, too. Are you sure you can't come down tonight?"

"I would if I could, but I'm so tired I don't think I should drive that far. After refereeing here, I went back to the store and helped unpack the suits and an order of luggage. I just got back to the house."

"Get some rest. You may need it tomorrow night," she said with that promising note in her voice.

"Sounds good. I'll see you then." He reluctantly told her good-bye and hung up.

The door opened and Amanda looked in. "I thought I heard someone talking in here. Are you on the phone?"

"I just got off. Come on in."

"I saved you some supper. Grace was all for making you eat at the Galleria but Evelyn and I are in cahoots." She brought him a plate of roast beef and vegetables. "There's cherry pie when you're ready for it."

He sat where he was and started to eat. "This tastes great. I'm worn out."

"Is that why you're not going on to Galveston?"

He nodded as he chewed. "I'll go down tomorrow."

"Grace is sure in a state, isn't she? I wonder what set her off this time."

"Who knows? How's the painting coming along?"

"Great for Dakota. I can't seem to make any progress at all."

"Maybe you're trying too hard."

"Maybe."

"I like him."

"Who? Dakota?"

Nathan nodded again. "The two of you go together. You know, like wine and soft music."

"That's very poetic," she said in surprise. "I never knew you thought about things like that."

"It's funny, isn't it? That we grew up in this house together and none of us really know each other. Grace could be speaking a foreign language as far as I'm concerned. I can't figure her out at all."

"I can, and it's not a pretty picture. She wants to be Mother when she grows up."

"That's sounds accurate. And have you noticed Todd is acting odd lately?"

"I said the same thing to Dakota this afternoon. What's going on with him? He acts as if he's off in his own world."

"Beats me. Let's leave him there, wherever it is." He thought for a minute as he ate. "I can't forget what you said to me on the lawn that day. How can you stand to be in the house with him?"

"I don't have any choice. We both have to be here. He won't try anything with Dakota around."

"No, he isn't that foolish. But really, Amanda. How have you managed to eat at the same table with him and sleep under the same roof and make conversation with him if he molested you?"

"It happened a number of years ago. I try not to think about it. That's one reason it takes me so long to put myself back together after a visit. I still have nightmares about him. Lately, he's tried to start things back up."

"It really pisses me off that you didn't tell any of us."

"Mother and Grace wouldn't have believed me and I thought you'd side with them," she said honestly. "I know now I was wrong."

Nathan shook his head. "We're a sad lot for a family, aren't we?"

"I think so. Yes."

He put his plate aside. "I may go down to Galveston after all. Eating gave me a bit more energy."

"What's down there that you can't be away from for more than a night at a time? I don't believe the work theory."

"There's quite a lot in Galveston."

"Named Cody?"

"That's only half of it." He regarded her thoughtfully. "Maybe one day soon I'll tell you about it."

"You could tell me now. I'm not one to pass confidences on to other people."

"No, when I explain about Cody, I'll want all the family to hear."

"It's that big a deal?" she asked curiously.

"It's definitely that big."

"Okay, but now you really have my curiosity up."

Amanda took his plate out to the kitchen and washed it. Her mind was turning over the possibilities. Cody might be a man, but she was still of the opinion she was a woman, probably a married one. But why would Nathan announce an extramarital affair to the entire family? They weren't a group to inspire confidences. She knew she would just have to wait.

As she was drying the dish, she heard someone come into the kitchen behind her and, thinking it was Nathan, she said without turning, "It's about time you came in here and told me the whole story."

Todd put his arms about her waist from behind and murmured in her ear, "I thought you might be waiting for me in here."

Cold chills spilled down Amanda's spine and she acted reflexively by jabbing her elbow into his ribs as hard as she could. He released her with a cry of pain.

"Don't you ever touch me again!" Amanda said angrily.

She turned on him, Nathan's steak knife in her hand and soap dripping from her clenched fingers.

"That's a funny game you're playing," he said angrily as he rubbed his bruised ribs. "First you welcome me, then you try to break my ribs. Put that knife down. You know you won't use it."

"I will if you touch me again." She was trying to remember if Dakota had already gone up to the studio. He must have or Todd wouldn't have risked coming near her.

"You know you still want me." He leered at her from a safe distance. "You remember what it was like between us."

"Why don't you tell me about it?" Nathan said from the den doorway.

Todd jumped and stammered as he tried to think up a plausible excuse for having said the words Nathan had overheard. "We were just joking around."

"She doesn't look as if she's joking to me. She's looks as if she's getting ready to carve you up and put you down the garbage disposal."

Amanda didn't lower the steak knife. She felt as if she were frozen. Her breath was coming in painful quick gulps and her heart was pounding with fear. For a few horrible seconds it had been exactly as it had been when she was a girl and Todd had her cornered. "Go away!" she ground out between clenched teeth.

Todd glanced from one to the other and backed out of the kitchen. As soon as the dining-room door shut behind him, Amanda could hear his footsteps making a fast retreat.

She felt all her muscles relax at once and then the trembling started. "Thanks for coming in. He didn't believe me when I told him to leave me alone."

"I know. I heard everything." Nathan came to her and took the knife from her cold fingers. He handed her a dish towel. "Here. You're dripping soap suds on the floor. Are you sure you're all right?"

She nodded. "He waited until he thought I was alone. He must have thought you left for Galveston from the store."

"You should tell Dakota."

"I can't. He already knows about what happened between Todd and me. If I tell him about this, he'll turn Todd every way but loose."

"That would be good for Todd."

"Maybe, but it would certainly get Dakota arrested. Grace is just waiting for an excuse to get him out of the house. She would call the police and have them take Dakota away."

"Not if Todd was attacking you."

"Maybe you believe in justice, but I haven't seen any evidence of it. No, I'll take my chances with Todd and stay as close to Dakota as I can."

"Okay."

She could tell he wasn't convinced she was doing the right thing, but she had already thought this through. Grace would love to have an excuse to have Dakota arrested.

Amanda left the kitchen and went up to the studio. Although she was too tired to paint, she didn't want to be alone in their room. Dakota was working without a shirt on and as he moved with each brush stroke, his back muscles rippled. He turned and nodded to indicate he was aware she had come in but was concentrating on his work. Normally, Amanda would respect his signal that he wanted to be left alone until he finished what he was painting, but her need to be held by him was too great to wait.

As she eased up behind him, she unbuttoned her blouse and opened the front clasp on her bra and pushed it aside.

Gently she brushed his back with her nipples, then pressed herself against his warmth. She heard him sigh, not in exasperation that she was interrupting but the way he sighed when he knew she wanted him. He dropped his brush into a jar filled with turpentine and with the other hand reached behind him and took her hand in his. She pulled her blouse back over her breasts as he turned around and walked with him in silence to their bedroom. Soon, all thought of Todd's sleazy touch would be erased from her mind as the man she cared for more than anyone in the world made passionate love to her.

Chapter Eleven

Amanda had begun her painting later than usual the next morning but with great enthusiasm, her memories of making love with Dakota so vivid, she could still feel the warmth of his skin, the strength of his sinewy muscles, and the satiny touch of his wet tongue all over her body. That always inspired her creativity. But in the light of day, her thoughts also returned to the incident with Todd the night before, and her recall of his repulsive touch was just as vivid. Within the hour, frustration with her work had erased all her enthusiasm.

Amanda threw her brush into the tray. "I give up. I'm never going to get this right."

Dakota came to stand beside her. By his silence, she knew he agreed but didn't want to say so.

"I'll never be as good as you," Amanda said with conviction. "You paint so effortlessly!"

"You think that? Most of the time, I'm filled with self-doubt." He put his arm around her. "You're tired. That's all it is. You've worked on this one until you've lost objectivity."

"I can't be tired. It's still morning." She sat on the wooden chair and frowned at the canvas. "It's still those damned wings that are giving me trouble. Maybe I'll paint an angel without wings for a change. A wingless angel. A 'muley'."

"Do it. It's your painting; you can interpret it any way you want to."

Amanda sighed. "Who do I think I'm fooling? I can't paint here. I can barely think." She hadn't told Dakota about what had happened with Todd, so he had no reason to know why her nerves were on edge.

"Honey, let's go home. You're right about not being able to paint here. You're not yourself at all."

"I can't leave," she snapped. She released the tension on the canvas and took it from the easel. "If you can work here, so can I."

"I'm not as emotionally connected to these people," Dakota pointed out. "Grace knows how to pull every wire to keep you off balance. Remember how you are after every visit? That's how you are now. You can't work like this, and being upset so often can't be good for the baby. I love you and I don't like to see you so unhappy."

"It's not a happy time," she said as she put a fresh canvas on the easel. "It would be rather odd if I were laughing my way through each day with Mother lying in ICU."

Dakota helped her center the canvas and snap the tension bar into place. "Expenses must be mounting like a tidal wave, as long as she's been in there. Is there any change at all?"

"No. We're supposed to meet with Dr. Hastings and Dr. Santon this afternoon. Apparently they met yesterday and reached an agreement that something has to be done. I'm afraid they'll expect us to make the decision soon."

"It's for the best."

"She's not your mother."

"I'll go with you."

Amanda shook her head. "It would only stir Grace up. Todd has flown back to Dallas for a few days. Maybe she'll calm down with him gone. No, you should stay here and work. I only wish I could do the same."

"You have to be able to put Grace and Todd out of your mind if you're going to get your work finished."

"Only the two of us know what we have planned for the exhibits. If I'm short by a couple of canvases, no one will know the difference."

"We'll know. We agreed that we would do the best we possibly could for these shows. You know how important they are to our career."

She turned on him. "And you know how hard I'm trying! I'm not taking the time off to go shopping or have my nails done! I'm working as hard as I can."

"I know. But you have constant interruptions. Let's go home and finish. We can fly back down then."

"You go. I'm staying. You just heard me say we may have to make the decision to remove Mother from life support any day now. I can't leave with that hanging over my head."

"We've also argued more since the beginning of this visit than we ever have."

She went to him and put her arms around him. "I'm sorry, Dakota. You're right about my nerves being raw. Everything seems to set me off. Maybe that also goes with being pregnant. Instead of morning sickness, I'm having temper fits."

"I hope that's all it is. You won't be pregnant forever."

"Maybe you should go with me to the meeting with the doctors. I really don't want to go through that alone."

"I'll be ready."

* * *

Nathan dressed in a sport shirt and slacks. He automatically corraled Nate as the boy whizzed by him, pretending to drive a racing car. "Slow down, partner. You nearly ran into the corner of the table."

"I'm going fast!" Nate announced happily as he squirmed to be put down. As soon as his sneakers hit the floor, he was off and running again.

"His batteries never run down," Cody observed as she watched their son dash out of the room. "He makes me tired just watching him."

"I know," Nathan said with a laugh. "I wish Amanda and Dakota could meet him. I like Dakota better all the time. I'd like for you to meet them, too. They don't strike me as bigots."

"I've met bigots before and survived."

"I was thinking of Nate. He's going to hear it eventually, but it doesn't have to be from his own family."

"Are you sure you don't want me to go with you to the meeting at the hospital? I could get a babysitter."

Nathan shook his head. "When you finally meet them, I don't want it to be at a time that may be traumatic. I expect the doctors to recommend that we take Mother off the machines."

"So do I. She's been in ICU so long! I've never heard of anyone staying there for this length of time."

"We have Dr. Santon to thank for that. Once Mother stabilized, Dr. Hastings would have moved her to a regular room." He put his wallet and car keys in his pants pocket. "Grace will be beside herself if I'm right."

"How about you? Will you be OK?"

Nathan thought for a minute. "It's not going to be an easy decision, but I think it's one that's overdue. My main concern is that Grace will refuse to be reasonable and let her go. I can't force her to agree to it. It wouldn't be right. We've decided it has to be a unanimous decision."

"You've said Grace never agrees with anyone about anything. Doesn't she realize how the bills must be mounting?"

"She says it doesn't matter. I think her primary reason, however, is that people will think less of us for removing the life support. Grace lives and breathes by public opinion."

"If you decide you need me with you, all you have to do is call. I'll leave Nate with a sitter and drive right up."

He bent and kissed her. "I know. Thanks, darling." He glanced at his watch. "I have to run or I'll be late." As Nate made another lap through the house, Nathan caught him long enough to kiss the top of his head. Nate struggled free and whooped gleefully as he resumed the race.

The meeting was in an office at the hospital. Neither of the men looked as if they were glad to be there. Amanda sat in a chair beside Dakota and held his hand. Grace and Nathan took the other two chairs.

"I'm afraid we don't have good news," Hastings began. "We've run some more tests and Elizabeth's prognosis holds no promise at all. I would be remiss as a friend of the family if I didn't tell you that I think it's time for you to accept the inevitable."

"No," Grace said in a low voice as she shook her head.

"There are no longer even sporadic brain waves," Hastings went on to explain. "For all intents and purposes, she has died. Only the machines are making her breathe and maintain vital signs."

"This isn't possible," Grace insisted. "Dr. Santon told me only a few days ago that he saw an improvement."

Hastings looked at his colleague in astonishment.

Santon quickly said, "You read too much into my words.

I only said your mother seemed to have better color. I thought you understood that she can't get well. I told you someone would have to care for her for the rest of her life.''

"I'll do it. I don't mind the sacrifice," Grace said stoically.

Nathan looked at Hastings. "You're positive? There are no brain waves at all?"

"No, I regret having to say this, but I'm declaring her brain dead."

The silence in the room was thick. Amanda found she was gripping Dakota's hand tightly and she tried to relax her muscles. Although she had known this would be the news, it still rocked her to hear the words spoken out loud.

Nathan looked at Grace, who seemed to be in shock. "We all knew she wouldn't get any better. I think we've all known that since the beginning."

"*I* didn't know it," Grace maintained. "I had faith that Mother would win this battle the way she always does."

Hastings spoke to her gently. "In the end, none of us wins this particular battle. It's your mother's time and I recommend that you allow her to go."

"What will happen when we turn off the machines?" Amanda asked.

"*If* we turn them off," Grace corrected. "Which we won't."

Hastings pretended not to hear her. "You won't see much difference at all. She will probably breathe a few times on her own, but her breaths will gradually grow more shallow and then stop. I can promise you, she will feel no pain. She's been beyond that for a long time."

"Dr. Santon," Grace urged, "tell me you aren't recommending that we do this!"

"I can't force you to make the decision. It has to be the

family's choice. But I now agree with Dr. Hastings that she's run out of options."

"I could have the life-support equipment moved to her house," Grace said wildly. "I'll move to Houston and see to it that she's cared for. I'll hire nurses around the clock."

Hastings gave her a long look. "That's not practical, Grace. Elizabeth's medical bills have already reached enormous proportions. Keeping her on the machines under these conditions would be foolish. Let her go gracefully."

"I can't kill my mother because she's running up medical bills!"

"You're not killing anyone," Hastings answered. "If she wasn't hooked to the machines, we wouldn't be having this discussion because she would have been gone weeks ago. You've had this time to become accustomed to the idea."

"We have to do it," Amanda told Grace. "She can't stay in ICU forever."

"We could move her to a private room until you all agree what's to be done," Santon suggested. "That would be less expensive."

"We're talking about Mother here!" Grace looked from Amanda to Nathan and back. "I can't believe what the two of you are saying. I refuse to give up."

"Grace, she's already dead!" Amanda said bluntly. "You're only prolonging the expenses. Mother is gone."

"One of these days you might be in her place," Grace said angrily, "and you wouldn't be quite so fast to pull the plug then, I'll bet."

Amanda stopped talking and looked ahead stonily. Dakota gave her hand a squeeze and she almost broke down into tears. The decision wasn't easy for her. She knew it was rough on Nathan, too, and he had no one to lean on. She had Dakota and Grace had Todd, however lame a support he might be.

Nathan turned to Amanda. "Let's go home and talk. I want to get it over with if there's no other choice."

"I'll have your mother moved into a private room until you agree on a course of action," Dr. Santon said. He wasn't looking in Hastings's direction because the older doctor was clearly against doing even this.

"I recommend that you reach a decision today if possible," Hastings said. "As I said, the costs are rising. Private rooms are cheaper than ICU, but they'll still run the bill up fast."

"Mother has insurance," Grace informed him icily. "We aren't paupers by any means."

They went out into the hall and stood awkwardly, waiting for someone else to speak. The doctors left to make their rounds. Amanda wondered if the two doctors had as much animosity toward each other under ordinary circumstances. "Dr. Hastings was upset with Dr. Santon. I think he's been telling him to have this conference with us for a long time."

"You're only guessing," Grace told her in an exasperated tone. "You can't possibly know that. I have far more trust in Dr. Santon than in Hastings. I had assumed Dr. Hastings was off the case once I hired the specialist."

"I asked him to stay on," Nathan said. "I never trusted Santon. He kept telling you good news that didn't seem to be based on facts. I never saw any improvement in Mother at all."

"I'm going to stay here and see to it that Mother is cared for properly," Grace said angrily. "You two can go home."

Amanda frowned at her but didn't argue. She didn't like being dismissed by Grace but she also didn't want to stay in the hospital. Dakota put his arm around her and led her toward the elevators.

* * *

Grace remained until Elizabeth was set up in the private room. It was far more private than the ICU ward but Grace wasn't pleased. "If something goes wrong, how will you be able to tell?" she asked the nurse who was regulating the glucose drip.

"We'll be reading the monitors at the nurses' station," the woman explained. "If any of the readings change, we'll know and come check her."

Grace made a doubtful sound. "I'll stay here with her for a while."

The nurse turned to leave the room. "Stay as long as you like. Visiting hours are over at nine o'clock."

Grace pulled up the stuffed vinyl chair and sat in it beside Elizabeth. Her mother did look terrible, she thought. She didn't know how the nurses managed to wash Elizabeth's hair with her in that condition, but she assumed they must do it somehow. It was hard to believe that shaggy mop with the gray roots was the same hair that Elizabeth had kept so immaculately styled. A dribble of saliva ran from the corner of her open lips but Grace didn't wipe it away.

"I'm doing my best, Mother," she said. "The others want to unplug the machines, but I won't desert you." She wished Elizabeth could hear her. Saving her life would certainly endear Grace to her.

She often wondered why Elizabeth had never loved her. She had arranged her entire life to be more like Elizabeth. As a girl, Grace's singing ability had been remarkable, but she had sung in public only one time. It had been a solo in the church choir and although the choir director had encouraged her to consider singing as a career, Elizabeth had referred to it as a "joyful noise." Grace had been crushed and had dropped out of choir that very day. Elizabeth eventually grew tired of needling Grace about her singing ability but Grace had never forgotten. If her singing offended Elizabeth, she would never sing again, and she hadn't.

In high school she had been infatuated with a boy who hadn't met Elizabeth's standards. The boy was good-looking and fairly popular with the other students, but he wasn't the most popular or the most handsome and his family had no connection with Houston politics or history. Grace had gone out with him once and Elizabeth had refused to let her date him again. They could have continued meeting in private, but Grace was too determined to earn her mother's love, so she had stopped speaking to the boy altogether.

"I've given up so much for you," Grace whispered. A tear, one that was real, escaped her eye and rolled down her cheek. "Why don't you love me?"

At least she had the satisfaction of knowing Elizabeth hadn't loved her siblings, either. It wasn't only Grace. And the will in the wall safe stipulated that the entire estate would go to Grace. Didn't that prove Elizabeth loved her better than she loved the others? Or maybe that will wasn't the most recent one.

That thought hadn't crossed her mind since the day she found the will in the safe. How had she let something so important slip her mind? Just because that was the document in the safe didn't necessarily mean there wasn't another, more recent one in the safe-deposit box or with the lawyer. Now that she thought about it, it seemed odd that Clay Bennett wouldn't tell her anything about Elizabeth's will if he knew she was the sole beneficiary. Bennett had known the family all her life, and wouldn't it be logical under the circumstances that he would tell her since someone had to make the decisions for Elizabeth now? "Is it possible that Amanda or Nathan have been named in a newer will?'' she mumbled.

"You didn't do that, did you, Mother?" Grace asked rhetorically. She looked around the room. The nurse had said there were monitors. Could the women at the station hear her speaking as well? Surely not. All the same, Grace said, "I love you, Mother, and I'm not going to let them kill you. There must be some way for me to care for you at home."

There was, of course, no answer. Grace got up and went to the door. She paused to look back. Elizabeth seemed so alone in the private room. At least in ICU she had been within sight of nurses at all times.

As Grace went to the elevator, she touched a tissue to her eyes as if she were crying. In reality, she was worrying that the will she'd seen might not have been her mother's last. It would be just like Elizabeth to have changed it. Nathan was the only son and the logical one to inherit. Amanda was the most needy. Of the three, she had the least money and Elizabeth might have taken that into consideration.

Grace decided no one must do anything irreversible until she knew if she was the sole beneficiary.

"I spent a lot of hours out here," Amanda said to Dakota as she ducked to go into the playhouse in the backyard.

Dakota followed her. "I can imagine you playing here."

"You should have seen it at the time. There was real furniture in the rooms." Her head almost touched the ceiling and Dakota had to duck to keep his head from bumping. "Grace had her tea set on that shelf and mine was over there."

"She didn't share then, either, I gather."

"Sharing was never Grace's strong point. Since she's ten

years older than I am, we never really played together anyway. She just didn't want to get rid of the tea set so it stayed on that shelf.'' Amanda opened a toy box. ''It's empty. I should have known it would be. Mother had Horace clear it out when we became too old to want to play here. Nathan's toy soldiers were kept in here. He had enough to start a war, but he seldom played with them. Nathan wasn't into war games, but Mother bought them for him, just like she bought dolls for Grace and me.''

''What did Nathan like?''

''Drawing. He was pretty good at it, too. He could have been an artist if he had been more willing to rebel. Since he didn't, he ended up with a business degree like Dad.''

''He seems to have done well with it.''

''He likes to do his own window displays whenever possible. Now that he has so many stores, it's not always feasible, so he also has a window designer. Personally, I think Nathan's displays are better than hers.''

''Your mother would have been pretty upset if she had two artists in the family.'' Dakota smiled at the thought. He sat on the toy box to straighten his neck.

''Especially if one was the only son. Nathan has had to work harder than either Grace or me. Even when he was a boy Mother expected so much more of him. I did pretty much as I pleased with respect to my education. Of course, I had to work my way through college since I did it without her approval, but I did do it.'' She sat on the small window ledge. ''I was earmarked as a lawyer.''

''Law? You?''

''Mother didn't take personalities into consideration. Grace was to be the wife of a successful man and I was to be a lawyer. Nathan was to follow in Dad's footsteps. Grace apparently never had ambitions to be anything else, so when she married Todd, Mother was relieved. The same was true when Nathan opened his second store. I'm the only failure in her eyes."

"You're far from a failure, Amanda. By this time next year, you could be famous."

"We have such high goals, you and I. It's a long way to the ground."

"We won't fail." His smile was full of confidence. "I'm basing it on our track record, not just idle speculation. Also, I've been thinking. We could diversify—find a commercial market for the angels you do so well. Perhaps as a line of Christmas decorations. I wanted to talk to you about it before I approached anyone."

"First I'll have to learn how to paint feathers," she said grimly.

"You make better feathers than a bird can. They aren't working in that painting because something else is wrong and you haven't figured it out yet. If I knew what it was, I'd tell you."

"We always said we weren't going to go commercial. That we wanted to be pure artists."

"I know, but two people can live on dreams easier than three. A commercial enterprise would build a good nest egg for the baby. My art doesn't lend itself as well to that as yours does."

"True. Yes, let's give it a try. I like that idea."

They left the playhouse and went to the large oak tree nearby. "Maybe someday we'll have a yard and you can build our child a playhouse. I'd love to have a yard."

"We'll find our house. You and I want exactly the same thing. I know it's out there somewhere."

"But we'll have to look for it in order to find it. We never take the time to look." She leaned against the tree. "I'll bet we live in that loft forever."

"I'll bet we don't." He came near her and pulled her

into his embrace. "We can't. The baby will eat our paint as soon as she gets old enough to get into everything."

"She?" Amanda asked with a smile.

"Or he. I'm not particular."

"We have to come up with a name. A real one, including a last name." She looked up at him expectantly. This was the perfect opportunity for him to take the hint and propose.

"How about Higgenbothem? That would go with anything."

She swatted at him and started to walk away. He caught her wrist and drew her back. "Or Thompson?"

"I like Thompson. I certainly don't want him or her to have my last name. I think a curse goes with it."

"Okay. So we're halfway there. Now all we need is a first name."

"You beat all. You know that? Most couples know the last name. It's taken us almost two months to agree. We'll never pick a first name in time. The baby will start to school as Baby Girl Thompson or Baby Boy Thompson."

Dakota laughed. "I'll buy us some name-the-baby books. We'll go through them one name at a time." He leaned his forehead against hers. "We've already established that we don't want to use a family name."

"At least not one from my side. Some of yours aren't so bad."

"You know, of course, my parents were flower children. You should have heard some of the names Mom said they considered naming us."

"I'm still reeling under the prospect of teaching the baby to say Aunt Shadow and Uncle Dune."

"You're beautiful when you laugh." He smiled at her, sunlight dappling his tanned skin. His hair was the color of a raven's wing in the tree's shade.

She felt love well up inside her. "You're the sexiest man in the world," she told him.

"Ever made out beneath an oak tree?"

"Here?" she exclaimed before she saw he was teasing. "Grace would have a field day with that!"

"She's still at the hospital."

"Nathan isn't."

"No, he's gone to one of his stores. He drove away while we were in the playhouse."

Mischief lit her eyes. "The neighbors could see."

"Not where we are. Today is Evelyn's day off and Horace won't be here until tomorrow afternoon. We're finally alone."

She put her arms around his neck and kissed him. "I guess we shouldn't waste the opportunity. I could probably fit you into my busy schedule."

He kissed her and she forgot to breathe. She held on to him to steady herself. Dakota kissed her forehead, the corners of her eyes, her neck. His hands were moving over her and seeking out the places he knew to be most sensitive.

Amanda's last objection dissolved. She pulled away long enough to say, "Let's go inside."

He laughed because he had known she wouldn't lie with him in the backyard in broad daylight, no matter who was or wasn't at home. He bent and scooped her up and carried her to the house.

Amanda buried her face against the strong column of his throat and kissed the warm pulse that throbbed there. "I love you," she said.

Once they were inside, he put her down and they ran hand in hand up the stairs and into the bedroom. Amanda turned the lock and rolled with him onto the bed as she covered him with kisses. This was the way they usually were. She hadn't realized what was missing until now— spontaneity.

"Our lovemaking will be more regimented once we have a child," she said as she unbuttoned his shirt.

"Children take naps. Older children go to school. We'll still have our time together."

She yanked off her blouse and threw it away from her. "This feels wicked! Making love in my bedroom here and in the middle of the day. Grace could come home at any time. So could Nathan."

"Then you'd better be quiet." He pulled her to him and silenced her with passionate kisses.

Amanda returned his kisses and let herself soar into their loving.

Chapter Twelve

Amanda looked out the front window, blinked and looked again. "Grace, why is Horace digging up Mother's shrubbery?" She asked her sister. "She's worked for years to get it all to the same height. I'll go out and stop him."

"No, I gave him orders to do it." Grace didn't look up from the magazine she was reading.

"You did what? You had no right to do that."

"That shrubbery is a pain in the neck. Every winter Mother lost a bush during the freeze or some bug would kill the roots. I'm having him put in azaleas. They thrive here and will flower pink in the spring and be evergreen the rest of the year. It's the most logical choice for Houston."

"Do you plan to turn the entire house pink?" Amanda was still reconciling herself to the rose confection Nicole Dupree was creating in Grace's bedroom. "You're certainly taking a lot upon yourself, especially since the house will be sold after Mother is gone."

"Sold? I have no plans to sell it." Grace finally looked up.

"It's not your decision to make. Besides, you live in Dallas and Nathan lives in Galveston. Who do you think will live in it? I'm certainly not moving back here. This house has too many bad memories for me."

"That's a very insensitive thing for you to say. Some of my best times were spent in this house." Grace looked around as if she had landed in heaven. "Why, we spent our entire childhood under this roof."

"I know. That's what I meant."

"Besides, I'm going to move here." She lifted the magazine again.

"You are? What about Todd's business? He can't just pick up and move. And Houston has more building contractors than it needs as it is. Todd is past the age when it would be easy to start over."

"You're talking about things that you know nothing about. As far as that goes, Todd could stay in Dallas during the week and fly down for weekends. Many husbands do that."

"What makes you so sure the house will be yours anyway? Do you know who Mother is leaving it to?"

Grace gave her a suspicious look. "No. Do you?"

"Of course not. She's never confided in me. I assume it will go to Nathan since he's the only son."

"I'm the oldest child. We have a matriarchal family, so it wouldn't necessarily go to the son." Grace gave her a tight-lipped smile. "I'd be willing to bet on it."

"Oh? You'd probably lose." Amanda turned back to watching the destruction of Elizabeth's shrubbery. Her mother hadn't been fond of flowers and only planted them because everyone else did.

"What do you know that I don't?" Grace demanded.

"Nothing."

"I don't believe you."

Amanda shrugged. "It's too hot to plant flowers. They probably won't live."

"If they don't, I'll have him plant some more." Grace was silent for several minutes. "Has Nathan mentioned that Cody person to you?"

"No. I haven't asked."

"He hasn't mentioned him to me, either."

"Why do you assume Cody is male?"

"Come on, Amanda. You weren't born yesterday. Nathan is thirty-three years old and never dates. Cody has to be a man. Mother thinks so, too. She told me that herself."

"Why don't you ask him?"

"Why don't you?" Grace countered.

"Because I know he'll tell us when he's ready. Whomever Cody is, is none of our business."

"I notice you're getting awfully chummy with Nathan these days. One might almost think you're cooking something up between you."

"One might also think you're paranoid. Nathan is my brother. It's high time I got to know him."

"When you find out who Cody is, I want you to tell me."

Amanda didn't bother to answer.

That night Todd returned to Houston and Grace went to the airport to pick him up.

"I could have taken a cab. I didn't expect you to drive out here."

"I wanted to talk to you alone. I never know if Amanda or that awful man will be listening to whatever is said in the house. He's attached to her like glue." Grace frowned as Todd drove down I-45 toward the Loop. "I actually caught him without a shirt on yesterday! Even as a boy

Nathan wasn't allowed to go around half naked. I told Amanda to see to it that Dakota stayed dressed if he's going to be out of her room."

"The weather was good in Dallas. Not as hot as here."

"And I think Amanda is gaining weight, too. Her jeans are so tight I could almost read the inside label from the outside. She's letting herself go now that she thinks she has a man. He'll leave her in a New York minute!" she prophesied with grim hope. "It will serve her right for living with him like some tramp. I'm just glad Mother never saw it."

Todd glanced at her. "Is your mother gone?"

"If Mother died, wouldn't I have called? She's no different than she was before you left. Dr. Hastings is trying to convince us that she's brain dead, but I don't believe it. When I visited her today, she fluttered her eyelids, and if her brain wasn't working, she couldn't do that. Eyelids don't move on their own accord. Watch out for that truck."

"I see it. Maybe Dr. Hastings is giving you good advice."

"He's a quack. He somehow convinced Dr. Santon to go along with him, but I can tell it wasn't Santon's idea to recommend turning the machines off."

"He said that? You have a lot of faith in him. Maybe you should think about doing just that."

"I won't sit here and listen to you plot to kill Mother." Grace tried to cross her arms but her plump middle spoiled the effect. She dropped her hands back into her lap. After a while she said, "I think when the time comes, I want Reverend Emmett to do the service."

Todd glanced at her.

"Keep your eyes on the road. It's tricky here. Mother always respected Reverend Emmett. He's been at the family church for many years now. I wonder if I should call him and make arrangements."

"How could you possibly make arrangements if she asn't died yet?"

"I could tell him that it's imminent. It's a large church nd he probably has a full calendar. I don't want some ssistant preacher officiating."

"As much money as she donated over the years, I'm ure Reverend Emmett will be glad to change his schedule ɔ accommodate her. When did you start planning the ervice?"

Grace glared at him. "I'm not planning the service. just don't want to be caught unprepared. Under the ircumstances, I want to be ready for the worst. Only a ool would do otherwise. If I wait until the last minute, I night make a decision I would later regret simply because would be in shock or deep in mourning."

"That doesn't seem likely," Todd said under his breath.

Grace glanced at him but she hadn't caught enough of is words to take issue with him.

"What do Amanda and Nathan think about having Rev-rend Emmett?"

"I certainly haven't asked them. It's up to me as the ldest and more logical to make these plans. Mother would vant me to."

"I doubt she would want anyone planning to bury her."

"That comment is in the poorest possible taste, Todd."

"Are you going to ask how the meeting with the investors vent?" he asked, ignoring her criticism.

"How was it?" She wasn't really listening to him. There vere so many more important matters to decide. Like who should play the organ and who should sing the hymns.

"It didn't go as well as I had hoped. We need to cut way back on our spending for a while."

"Not now, Todd," she said impatiently. "We can't stint on Mother's funeral. What would people think? It's bad enough that you flew off to Dallas for some meeting that

Fred Willis could have handled without you expecting me to look bad.''

"I only meant that we should be careful. I'm assuming the Wainwright estate will pay for the funeral, not us. Besides, Nathan and Amanda would help, too, if it came to that.''

"Mother has insurance, naturally. As for the others, doubt Amanda has a penny to her name. Artists never do. Why, I'll bet Dakota has never seen a house as nice a Mother's. That's probably why he refuses to leave.''

Todd brightened. "Yes, that could be it.''

Grace shuddered. "I don't know how I'll explain him at the funeral. He's sure to wear that earring, too.''

When they reached the house, Grace went upstairs and Todd went to the den. He was thrilled to find Amanda there alone. When she saw him, she jumped.

"I didn't know you were flying in this early,'' she said.

"I caught an earlier flight.'' He sat opposite her in the leather chair. Grace was right, Amanda's jeans were tight. Her breasts looked larger, too.

She shifted under his stare. "I was just going upstairs,'' she said as she put her book aside.

"Don't go yet. I need to talk to you.''

"What about?'' Amanda asked warily.

"Your mother. Grace tells me the doctors both agree she's brain dead.''

Amanda nodded. "We had a conference with them yesterday. Grace refuses to take Mother off the machines. Can you talk sense into her?''

"I've never been able to yet,'' he said with a humorless laugh. "I'm on your side. It's time to let her go.''

"We haven't exactly chosen sides.''

"I didn't mean anything bad by it. You always think the worst of me.''

"I wonder why.'' She was watching him closely.

Todd liked her to look at him. He couldn't tell if she was tense because she was afraid Grace or Dakota would barge in and spoil their conversation or if it was the sexual tension between them. He decided it was both. "I had a terrific meeting in Dallas. Several of the chain stores are interested in my mall. I'll probably come out of this a millionaire." It was a lie. None of the chain stores had been interested. As soon as they heard the amount he was asking from them, they had backed away.

"Good for you."

"Maybe I'll buy one of your paintings then."

"I may not have any for sale at the time."

"Nonsense. Artists have to sell their paintings in order to make ends meet. Even I know that." He grinned at her. "By the way, I'm sorry you misunderstood that little incident the other night. I don't know what you thought I was going to do, but you were wrong. You nearly cracked my ribs."

"I meant to do exactly that."

"I was only hugging you. Brothers-in-law hug sisters-in-law all the time."

"Not the way you were hugging me. I've told you before, don't ever touch me."

"I like it when you play hard to get."

"I'm not playing hard to get. I'm telling you I'm impossible to get."

He laughed again. "We both know better than that, now don't we? You have a short memory."

Amanda was off the couch and storming toward the door when he stopped her by grabbing her wrist. She glared at him as she tried to pull away.

"You're welcome to play your little game. I kind of like it. But you're taking it too far. I know a lot about you, Amanda. I'll use it if I have to."

She jerked her hand away and ran out of the den. Todd

watched her go. Yes, she filled out her jeans nicely. They were skintight. If she had put on some weight, it wasn't unflattering. Not like that roll around Grace's middle. Amanda had been too thin before, in Todd's opinion.

Amanda didn't stop running until she was in her bedroom. Dakota was reading in bed. She was trembling as she started to undress.

"Amanda? What's the matter? Are you feeling sick?"

"Grace and Todd are back."

He sat up and the sheet dropped to his waist. His bare skin was bronze in the lamplight. "Did Todd say something to upset you?"

She shook her head and didn't meet his eyes. If Dakota knew what Todd was doing, he would, at the very least, hit him and probably throw him out of the house as well. Grace would have the police on the scene before Todd hit the ground. "I just didn't expect them so early. That's all."

"There's more than that. You're shaking."

"I guess I took the stairs too fast." She turned her back and put her clothes in the bag she had used for laundry since her college days. "I thought I would come up here and read."

He moved over and made room for her beside him.

Amanda got into bed and pulled the pillows into a mound behind her. The book was a good one, but she didn't think she would be able to concentrate enough to make sense of it tonight. She heard a sound in the hall and wondered if Todd had come upstairs.

"I like your reading apparel." Dakota ran his hand over her bare stomach. "Let's start our own nudist camp."

She smiled. "In a few months I would be a sight to behold."

"I'm looking forward to it. I can't imagine you with a round middle."

"I'm getting there. We'll have to tell everyone soon. My clothes are getting tight."

"We won't be here that long. If you don't want your family to know about the baby, you don't have to tell them."

"You changed your tune on that one."

"That was before your mother was terminal. There won't be anyone to hold the family together. Grace certainly doesn't have that control over you."

"No, but she would like to. I may tell Nathan."

"I like him. I want to stay in touch with him after this is all over. Grace can jump off a cliff."

"It's a good thing you never really met Mother. Grace is the faded version."

"That's a scary thought."

"I read once that all women become like their mothers as they get older."

"You're nothing like that. If you get that way, I'll have you put to sleep." He put his arm around her and she leaned back against him.

"You can't read this way."

"That's okay."

She put her hand on his bare thigh. "I love living with you. I love being in love with you, too. I don't know how I would be able to get through this if I didn't have you to lean on."

"It's my job, ma'am."

She smiled. She felt perfectly safe now. "Grace had Mother's shrubbery dug up and replaced with pink azaleas. When we have a lawn, I don't want a single pink flower on it."

"I wondered what Horace was doing."

"I'd like a big tree, too." This was her favorite fantasy these days, planning the house she would have someday.

"A big oak like the one in the backyard. With limbs that reach to the ground so our children can climb it easily."

"Naturally. And water. I'd like a stream nearby. The house where I grew up has a stream and we used to wade in it during the summer. It wasn't deep enough for swimming, but it kept us cool."

"Okay. We'll have a stream. And a big rock. A flat one that gets warm like an oven in the winter. I'll sit on it and sketch when I get tired of being inside."

"One rock, suitable for sitting. I'll add that to the list."

"And room for a horse. I think all kids want a horse. I know I did. I had to settle for renting one at Hermann Park. We never had pets, and a horse was certainly out of the question."

"A horse and pets. Got that."

"But I'd settle for just a house of our own." She stroked his leg as she wished. "Do you really think it will happen someday?"

"I promise." He nuzzled her ear and she leaned her head back.

"I love it when we're like this."

"Naked and in bed?" he asked.

"That, too. I meant, I love building dreams with you. You never tell me it's impractical or that you're allergic to pets."

"I'm not allergic to anything."

"But you might have been. See? We're perfect for each other."

"I've been telling you that for over a year now."

"I can hardly wait to go home."

"We can leave in half an hour."

"Be serious."

He sighed and wrapped his arm around her to cuddle her close. "I know this has been rough on you."

"I have a feeling the worst is yet to come. Can you picture

the scene Grace could throw at the funeral? And there has to be one eventually."

"I know. She'll be in her element. I'm telling you, she's evil and must be destroyed. At least she doesn't have children."

"None of us do. At least not yet. That's unusual at our ages. Nathan isn't married, either. Most people marry by their mid-thirties. I wonder why he hasn't."

"Maybe he never found the right person. I haven't been married before either."

Amanda didn't want to spoil the tender moment by bringing marriage into the conversation so she steered it back to Grace. "Not long after they married, I asked Grace about children and she said she absolutely didn't want any. As far as I know, Todd never did, either. Of course it wouldn't have mattered if he did. Grace rules him completely."

"I've always wanted children. I was about to give up on finding their mother, though."

"You romantic devil," she said with a laugh. "So that's why you keep me around. I'm the supplier of children."

"I have other reasons, too."

She tilted her head back to kiss him. His lips were warm beneath hers. Amanda loved to kiss him.

When he lifted his head, he rested his cheek on top of her head and picked up his book again. Amanda snuggled close and opened hers. Until she met Dakota, she never knew reading could be so much fun.

Chapter Thirteen

Grace dropped the magazine on top of the one she had finished reading and picked up another. When she visited Elizabeth, she read articles or looked at the pictures or otherwise amused herself. She had ascertained that words spoken in the room couldn't be heard at the nurses' station and that the women were only aware of Elizabeth's vital signs coming through the machine. Since that time she hadn't bothered to talk to her mother and seldom even looked her way.

When the door opened, Grace was startled. As she recognized Clay Bennett, she put the magazine aside. "Hello, Mr. Bennett. I was just looking for an article to read to Mother." She gazed fondly at the figure on the bed as she came to shake the lawyer's hand. "We don't know if she can hear us, but I like to keep her senses stimulated. When a person is in a coma, no one is too sure what they may or may not be aware of."

"I just dropped by to look in on her." Bennett stared

down at the woman. "You'd never recognize her for the same woman, would you? Mrs. Wainwright was always so careful about her appearance."

"I hope she can't hear that," Grace said rather sharply. "We do the best we can, but with these terrible machines it's difficult to keep her hair neat."

"Of course," Bennett said hastily. "I didn't mean anything against you. It's just a shock seeing her like this. No one was more vital."

"You needn't speak about her as if she were already dead. We haven't given up the fight yet." Grace smiled beatifically at her mother and reached out to pat her foot.

"Such a shock," Bennett repeated.

"She has always been so involved," Grace said as if she were speaking of a saint. "No charity was too insignificant for her to notice it. She donated large sums of money to many a cause."

"I'm fully aware of that. She was—*is* a generous woman."

Grace wondered if that was true of Elizabeth. She certainly had donated money to charities, but Grace wasn't sure she had ever cared much one way or another if her money really helped the cause. Philanthropy bought a secure place in society. "This has been so difficult on all of us. We've worried so much about her."

"Yes, one would. What does the doctor say about her condition?"

Grace mutely shook her head as if she were too overcome to speak for a moment. "It's not good, I'm afraid. There's talk of removing her from life support."

"Such a pity."

"She never left any instructions with you as to what we should do in this circumstance, did she?"

"No, as I told your sister, Mrs. Wainwright never considered such an alternative."

"It was as if she thought she would never die."

"To some extent. She did keep her will up to date. In fact, she had been in to put her signature on the most recent changes the day before the accident. She was supposed to come back for her copy the next day. I still have it in my file."

"Oh?" Grace said sharply. Then in a more moderate voice, "I was surprised when she told me she was going to make some changes." Elizabeth had never confided in Grace, but she knew Bennett wasn't likely to know that.

"Yes, it surprised me, too. I told her it wasn't a good idea to change it so often, but she was a strong-willed woman. I'm sure you know that."

"She was very independent in her ideas, but we were all surprised by the change." She waited to see if he would take the bait.

"I told her it wasn't advisable to make only one of you the sole heir, since she has a good relationship with all of you, but she wanted to keep the estate together."

"Yes," Grace said slowly. "She would want that." The will in the wall safe had been dated in December. That left six months for Elizabeth to have altered it and changed it back again. It was possible that Grace was still the heir. "I don't suppose I could see that will, could I? I want to prepare my brother and sister."

Bennett looked at her more closely. "I thought you said Mrs. Wainwright confided the contents of her will to you."

"She did, but I don't know the particulars. The details." Grace tried not to sound too eager.

He backed toward the door. "No, I've already said more than I should have. I'd better be going."

"No, wait. I want to talk to you." She was too late. He had already gone.

Grace stared down at Elizabeth. There was a good chance that she wasn't the sole beneficiary after all. Six months was long enough for Elizabeth to have changed the will several times.

She left her magazines scattered over the floor around the chair, got her purse, and left. She had to make certain that she would inherit the fortune before Elizabeth was pronounced dead.

When she returned to the house, she went straight to the wall safe. The will lay exactly where she had left it. She sat at the desk and read it again. The date was December 28, just as she remembered. Since then, the family had been together twice—once on Elizabeth's birthday in April and again on Mother's Day. If she changed the will according to who was least in her good graces, she could have changed it twice, and there was no guarantee that Grace was still the beneficiary.

She opened the desk drawer and found the White-Out. She eradicated the date carefully and blew on the paper to dry it. Then she put it in the typewriter and typed in the date of the accident. As she was taking it from the typewriter, Todd walked into the room. Grace jumped guiltily.

"What are you doing?" he asked.

"You frightened me half to death! I thought I was alone in the house."

"Amanda is upstairs painting. I used her car to run to the store and I just got back." Like Grace, he never mentioned Dakota unless it was absolutely necessary. "What are you doing?" he repeated. He looked from the blue-backed legal paper to the open wall safe.

Grace had no choice but to tell him the truth. "I'm making certain the estate goes to me."

He came to look over her shoulder and she moved away irritably. She read the date again and folded the paper the way it had been before she altered it. "I talked to Mr. Bennett today and he said Mother changed her will the day before her accident. I want to be certain that I'm the one to inherit it all. As the eldest, it's my right."

"I won't argue with that."

"No, I suppose you wouldn't. After all, if I inherit Mother's money, you profit." She put the will in the safe and closed it. As she twirled the dial, she added, "You're not to tell anyone you saw me do this."

"I'm not that big a fool," he said testily. "What you just did is illegal."

"Yes, and now you're a part of it, so just keep quiet. It's not really illegal in this case," she added. "I was the one named in this will. Mother did intend to leave everything to me."

"But if Bennett has the real one, he'll know this one has been tampered with."

"Not if I can convince everyone that Mother changed this one before she left the house the day of the car wreck."

"Why would she do that, Grace? You just said she changed it the day before. She would telephone Bennett and tell him to do it for her."

"I can say she was in a hurry. Or that she had some sort of premonition. I don't know." Grace paced as she frowned. "But if you know what's good for you, you'll help me convince the others. But maybe it won't be necessary. It depends on how often she changed it. I'm probably still the beneficiary. This is just insurance."

"If you say so."

She looked at him suspiciously. "You don't seem all that surprised to learn that my name is on that will."

"How could I possibly know?" he asked. "Your mother never confided in me and she certainly never gave me the combination to that safe. It's just that I've always assumed you would be the one to inherit it all. Like you said, you're the eldest. You're also the one who is most like her.''

Grace nodded, slightly mollified. "True. If the other will is in my favor, no one ever need know I touched this one. I'll destroy it and that will be that.''

"Does this mean that you're now willing to take your mother off life support?'' he asked hopefully.

"Certainly not! I can't possibly do it now. Bennett would remember our conversation and become suspicious. So would the others. No, time has to pass. I've been so adamant that Mother will recover, Amanda and Nathan would wonder if I suddenly changed my mind. I have to handle this carefully.'' She thought as she paced. "I have to weigh all the possibilities.''

"It seems to me you've just taken care of that.''

"No, there's still a chance that I won't get the things I'm due.'' She looked around the room and smiled. "But I have an idea.''

That night after dinner, Grace told the others of her decision. "We need to divide Mother's belongings.''

"Divide them? Why?'' Amanda asked.

"I still say she will recover,'' Grace said. "But it's occurred to me that if she doesn't, we'll have a great deal to decide at a time when we're least capable of doing it. Look around you. This house is packed with belongings, all of which will have to be disposed of.''

"I thought you wanted to move here,'' Amanda said suspiciously. "Why would you want to break up the house if you think it's going to be yours?''

"I'm hurt that you have such a low opinion of me,'' Grace replied. "To think that I would want to cut you and Nathan out of anything that might come to you! That's a terrible thing to say, Amanda.''

Amanda didn't answer but she was still suspicious.

"I don't think that's a good idea," Nathan said. "If Mother has named which of us is supposed to get a particular item, we should abide by that."

"If you're so certain Mother is going to recover, why do this?" Amanda pulled her leg under her on the sofa and let her hand rest on Dakota's leg. "Can you imagine how angry this would make her?" She knew there was no chance that Elizabeth would recover, but she couldn't understand Grace's abrupt change of direction.

"If she does, no, *when* she does, she need never know we did it. We won't remove anything from the house, so she won't have any way of knowing. And if she left everything to only one of us, the other two will be assured of having something of the estate."

Nathan frowned. "Why would she leave everything to only one of us? That doesn't make any sense. I'm sure it's to be split three ways."

"I wouldn't be too sure," Grace said with a small smile.

"Do you know something we don't?" Amanda asked. She knew Grace well enough to know something wasn't right about her suggestion.

"How could I? Mother certainly couldn't have told me."

"You sound pretty defensive," Amanda commented. "I don't like the idea of us dividing her things anyway. Let's wait and see what the will says."

"No, I feel very strongly about this." Grace produced a pen and paper. "I'll take notes so we can remember it correctly later."

"And so you can change it more easily if things don't go as you plan?" Nathan was just as suspicious as Amanda.

"If you can't trust me any more than that, you're a fine excuse for a brother," Grace snapped. "Now. What about the furniture in this room?"

Dakota stood. "I'd rather not be a part of this. I'm going upstairs."

"So am I," Amanda said as she stood to go with him.

"No, you're not," Grace commanded. "Sit back down and let's do it."

Amanda reluctantly obeyed. Curiosity was getting the best of her.

"I'll take the silver candlesticks," Grace said, writing on her notepad. "Nathan, do you want the furniture?"

"No. I have furniture."

"Okay, the furniture goes to Amanda." Grace's pen moved over the paper.

"I feel like a vulture. I don't want the furniture, either."

Grace made another notation. "The furniture stays with the house. All right. I want the brace of dueling pistols."

Nathan looked at the framed set. "Dad paid a lot for those. Their value has increased a lot since then."

"Dueling pistols," Grace said as she wrote the words.

"Have you noticed anything odd about that list, Amanda? Grace now has two expensive items under her name and we don't have anything at all under ours. This is starting to make sense to me." Nathan frowned at his older sister. "You're counting on us not wanting to do this, aren't you?"

"There's no reason for you to insult me," Grace told him coldly. "I'm only trying to be fair. If you two don't want anything, that's up to you."

"Okay," Amanda said. "I want the cottage."

"What cottage?" Grace said.

"That one on the shelf. The only cottage in the room." Amanda went to it and took it off the shelf. "I've always loved it. Dad used to tell me stories about the imaginary people who lived inside. He promised to give it to me when I was grown." Her voice was soft as she remembered the happy times with her father.

"You have no more right to the cottage than Nathan or I do," Grace protested.

She didn't list the cottage under Amanda's name. "That's not just a pretty piece of bric-a-brac, you know. It's a signed piece and worth a great deal."

"I don't care about that." Amanda stroked her fingers over the delicate porcelain lines of the miniature thatched house. "Dad built the playhouse on this same design."

"Then I suppose you want the playhouse as well?" Grace asked.

"It might be a bit hard to pack and fly home," Amanda retorted. "All I want is this one piece. You and Nathan can divide all the rest."

Nathan was watching them dispassionately. "Don't lump me in with this. I don't want to divide the house, either. It's a bad idea, Grace. We aren't going to do it."

Grace slammed her pen down on the notepad. "You two beat all! You say you want to take Mother off life support and you won't do the things that will be necessary once we've done it!"

"There's plenty of time to do all this after she's gone." Amanda crossed her arms stubbornly. "I agree with Nathan. We're not going to do this."

Grace stood and motioned to Todd. "All right. Fine. I'll remember this when we have to sort out everything at the last minute. Of course, you two won't be all that broken up if we lose Mother, but I will be!" She turned and stalked from the room with Todd following close behind.

"I wonder what prompted all that," Nathan said.

"Got me. And it's not that I don't love Mother." Amanda put the cottage back in its customary place. I do love her. She doesn't love me." The admission brought tears to her eyes. "It really is going to hurt to turn off that machine. Perhaps more than it might if I knew she had cared for me all these years. Once that machine is off, there's no chance of anything changing that.''

"I know. I've had the same thoughts.''

Amanda looked at him. "Has she ever loved any of us? Really loved us, I mean.''

He slowly shook his head. "If she did, she wouldn't have done half the things she's done. It may even be her fault that we've never been closer. I've been thinking a lot lately. She's frequently told me things she claimed you said that have hurt me or made me angry. I don't know for a fact that you ever said any of them.''

"Things I said? I don't talk to Mother about you or Grace. Not other than to ask how you are or if you're coming to the next visit.''

"It hurt me that you came to Houston last March and didn't want me to come up.''

"Mother told me you couldn't come because you were sick, but from the way she phrased it, I thought you just didn't want to see me.''

"I wasn't sick. I didn't know you were coming until after you left. Mother said you wanted it that way.''

Amanda stared at him. "She must have been doing that all these years! Why didn't we see through it before now?''

"Probably because she discouraged us from talking to each other. I don't have your unlisted phone number and when I write you, you don't write back.''

"I've never gotten a letter from you.''

"Is your address 364 North Palm Street?''

"I never heard of Palm Street. We live on Hampton Drive.''

Nathan laughed incredulously. "Can you believe it? She gave me the wrong address!''

"Why didn't your letters come back?''

"I didn't write all that often. I guess there really is someone living at 364 North Palm who just throws them in the trash."

"This is too weird. I wonder if she's done the same thing between both of us and Grace."

"No, I don't like Grace on my own."

Amanda smiled. "Me, too." She put her head to one side. "I'll give you my address and phone number if you give me yours."

Nathan's smiled faded. "I may do that. I need to think about it."

"What's the big mystery? I can understand if you have some illicit lover hidden in your closet."

"I don't have a lover. Not an illicit one anyway." He shook his head. "This isn't the right time to explain about Cody."

"Okay. I'm not going to try and fish it out of you." All the same, curiosity was eating her alive. "Will you promise to tell me before I leave?"

He hesitated, then nodded. "I'll tell you before we go our separate ways. I want to stay in touch with you."

She tore some paper off Grace's pad and wrote down her phone number and address. "Here's mine. I can always find you through your stores. Right?"

"Right. It's not that I don't want you to know about Cody, it's just that it's hard to tell a secret I've kept for so long."

"Toss me many more crumbs like that and I'll go back on my intentions not to fish it out of you," she threatened.

He smiled, but said no more.

She went upstairs and found Dakota in the studio. He wasn't painting, only studying the canvases. When he saw her, he said, "Are you through dividing up the spoils?"

"We talked her out of it." She drew the chair up beside his stool. "Grace reminded me of a circling vulture."

"Has she agreed to take your mother off the machine?"

"No. That's why I don't understand her wanting to divide up the belongings. One contradicts the other."

"I noticed that."

"I learned something interesting." Amanda was eager to share the information with Dakota. "When I was talking to Nathan, we discovered that Mother has been deliberately keeping us apart all these years. He wasn't sick when I came down in March and she even gave him the wrong address for us."

"What about this surprised you?"

"It's so calculating! What difference could it possibly make to Mother if Nathan and I wrote each other or talked on the phone?"

"She wouldn't have direct control of the conversation. If you only have contact under her roof, she's better able to control all of you."

Amanda considered his words. "That's true. But we're a family, not some business conglomerate. Families don't operate like this. Your family certainly doesn't."

Dakota laughed. "Our mothers are nothing alike."

She smiled. "That's the understatement of the year."

She narrowed her eyes to study the paintings. "I've given more thought to what you suggested about angel decorations. I'll make some sketches tomorrow."

"Sounds good."

"What do you think about the canvases?" She could see her efforts weren't paying off as well as his. "Mine stink."

"No, they don't. They just don't soar."

"I was hoping you'd convince me they're better than I thought."

"You don't do your best work here. We both knew you wouldn't."

"I can't leave. Not when we're at the point of making the decision about Mother."

"I know. I just wonder how long it will take you to bounce back once we're at home?"

"I have no way of knowing that," she said with exasperation. "Have some compassion. Okay? This is a traumatic time for me."

"I'm aware of that. I understand. It's just that the dates are set for the exhibitions and they can't be changed. Advertisements have gone out."

"I know. I know!" She stood and went to the picture of the angel she couldn't complete to her satisfaction. "I'm being pulled in two directions. Mother and I aren't on good terms, but in a way that makes this decision harder. I have to be sure I'm not acting from personal motives."

"You'd never do anything like that."

"Not consciously, but I'm afraid to put any effort into convincing Grace to do what we all know is necessary because I'm afraid she or Nathan will think I'm doing it in order to get back to my life."

"Grace will probably think that anyway. Nathan seems smarter than that."

"I'm the one she never loved. Nathan doesn't think she cared for him, but I know she did in her way. Grace was her favorite, but she hasn't made life easy for her, either. But me? I'm the one she considered a tossaway. I think I was a big surprise to her and she never forgave me. Before I came along, she had the perfect family: one boy, one girl. I messed up the balance."

"That's a hard burden to carry."

"It's something I've always known. But that doesn't make it any easier." She sighed. "We can't keep prolonging it. Can a person be kept on life support forever? Surely there must be some limit."

"I imagine finances take care of that. It's too expensive to last forever."

"That's another thing. I have no idea how much money

Mother has. Grace has told me we've already reached the maximum the health insurance will cover. That means all the rest has to come out of the estate. No fortune will last forever. What happens if it's depleted? You and I don't have enough money to contribute much.''

"Not yet at any rate."

"Maybe not ever. Artists don't become millionaires. If the tour is successful, it will help a lot, but it won't land a fortune in our lap. Grace and maybe Nathan, too, will resent me not being able to contribute my share."

"Now you're borrowing trouble. Can't you find out how much money there is?"

"I don't know how. Short of us declaring Mother incompetent, the bank isn't going to give us any figures. Besides, it's not a matter of money alone. It's the principle. We can't leave her on the machine in good conscience. Not when both her doctors say there's no hope."

"Grace has to listen to reason. She's not a stupid person. She knows the doctors have ways of determining when a person is brain dead. There is a time when a person has to give in to the inevitable."

"I know. Tell it to Grace." She put the angel picture beside the others. "It really doesn't soar, does it? An angel has to do that, at least."

"The composition is good. So is the theme. The major problem as I see it is that you're trying to paint with your mind and not your heart. You have to feel what the angel feels."

"I know that as well as you do," she retorted. "I just don't feel like an angel lately."

"The castle one has a lot of promise. If I were you, I'd stop working on it and let it dry so we can fly it back to L.A."

"I had already decided to do that. In fact, it should be dry by tomorrow. Maybe working on the angel sketches

will blast me loose so I can finish this painting." She put
the angel canvas back against the wall, its face turned
inward. "I never considered becoming a commercial artist.
That's what these sketches may mean if they sell."

"Commercial art isn't a dirty word. It's a different sort
of art, but a commercial venture may bring in enough
money for us to continue to paint what we want."

"I guess. I'm going to look at it that way." She knelt
and studied her painting of a castle. Each painted stone
had centuries of lichen growth and every turret was logically placed. But the castle was rising from a cloud bank
and in places the walls were almost transparent to reveal
lords and ladies in elegant clothing whose eyes urged the
viewer to intuit their secrets. "I like this one."

"So do I."

"I can add the touches of gold and white when we're
back home. I want better light before I try that. It has to
be done just right or I'll have to repaint it." She thought
for a minute. "I wonder what would happen if I were to
use gold leaf instead of the paint I had intended to use.
It would put it in a different medium, but the effect might
be worth it."

"It's a thought." He knelt beside her and studied it
intently.

"I'll try on a practice canvas first." Her mind was racing
at the possibilities. "There's really no reason for sticking
entirely with oil-based paints." She looked at him in tri-
umph. "See? I can still create."

"I never doubted you. Only your surroundings."

"I'll be glad to get home." She sat on the floor and
started making notes on a sketch pad for what she intended
to do with the canvas.

Chapter Fourteen

As Todd and Grace sat in Elizabeth's hospital room, Grace was making funeral plans in the leather-bound notebook she used for social engagements. "I want a lot of flowers," she said. "I don't see any reason to ask mourners to donate to some charity. Mother gave plenty when she was . . ." She glanced at the woman on the bed. "Able," she amended.

"That's up to you." Todd had been on pins and needles since they arrived. He had told her he needed to return to Dallas and Grace was refusing to allow it.

"I'll specify pink if anyone asks. You do the same. The church will be gorgeous in different shades of pink. I wonder if Mother has a dress that color. Her dress should go with the color of the flowers. Maybe I could buy her a pink one."

"I heard Nathan talking to that Cody person again this morning."

"You did? What did he say?" Grace's pen poised over the paper.

Todd chuckled. "I'd say they're lovers all right. I never heard anyone talk like that to someone if they weren't sleeping together."

Grace nodded as if she had known it all along. "It's a shame Mother didn't know about them. You know how she felt about homosexuals. She would have disowned Nathan if she had been positive he was that way. He was sneaky long enough to put it past her but apparently he's not being so careful now."

"There's no reason for him to be. Your mother can't do anything about it now."

"No, but I can. If she left the estate to him, I'll use that as a reason to contest it along with the altered will."

"No judge would rule in your behalf. That would be discrimination."

"I don't care. Nathan has no business flaunting his sick lifestyle under our noses. Doesn't he realize I'll find out about it and that I feel as strongly on that issue as Mother did?"

"I doubt he cares."

"He would do well not to underestimate me." Grace went back to her notes. "Someone should sing 'Amazing Grace.'" She smiled almost happily at the coincidence of names. "Don't you think? I don't know Mother's favorite hymn, but everyone seems to like that one." She wrote it down. "Who can sing it?"

"I don't now. Ask Reverend Emmett."

"I suppose I could do that. I wonder if there's some way to hear the person sing before the ceremony itself. It would be terrible if he chooses someone with a bad voice."

"Ask him about it."

"What did Nathan say to this Cody?"

"I was wondering if you'd ask. He talked about his house

as if they're living together. And get this! There's a third person named Nate."

"Nate? That's odd. Nate isn't a common name and its very similar to Nathan."

"I wondered about that, too."

"Somehow that makes it more decadent."

"Apparently Cody wanted to come to the house because he told him it wasn't a good time."

"As if any time would be!" Grace frowned. "He had better not bring any of his boyfriends to Mother's house."

"I'm sure he knows that would upset you. I'm surprised he hasn't done it before now."

Grace tapped her pen against her red lips. "Mother didn't know for certain about Nathan, but even a doubt could have been enough. She was so adamantly against deviant behavior. She might have written him out of the will on the suspicion alone."

"It's possible," Todd said thoughtfully.

"I've given it a lot of thought," Grace continued. "She may have turned against me last Mother's Day. She overheard me threatening to divorce you and she was against divorce, too."

Todd shifted uncomfortably in the chair. "I told you, nothing was going on between Amanda and me. We were only talking."

"Are you forgetting I was listening to the conversation?"

"I didn't mean to sound argumentative." He didn't meet her eyes.

Grace wasn't sure what that meant. She knew Todd through and through and she knew he was hiding something. Surely he and Amanda hadn't found a way to get together with Dakota in the house as well. Grace didn't think Todd was that foolish.

"I'm glad you didn't follow through and leave me."

Todd gave her that placating smile that hadn't worked since the first years of their marriage.

It's not over yet, Grace thought to herself. To Todd she said, "Regardless of all that, Mother might have changed the will to keep me from divorcing you. She would have told me once she had the will in her possession." Elizabeth had used that tactic before to get Grace to do what she wanted.

"That means everything goes to Amanda," Todd said as if he were thinking aloud.

"Yes. It would mean that." Grace couldn't believe Elizabeth would make a mistake like that. Amanda was the least deserving of them all. She lived openly with a barbarian and was an artist.

"I need to make a phone call," Todd said.

Grace was hardly listening to him. "Don't use this phone. I'm trying to think. Go to a pay phone." She watched him leave.

She would be glad to get rid of him. Once Elizabeth was dead, there would be no reason to stay married to him. Unfortunately she couldn't do it now or people would talk. Once she had her fortune, she could divorce Todd. She didn't want another man in his place. She would be much happier by herself.

She decided it was fortunate that neither Nathan nor Amanda had wanted to divide up the furniture. She could tell the judge they had been offered the belongings and had refused them. That could go in her favor.

Nathan came from the back room of his Galleria store and into the showroom. As always, the store was running smoothly and quietly. Salesclerks were attentive to the customers and the wares were elegantly displayed. Nathan walked closer to one of the shadow boxes used to show merchandise and looked to see if it had been dusted recently. It had.

"Hello, Mr. Wainwright," a voice said behind him. Nathan turned to see Clay Bennett.

"Hello, Mr. Bennett. What can we do for you today?"

"I came by to get some shoes I ordered and wanted to speak to you while I was here. Such a shame about your mother. You have my sympathies."

"Thank you. We're facing a difficult decision but the doctors agree that it's time to act." He kept his voice low so he couldn't be overheard by the customers.

"Yes, I heard that. Mrs. Hillard is taking it hard."

"Yes, she is." Nathan wondered when Bennett had seen Grace. She hadn't mentioned it.

"I hope none of you are upset with me. About what I told her at the hospital, I mean."

"No," Nathan said slowly. He had no idea what Bennett was talking about.

"I let the cat out of the bag, I guess. I just assumed that Mrs. Wainwright would have told you when she changed her will."

Nathan managed to keep the surprise from his face.

"Mrs. Hillard led me to believe you knew all about it or I wouldn't have spoken so freely." He shook his head. "I advised your mother against leaving everything to only one of you. It would be different if you had nothing to do with each other or if there were hard feelings between you, but that wasn't the case."

"Mother's money goes to just one of us?"

Bennett paled. "Damn! I've done it again!" He turned on his heels and hurried from the store.

Nathan watched him leave. The words were still sinking in. The estate was to go to only one of them? *Not to me,* he hoped fervently. He knew Grace would battle that for years to come and it might cause hard feelings between him and Amanda as well. He was only now getting to know his sister and he didn't want the relationship to be destroyed by their mother—even from the grave. He had his own fortune, earned by his own endeavor. He didn't need the family money.

He left the store and went directly to the house. Amanda was in the studio. As soon as he greeted her and Dakota he told her they had to talk.

"Go ahead. I'm just drawing. I can do that and listen at the same time."

"I think I know what was behind Grace wanting to divide up the furniture last night. Clay Bennett came to the store and let it slip that he told Grace the whole estate is going to one of us."

"What? It is? Grace never told me that."

"She didn't tell me, either. But if she found out somehow that it wasn't going to her, doesn't it make sense that she would try to lay claim to whatever valuables she could?"

"Surely even Grace isn't that bad." Her pencil went back to moving swiftly and surely over the paper.

"Are we talking about the same Grace? Of course she is."

Amanda stopped working. "I guess she would stoop to that. So who got it? You or me?"

"I don't know. He realized he had made a blunder and practically ran out of the store."

"It won't do any good to call and ask him. He's already told me that it can't be revealed until the will is officially read."

"If it's me, you can have it."

"No thanks," she said. "Grace and lawsuits would come with the money. Besides, I want to make it on my own. It's a matter of pride, but that's how I feel." She looked across at Dakota. "Do you feel the same way?"

"Absolutely." He didn't stop painting.

"I don't want it, either. I'll give it to Grace. That would solve everything."

Amanda stared into space as she gave the matter thought. "On the other hand, it would make a nice nest egg for the future. It would pay for college educations." She looked back at Dakota.

"No," he said without elaboration.

Nathan didn't follow what they meant, but it didn't matter. "I just thought you should know. I wonder why Grace didn't mention it. I would have expected her to still be complaining over it."

"So would I. She complains enough about everything else." Amanda went back to her detailed angel drawing. Several others were taped to her drawing board. "It's just like Mother to leave it to only one of us."

"How do you figure that?"

"What else would be as likely to divide us?"

Nathan nodded slowly, realizing his sister was right.

Todd hung up the telephone and paused for a minute to gather his thoughts. Then he walked to the plate-glass window and looked out at the traffic. His mall was about to go under and take everything he owned with it.

It wasn't unexpected. When the major department stores hadn't signed up, the handwriting had been on the wall. Somehow, though, Todd had thought the calvary would come over the hill and save the day.

The end hadn't come yet, however. According to Fred Willis, if Todd could find committed investors to put money into the project, the smaller chain stores might be approached. If commitments could be made for most of the store slots, they might be able to get by without the giant department stores. The investors would have to be found immediately, however. Creditors were already sending moderately polite demands for their money.

Todd already had bought all the supplies he would need for the mall construction so there was no problem about not being able to complete the building if he could continue paying the workmen. Several small stores had signed rental agreements. He wouldn't have a half-completed, empty mall. He just wouldn't have the backing he needed to stay open.

There had to be other investors he could contact. He sat on a vinyl chair and tried to think clearly. He had called or written everyone he had ever worked with in the past. All the answers had been the same. No one wanted to risk money on such a large mall that was so close to two others.

Grace might know of someone in Houston, but there was no way of getting their names without telling her the predicament they were in. Grace would be furious if she knew how close they were to financial disaster.

Todd tried to think. He had to think. There was a way out of all problems. There had been in the past. He had often gambled on a project, though not as heavily as he had this one. Somehow he had always managed to pull through.

The inheritance. That was the answer. He could put more money in the project and not have to split the profits with anyone else.

To get the inheritance, Elizabeth had to die.

Todd's mind skittered off on a tangent. Anything to keep from thinking of unplugging Elizabeth's machine himself.

Amanda would inherit the fortune. Even Grace thought so. If he could marry Amanda, he could get the money without Grace and her falsified will. To marry Amanda, he would have to divorce Grace.

He knew Amanda wanted him. There was no doubt in

his mind. She was only hanging out with that artist to make Todd jealous. No woman would want an artist when she could have a man with one of the largest construction companies in Dallas. Amanda had no way of knowing Todd's financial condition, and on paper he looked good. Artists made almost no money at all. He could promise her a lot. If she married him, he could build her a gallery all for herself.

A gallery in the new mall. That might sway her. Amanda had said one of the largest career obstacles she faced was to be able to get her work where the public could see it. Todd didn't care for her recent work, but he knew she had talent. Having her own gallery might be incentive for Amanda to invest in his mall now. That would give him time to get a divorce, then he could marry her. Yes, that would work.

What if Grace managed to push through her faked will? That wasn't impossible. Todd had seen other less likely things happen in the courts. He didn't want to divorce Grace and marry Amanda, only to find out Grace got the money after all. This had to be handled very carefully.

He had to make Amanda his mistress. That would solve several matters. It would get rid of Dakota and ensure that Amanda was waiting for him as soon as he divorced Grace. If it happened right away, it would give him the pleasurable convenience of having Amanda at his beck and call when Grace and Nathan were away from the house.

The memory of the days when he had Amanda at his bidding made his mouth water. She had been so luscious then and she was even better now. She was older than he preferred his lovers, but she was still his beautiful Amanda and that would make up for the years. Without makeup and in the right clothes, she could still pass for a teenager.

He went back to Elizabeth's room and sat back down in

the chair he had used earlier. Grace looked up but didn't bother to speak. That was fine with him.

As he stared at Elizabeth, he made his plans.

Amanda completed a series of angel drawings and showed them to Dakota. He grinned as he thumbed through them. "I think you've got something here."

"Do you?" she asked doubtfully.

"Picture these as Christmas ornaments and this group on the top of music boxes. What do you think?"

"They would do for either. I drew them with the idea in mind of making them three dimensional."

"Wood. They should be made of wood."

"The only sculptor we know is Jerry Kinsington. He wouldn't be interested at all in something like this."

"No, it has to be sold by the drawings alone. There's no need to wait for a prototype to be made." Dakota sat on the stool and thought as he looked at them. "You know, these drawings are terrific in their own right. There might be a market for them just as they are. Remember that man we met at the Loftners' party?"

"The one with the card company? Yes."

"He's the one who needs to see these." Dakota looked at the clock on the wall. "I think I'll give him a call and see if he's interested. What was his name?"

"Joe Simon." she watched him with growing enthusiasm.

Dakota brought the phone into the studio and called Information for the number of Simon's company. When he was connected with the man, he identified himself and reminded him where they had met. Then he got right down to business. "Amanda and I have an idea for something new and I thought you might be interested." He paused while he waited for Simon to finish speaking.

"Amanda has drawn a series of angels that I think would be perfect for Christmas cards and ornaments. Right. Three-dimensional ornaments. I can see them in wood and marketed as Victorian nostalgic items."

Amanda sat on the stool and tried to imagine what Simon might be saying.

"No, I'm not in town right now and I'm not sure when I'll be back. Sure. I'll call you when we return and make an appointment. I understand. No, I won't wait too long. Bye." He hung up.

"Well?" she asked impatiently. "What did he say?"

"He remembers us and is familiar with our work. He's interested in seeing the drawings but naturally he can't make any commitments without seeing what we're talking about."

"Did he think it was a crazy idea?"

"No, he sounded enthusiastic. He's buying for Christmas a year from now and cautioned me not to wait too long before showing him the work. With your track record, he thinks this could be a profitable venture for us both."

Amanda told herself to stay calm. "All this is so new to me! I never thought of using my art for something other than paintings. Will we cheapen our work by doing this? What effect will it have on the exhibitions?"

"None of these angels are taken from that series. It won't harm the shows at all. It might even help them if we can get a commitment from Simon and use it in our advertising."

Dakota grinned at her. "We shouldn't set our expectations too high. It might not work out. We won't know until he sees the drawings."

"But if he likes them, it could help us a lot financially," she finished for him. "Why didn't we think of this before?"

"Beats me. I only considered painting and I know that's all you've wanted to do."

"I'm tired of just making ends meet. Making some money right now sounds good. It would relieve a lot of worries. I wonder how much we could get from this."

"From what Jed Loftner has told me, it could be very lucrative."

"Maybe so much that you wouldn't have to teach art classes at the college next semester?" she asked. "Or that I wouldn't have to give private lessons? I'd like that." She disliked teaching as much as Dakota did, but neither had ever admitted it aloud. Like many artists, they taught when funds were running low or when their painting was in a slump.

"We're not going to place too much hope in this," he cautioned her. "I don't want you to be disappointed if it doesn't pan out."

"The same goes for you."

"Okay. As soon as possible, we can make an appointment and show him the sketches. Until then, we should put it out of our minds and work on our canvases for the shows. Agreed?"

"All right." She didn't think she would be able to put it out of her mind, but she would try. Even if the angels brought in only a few extra dollars, it would be a help with the baby on the way.

To prove to Dakota she could control her thoughts she picked up a paintbrush and put a fresh canvas on the easel.

"You look as if you have an inspiration," he observed.

"I do." She quickly started blocking in a picture of another castle. This one would rest on the back of a semi-transparent dragon. Her castle pictures had often been successful and she enjoyed painting them. As she worked she said, "Evelyn told me today that she's definitely decided to retire."

"Oh?"

"It's for the best, really. Mother will never come home

from the hospital and Evelyn would be out of work. She says she's too old to find a position elsewhere, so she's going to move to Austin and live near her younger sister. "It won't be for a while yet. She's going to wait until we get past the funeral, of course. She worked for Mother most of her life. It's going to be a hard adjustment for her."

"Did your mother treat her that well?"

Amanda smiled. "Like one of the family." Their eyes met over the top of the canvas and they both laughed. "But Evelyn will miss her anyway. I told her we'll stay in touch."

They worked in silence for a while. Then Amanda said, "I think we should build the baby a room in our loft. You know, one with real walls. He shouldn't breathe too much paint and turpentine fumes."

"You're right."

"It will look funny to have walls in there."

"There are walls around the bathroom and the elevator stop."

"Those don't count."

"We can start on it when we go back home. If we work evenings, it shouldn't take us too long."

"It might be fun. Sort of like having a house of our own." Amanda's muscles were strong from stretching canvas, lifting heavy frames and paint boxes, and from painting for hours on end. She had no doubt they could do it.

"You really want a house, don't you?"

"You know I do. Don't you?"

"Yes, but I hadn't really thought much about it until lately. a lot of things are different these days."

Amanda gazed at him over the top of her canvas. "The baby, you mean?" She hoped he wasn't referring to the panic attack she'd had two nights before that forced their lovemaking to end abruptly. She hadn't been able to explain what had happened to her because she didn't really understand it. She was sure it had left him sexually frustrated and she'd hoped to make it up to him the following night, but there had been too much tension between them then for either to make the first move.

He nodded. "And us. We're changing. Have you noticed it?"

"No," she lied. She was afraid to even acknowledge the change she had seen in herself. A therapist had told her once that the unexplainable fear, the panic attacks, that hit her on rare occasions stemmed from having been sexually abused by Todd and that there was little she could do about it but pray that the frequency of the attacks would abate when she no longer felt Todd was a threat. Since the incident in the kitchen, she felt she had lost a lot of ground in her struggle to view his inappropriate behavior as more of an irritant than a threat. She was sure that once they were back in L.A., far away from Todd, all her thoughts of him would drift into the recesses of her mind and not cause further problems between her and Dakota.

It wasn't only the change in her he was talking about because he'd said, *"we're* changing." Did that mean that his feelings of love for her were diminishing? She hoped not, but only time would tell.

Chapter Fifteen

Todd watched Grace and Nathan drive away toward the hospital, then made himself a drink. Lately he had been drinking more. It helped dull the panic he felt over the financial ruin that seemed imminent. He knew of no other backers and to ask Grace for names of potential investors in Houston could be catastrophic. He couldn't risk being divorced before Elizabeth's death.

He heard splashing and went to the side window. Elizabeth had installed a pool while her children were still living at home. Because she was Elizabeth, she had put it on the side of the house where it could be seen from the street and enclosed it in a luxurious glass room. Dozens of plants provided a screen from the view of the street, but all the neighbors knew it was there. In recent years it was rarely used.

Dakota was swimming laps, his strokes sure and strong. Todd stood there watching him without being seen from inside the house. He hated that man with passion. The thought of Dakota's hands on Amanda made him tremble with rage. Why would she want to give herself to a man with an earring and long hair? The answer was obvious. She wanted to make Todd jealous.

He looked up toward the ceiling. With Dakota in the pool, they were virtually alone in the house. He smiled and tossed down the rest of his drink and started upstairs.

Amanda was painting in the studio. Since finishing the angel drawings she had felt a burst of creativity and was making the most of it. She didn't look up when the door opened. "Back so soon? I expected you to swim for half an hour at least."

The door closed but there was no answer.

"Dakota?" she asked, peering around the canvas. At first she didn't see anyone and the hair prickled on the back of her neck. "Who's there?"

The sound of a soft footstep jerked her head around. Again. He had come up behind her again. "Todd! What are you doing in here?"

"I came to keep you company."

"I don't need company. Go away." She was determined not to let him see she was nervous at being alone with him. With the door closed and Dakota down in the pool, no one would hear her if she called out. Todd knew that.

"I saw him swimming, so I said to myself, that means Amanda is all alone up there."

"You'd better go back downstairs before Grace or Nathan finds you in here."

Todd smiled and shook his head. "No way. They've gone to the hospital. It's just the two of us. Just like old times."

"No, it's not," she said firmly. He stepped nearer to her and she backed away. "Todd, I'm warning you. Don't come any closer."

"You didn't say that at one time. Then it was " 'Closer, Todd, come closer.' "

Her insides twisted. "You've been drinking. Isn't it rather early for that?"

"Not for me. Grace doesn't care what I do."

"She would definitely care about you being in here with me. You know how angry she was last Mother's Day when she found us together in the kitchen." She hoped the reminder would send him away. In spite of his bragging words to the contrary, Todd was afraid of Grace.

"She's never going to know."

"Yes, she is. If you don't leave right now, I'll tell her."

"If you do, I'll tell about that mole you have right there." He reached and touched the side of her breast.

Amanda slapped his hand away. "I'm warning you, Todd!" Furtively she glanced around for anything she could use as a weapon to defend herself. Her pallet knife was honed to a sharp edge from having been used to mix paint for years but it was out of reach.

He reached out again and touched her other breast. "Go ahead and play hard to get. I like this game as well as the bashful teenager you used to play."

"You should never have done what you did to me."

"You asked for it. That first time you practically ripped my clothes off. Remember that? Remember my apartment, Amanda?"

"I was only a kid and you knew it. You had no business taking advantage of me! I didn't know what I was doing!"

"Oh, you knew what you were doing all right. Even then you were better than Grace ever became. If you hadn't been so young, I would have married you instead. I've never stopped wanting you."

"You're married to my sister. I wouldn't want you even if you weren't."

"You're jealous of Grace. That's it, isn't it?" He grinned and reached out for her again.

Amanda almost fell over the legs of an easel as she moved

to avoid his groping fingers. She was becoming more frightened by the minute.

"You see us sharing a bed and you think we're doing it. Well, you don't need to be jealous of that. This is the first time Grace and I have shared a room, let alone a bed. I haven't touched her in the past five years."

"I don't want to know any of this. Get out of here!"

"Not until you know how it is. I'm still married to her but that's going to change. Then it will be you and me. You'd like that, wouldn't you?" He reached out and pinched her.

Amanda cried out and struck at him but missed. Her heart was hammering and she was afraid to take her eyes from him. Where was the door? She had to be near it. If she was fast, she could open it and run to Dakota before Todd could catch her. She was younger and faster, and he had been drinking. "I love Dakota," she said to stall him. "I don't want you."

"You need a real man. I know about artists. You need somebody like me—a man who knows how to please a woman."

"If you don't go away, I'll start screaming and I won't stop until Dakota hears me. You really don't want Dakota to know what you're doing!"

"You won't tell him. Want to know how I know? Because you didn't tell him about the night I surprised you in the kitchen. You don't want him to know about us."

"That's where you're wrong. I told him all about us. He knows what a vile person you are." She tried to reach behind her for the door but Todd stepped closer and she had to move away. He was enjoying this game.

"Come here, baby. Come let me touch you."

The words were the same ones he had used when he was forcing himself on her so many years ago. Amanda started shouting for Dakota. The sound caused Todd to leap forward and pin her against the wall. He yanked at her blouse with one hand as he gagged her with the other. His breath was rasping in her ear and his thick body was pressed painfully against hers.

Suddenly the door burst open and Dakota was there. He jerked Todd away from her and spun him around. Water beaded his tanned muscles and his hair hung wetly on his shoulders. Without thought he knotted his hand in Todd's shirt and thrust him against the wall. Todd yelped in fright.

"If you ever touch Amanda again, I'll kill you," Dakota said, his black eyes boring into Todd's. "Do you hear me?" When Todd didn't immediately answer, he shook him and shoved him harder against the wall. "I said do you hear me!"

Todd nodded. "Okay, okay! I didn't mean anything by it! We were just playing around."

Amanda caught Dakota's arm and pulled at him. "No, Dakota! Don't hurt him!" She had visions of Dakota beating Todd soundly and landing in jail. "I'm not hurt. I'm all right. Turn him loose!"

Todd's eyes were round with fear and his face had a greenish pallor. Sweat beaded his forehead.

"I know what you did to her when she was a girl," Dakota said, his face bare inches from Todd's. "If you ever even look at her again, I'm going to beat the shit out of you. Now get out of here!" He lowered Todd to the floor and shoved him toward the door.

Todd stumbled as he ran out.

Amanda leaned against the wall in relief. "Thank God you heard me! How did you get here so fast?"

"I didn't hear you. All of a sudden I knew you needed me." He was glaring at her. "I didn't hear you make any sound at all."

"I shouted for you!"

"And then you stopped me from hitting him. Why did you do that!"

"Because Grace would have you arrested! Can't you see that's just what she would want?"

"I wouldn't be arrested for protecting you."

"Yes, you would!" She was shaking so hard she was finding it difficult to speak coherently.

"All I know is I came in and saw him kissing you. Look at your blouse! It's torn half off!"

Amanda looked down and saw Todd had ripped the buttons loose and the fabric had split from the collar. She pulled it in place to cover herself.

"Did you encourage him?"

Her head snapped up. "What!"

"I asked if you encouraged him? Todd is a coward. I can't believe he would take a chance like this with me in the house!"

"No! Of course I didn't do anything to encourage him! How can you ask me such a thing?"

"We never let anyone in our studio, but here he was."

"He came in because he knew you were swimming!"

"I didn't hear you call for help. If some guy was ripping her clothes off, a woman would shout for help and fight back."

"I *was* fighting back!"

He gestured at the room. "Nothing is turned over. Canvases would be all over the floor if you put up a real struggle."

"I can't believe you're saying these things to me!" She stared at him as if he were a stranger. "Don't do this to me!"

"Maybe next time I should let you protect yourself. You've told me for a long time that you can take care of yourself. That I didn't need to come to Houston with you because you could keep Todd at bay. It seems to me that something is wrong with this picture!''

"He surprised me. Until this visit, we've never been alone in the house. The other visits weren't like this!'' Her nightmare was coming to life. When Todd had been forcing her to let him do as he pleased with her body, he had used the threat that no one would believe her if she told. "Dakota, don't say these things to me! Please!''

He gave her a last glare and turned and stalked from the room.

Amanda sank into the chair. Although she was cold all over, a fine sweat slicked her brow and she felt as if she was going to be ill. Her world had crumbled. Dakota didn't believe her! Hot tears ran down her cheeks but she didn't make a sound. She wrapped her arms about her body and hugged herself the way she had years before when Todd was finished with her.

Dakota went to the bathroom and dried himself off with a towel. He was so angry he was shaking. That bastard had tried to all but rape Amanda! He hardly remembered what he had said to her afterward. Anger was pounding in his veins and he wanted to find Todd and take him apart, piece by piece.

Why hadn't she called out for him? He had acted on instinct when he came upstairs, trailing water behind him. Something deep inside him had set off an alarm and he had listened to it. If he hadn't, Todd could have done anything at all to her—since he had been staying at the Wainwright house Dakota customarily swam for at least half an hour.

As his anger became more controllable, he remembered that he and Amanda had exchanged heated words, but he couldn't exactly remember what had been said. He had been so angry at Todd that he might have said anything.

He dressed and went back to the door of the studio. Amanda stood behind one of her canvases, her raised hand holding her paintbrush. Whatever he had said must not have affected her too much if she was painting. He came into the room. "Are you okay?" he asked awkwardly.

"I'm just fine," she snapped.

"I'm sorry I lost my temper. I wanted to smash Todd and you happened to be the one standing in front of me."

"Don't give it a second thought." Her words were icy.

Dakota frowned. She was still angry. He went to her and took the brush from her hand. When he tried to embrace her, she shoved at him.

"Don't touch me! I don't want anyone to touch me!"

"I said I'm sorry. I probably said some things I shouldn't and I'm trying to make up."

"You 'probably' said some things?" she said angrily. " 'Probably'?"

"Give me a chance, Amanda!"

"Oh, sure. I'll give you a chance. I'll give you the same consideration you gave me! Leave me alone!"

"You don't mean that!"

"Yes, I do! Go back to L.A. and get out of my sight!"

Dakota backed away. He hadn't expected this. "You want me to go?"

"Are you deaf as well as insensitive? Yes! I want you to go!"

He turned and left the room. He had no intention of leaving Houston, but he knew the argument was only going to build if he stayed where he was. As he stalked down the stairs and headed toward the den, he saw Todd scurry out of his way. He glared at him until Todd retreated into the living room and was out of sight. It would be a long while

before Todd tried to hurt Amanda again, but Dakota still
ached to hit him.

He went into the den, dropped into the leather chair
and propped his foot on the coffee table. What the hell
had he said to Amanda? No matter how hard he tried to
remember, he couldn't recall the exact words.

Usually when Amanda's temper flared, it soon receded.
He decided it would be a good idea to wait a while before
trying to make up with her again. Whatever she had read
into his words, she was in no mood to listen at the present.

Nathan was glad to return to the house. He hated seeing
his mother look the way she did. Now that he knew there
was no hope of her recovering, it was like watching a dead
person being made to breathe by machines. She didn't
even look like Elizabeth any more. The muscles were atro-
phying on her bones and the skin hung slack on her face.
He couldn't see why Grace continued to hold on to the
hope that a miracle would happen. Elizabeth was beyond
miracles.

Todd was in the living room, which was unusual since
he almost always sat in the den. Nathan nodded to him in
greeting. Todd looked away and shifted uneasily.

"You should have gone with us," Grace said to him.
"People are going to wonder why you hardly ever visit
Mother. While we were there, Reverend Emmett stopped
by. He's such a nice man. Maybe I'll start going back to
church when I move down here."

"Whatever you want to do is fine." Todd wouldn't make
eye contact with her.

"What's wrong with you?" Grace asked suspiciously.

"Nothing. Nothing at all."

Nathan leaned against the doorframe. Todd was acting

as guilty as a kid caught with his hand in the cookie jar. "Where's Amanda?"

"How should I know?" His tone was stringent. He stood and went to make himself a drink at the wet bar in the next room.

Nathan watched him. Something had happened.

Grace was right behind Todd. "You've been up to something. I can tell."

"No, I haven't!"

"Did you talk to Fred Willis?" she demanded.

"Yes. That was it. I talked to Fred."

She waited. "So? What did he say?"

"He just gave me an update on the mall's progress."

Nathan didn't believe him but Grace apparently did. She turned away. "I wish you wouldn't be so involved in that business of yours. I'm in a crisis here and I need some moral support from you."

Nathan straightened and went upstairs. He found Amanda in the studio alone. "Hi. What's going on?"

She jumped as if the sound of his voice startled her. "Nothing." She clearly wasn't encouraging communication.

"Where's Dakota?"

"How should I know?"

"Is something wrong?"

She frowned at him. "What could possibly be wrong? This family is too wonderful for anything to be wrong."

"Why are you angry?"

"Leave me alone, Nathan. I'm trying to work."

He backed out. Something had happened while they were gone. He went in search of Dakota and found him in the den. "What's happening? Todd is acting as if he's committed a crime and Amanda is mad enough to bite nails in half."

Dakota frowned. "Todd tried to force himself on

Amanda. I caught him and wanted to beat the hell out of him but Amanda stopped me. Todd ran like a scalded cat and somehow Amanda and I ended up in an argument."

"He touched her?" Nathan was shocked at Todd's boldness.

"He nearly tore her blouse off!"

"I'm surprised we aren't having to carry him out in parts!" He sat on the couch and leaned forward. "Why did you and Amanda argue?"

"Damned if I know." Dakota frowned at the opposite wall. "I went back and tried to apologize but she told me to go back to L.A."

"That must have been some argument!"

"Not really. That's what I can't figure out. Maybe she misunderstood something I said. I'm giving her time to cool down and try to talk to her again."

"Anything I can do to help?"

"Not unless you want to beat up Todd for me. Amanda says if I touch him, Grace will have me arrested."

Nathan nodded. "She's right."

"It might be worth it."

"Not with those exhibitions coming up. You don't want any bad publicity now. Besides, if you're in jail, you won't be here to keep an eye on Todd."

Dakota made an angry sound. "I shouldn't have to guard her in her own family! Why don't we make him leave?"

"We won't be here much longer. Grace will surely come around in a day or two. You haven't seen Mother lately. I don't know how Grace still holds out hope."

"Maybe she doesn't. Maybe she's just doing this to torture the rest of us." He sighed. "I'm sorry. I seem to be saying all the wrong things today. I was out of line."

"I've thought worse about her." He studied the floor between his feet. "I never thought Todd would try something like that with you in the house."

"He used to molest her when she was a girl. Did you know that?"

"Not at the time. Amanda told me on Mother's Day."

"For all I know, he's never stopped. Men like that ought to be locked up. Or better yet, castrated."

"I agree."

"This family has too many secrets."

"I agree about that, too. Until Mother's Day, I didn't know you existed and apparently you've lived together for a year."

"About that." Dakota looked at him. "Who's Cody?"

Nathan hesitated. "My wife."

Dakota stared at him. "Your wife? You're married and you haven't told anyone in your family?"

"Not until now." He added, "I'd appreciate it if you don't tell the others. This isn't the right time to break news like this. Mother is about to die and all our tempers are on edge." He grinned. "I also have a son."

Dakota leaned his head back and laughed. "You've been married long enough to have a son? That's rich, man!"

"It's one of those secrets that's gotten too big to tell. I might be able to explain a wife, but not a two-year-old boy."

"He's two? This gets better and better!" Dakota shook his head in amazement. "Why the hell haven't you told anyone?"

"If you knew Mother you'd understand. Or if you had met Cody. There's nothing simple about this family."

"I agree with you there. I don't feel so bad about Amanda keeping me a secret now." He laughed again. "I wonder if Grace and Todd also have something they're not telling."

"I think Todd's behavior toward Amanda qualifies. Grace certainly doesn't know what he did to her. I haven't known that long myself. But even if she hadn't told me, I would have figured it out the night I caught Todd trying to force himself on her."

"What? When did this happen?" Dakota exclaimed.

"She didn't tell you? I was certain she would have gone straight to you. It was about a week ago."

Dakota's frown darkened. "I ought to kill that bastard!"

"It wouldn't solve anything. With the two of us keeping an eye on him, he can't hurt her."

"I don't think we're doing that good a job of it."

"We'll try harder. In a few days we'll all go our separate ways and Amanda never will never need to see Todd again. Believe me, it's better this way than to get Grace stirred up."

"Sweep it under the carpet? You're going to run out of room under there."

"I'll have a talk with him. I don't think he'll try it again since he knows now that you'll be watching. I know I wouldn't want to mess with you."

Dakota nodded. "Maybe. But I'm not going to back away next time."

"I'll see to it that he knows that, too." Nathan hoped Todd was smart enough to listen to the warning.

Amanda was still angry and hurt the next day. She dressed in a silence that was painful in its intensity.

"Will you at least tell me why you're not speaking to me?" Dakota asked impatiently.

"I don't want to talk about it." The night had been terrible. A full-size bed wasn't large enough to accommodate Dakota comfortably and Amanda had frequently found his leg pressed close to hers or her arm resting against his chest. Last night had been the first night since they fell in love that she had worn a nightgown to bed.

That he had been able to sleep when she couldn't hadn't made matters any easier.

"Do you really want me to leave?" he asked.

She turned her back. The last thing she wanted was for him to go back home, but she couldn't swallow her pride long enough to tell him that.

"I gather by your silence that the answer is yes?"

"Do as you please." She yanked a brush through her hair and avoided looking at him.

"Amanda, don't let this get between us."

"It's already there. You put it between us yesterday."

"What the hell did I say to make you so angry?"

"You know what you said as well as I do! I'm certainly not going to repeat it for you!" Just thinking that he had accused her of encouraging Todd and of giving in to him on her visits to Houston made her physically ill.

"We always said we would talk out our problems. You know how I hate it when people refuse to communicate with me!"

"Tough."

"You're making me wonder if you're angry with me for what I said or for coming to your defense."

She whirled on him. "You're accusing me of enjoying what was happening?" She was so angry her voice broke.

"That's not what I said, damn it! And while we're on the subject, why didn't you tell me Nathan interrupted the same thing before? You never told me about it!"

"I was trying to protect you!"

"Protect me? I don't need protection!"

"Well, then I guess I was just encouraging Todd again. What a slut you must think I am!"

"What? What are you talking about? I don't think any such thing!"

"I told you I don't want to talk about it!" She slammed out of the room and went down to the kitchen.

Evelyn smiled when she saw her, then looked concerned. "You, too? What did all of you do yesterday? Start World War III? Nathan and Todd aren't speaking and Grace is angry with everybody. I'm not going to take any more days off if you all can't behave while I'm gone."

Amanda dropped into a chair and frowned at the table. "Yesterday was awful. I don't ever want to have another day like it." She took the glass of orange juice Evelyn poured. "I'm so mad at Dakota, I can't stand it."

"Is he mad at you, too?"

"I don't know. Probably." She traced a pattern in the frost on the glass. "I can't talk about it."

"Okay by me. I think talking is overrated, personally. I've found it's better to let good old-fashioned silence reign until everyone is cooled down and avoid bringing it up again."

Amanda finally smiled. "A psychiatrist would have a field day with you."

"Probably. Maybe that's why I never remarried. It's easier to live peacefully if there's only one person under the roof."

Amanda was silent. She wanted to make up with Dakota but she didn't know how to do it if he really thought she had encouraged Todd. The idea that Dakota could think that of her made her sick inside. She wished she could erase yesterday and start all over. "I told him to go back to L.A."

"Why would you do a fool thing like that?"

"I'm just so angry with him. We had a terrible fight."

"Have you tried apologizing?"

She tossed Evelyn a glare. "I'm not the one at fault."

"Okay. So let him go back and get ready for that show. By the time you're finished up here you can join him and everything will be dandy again."

"I don't think we'll ever be finished here. Grace won't

listen to reason and we can't do anything without her agreement. She would hound us over it forever.''

"That she would.''

"Maybe I should go back home with Dakota. It's just that I keep thinking that any day now Grace will accept the inevitable and the doctor can take care of matters. I don't want to get home and have to take the next flight back.''

"No, that wouldn't be any good. I don't trust airplanes. Never have.'' Evelyn began drying the dishes she just washed. "You want some cereal? Or I could make you some eggs and bacon.''

"I don't want anything but juice. I just came down to keep from starting the fight with Dakota again.''

"Wise decision. Just stay clear of each other until the air clears. That's what I would do.''

Chapter Sixteen

"We're going to talk," Dakota said, blocking Amanda's way out of the studio.

She crossed her arms over her chest and said, "Talk."

"Not here. I want you out of this house. Let's go out to eat."

"I have paint all over me." She hadn't been able to get much done that day, but her hands didn't show it. Oil paint in several colors stained her skin and the clothes she wore to paint in.

"You were about to clean up. I'll tell Evelyn we won't be here for dinner and you take a shower."

She gave him a frosty look and brushed past him. Although she didn't want to admit it, she wanted to talk to him, too, and she especially wanted to get out of the house. Being hurt and angry for so long was making her feel ill and she was fighting a black cloud of depression.

She took her time in the shower, letting the hot water wash away all the lingering turpentine and paint. All the creativity she had felt the morning before had vanished and her self-doubt was back. Dakota hadn't been able to get much done that day, either. It would be best if he went back home so at least one of them could work.

As she dressed, she wondered how long she would be in Houston. She hadn't dreamed she would still be here a month after she had learned of her mother's accident. Would she be there the following month as well? No, she resolved. She wouldn't do that to herself.

Dakota had used the other shower and was waiting for her when she went to their room. Barely speaking, they left the house.

The silence was so strong she wanted to scream. He was still angry. She could tell by the way he drove as well as by his silence. It wasn't like him not to talk. By now her own anger was gone, but the hurt feelings remained. How could he have said those things to her?

After what seemed like forever, they got to the restaurant where they ordered and waited in more silence for the food to come. "We aren't talking," she observed at last.

"I'm afraid I may say the wrong thing by accident."

"I'm not that unreasonable." She knew she wouldn't be able to eat past the lump in her throat.

"Maybe it would be best if I go back to L.A. I'm asking you to come with me."

Amanda thought for a minute. "I don't know what to do," she admitted.

"Amanda, being in your mother's house and around your family is tearing us both apart. We've never had an argument like this. I can't leave you here alone with Todd. Nathan can't be with you all the time. Next time he could rape you."

She glanced at the neighboring tables. "Say it a little louder. I think some of the people in the back may have missed it."

"I mean it. You're not safe in that house."

"I know that."

"Will you come back with me? I want to work out this problem between us and get on with our lives. If we stay here much longer, it may never happen."

The hurt built inside her. He didn't love her enough to keep her family from destroying them? "It's not easy for me, either."

"If your mother dies, you can fly back down. That's what we should have done weeks ago."

"I keep thinking that each day could be the one. You know how I dislike flying."

"You dislike being here more. Or at least I thought you did."

"I have so many mixed emotions about being here. Nathan and Grace are my entire family now. I'll never see Evelyn again after the house is divided up. I'll never be inside the house where I grew up. It wasn't a happy house, but my roots are here. Can't you understand that?"

"I guess roots aren't that important to me."

"No. I guess they aren't."

"Are you saying you won't come back with me?"

"I don't know. I can't make that decision over a salad. I have to think about it." She looked at him. "Is it all right if we go by the hospital when we leave here? Maybe if I see her again I'll know what to do."

"Okay." He sounded reluctant.

She wasn't looking forward to going there, either.

Todd waited until Dakota and Amanda had left, then slipped upstairs and into the studio. He was still furious at Dakota for interrupting the day before and for making him look like a fool in front of Amanda. She had tried to come to his defense. He had to give her that. If it hadn't been for her, Todd was certain that Dakota would have hit him.

Amanda had stayed angry with Dakota for the rest of the night and all day as well. He could tell by the way she carried herself and by the silence between them. Todd had watched Amanda for so many years he could tell her mood before she said a word, just by her body language. It made him feel almost vindicated to know she had stepped in to protect him. Almost, but not quite.

He turned on the lights and walked among the paintings as if he were in an art gallery. He didn't understand any of them. There was one painting of a castle that was pretty, but it was almost as if the walls were transparent in places. Todd didn't get it. He was fond of landscapes, personally.

Their styles were remarkably similar, at least to Todd's undiscerning eye, and he wasn't sure who had painted which canvas.

Dakota had definitely painted the one of the cliff, however. He had already signed it in the lower right-hand corner. Todd took out his pocket knife and stood smiling at the canvas for a last moment. Then he jabbed the knife in the canvas and ripped it from top to bottom. The sound was most pleasing, so he did it several more times as well. Then he turned to the next one . . .

He had been at his work for several minutes when he heard Nathan's footsteps on the stairs. Todd hurried to the light switch and turned it off before his brother-in-law noticed the crack of light beneath the door. When he heard Nathan go into his room and shut the door, Todd opened the studio door a crack and peeped out. No one was in the hall. Since Nathan's room was next door to the studio, he couldn't destroy the rest of the paintings, but he had the satisfaction of knowing he had paid Dakota back.

Todd left the studio and went downstairs to tell Grace

he was going out to a local bar he had started frequenting. She wouldn't care. She didn't want to be with him any more than he wanted to be with her.

Dakota stayed in the waiting room while Amanda went into the room.

Elizabeth lay as she always did. Her chest rose and fell to the machine's rhythm. The only sound in the room was the low snore of escaping air as she exhaled and the monotonous sound of the machines that were monitoring her body's functions.

Amanda sat beside the bed and took Elizabeth's hand in hers. "Mother, I just wanted to talk to you one last time. I'm going back to L.A. with Dakota so I won't be here when it happens. I'm sorry and I know you wouldn't understand, but being in the house with Grace and Todd is destroying our relationship." She paused. "I haven't told you about Dakota. I love him and he loves me. At least I think he still does. If I go back home with him we may be able to patch this up. It's only going to get worse if we stay here.

"I more than just love him. I've been living with him for a year. You wouldn't approve of him at all. He's an artist, too, and if you think I'm flamboyant, you should see Dakota." Amanda smiled at the thought. "Grace nearly had a seizure when he showed up on the doorstep. But the point is, he's right for me. I told you about the upcoming exhibitions. Well, I yelled it, actually, but you know about them. Dakota is the other half of the exhibit. He does New Age paintings. You wouldn't approve of them, either."

She squeezed Elizabeth's hand in an effort to convince herself that her mother was somehow listening and understanding. "That's not all. Not only have we lived together for a year, but we're going to have a baby. Your first grandchild. The only problem is that we don't have any plans to be married. Maybe we never will after what happened with Todd yesterday. But whatever happens, I'm going to bring my baby up in a world of love. It's not going to be much like my own upbringing. I don't know why you never loved me, but my baby will never have to ask that question of me."

Suddenly, unexplainably, Elizabeth's hand tightened.

Amanda's eyes opened wide. Elizabeth was gripping her hand!

She leaped to her feet and ran to the door and down to the nurses' station. "You've got to come quick! I think she's waking up!"

The nurse stared at her, looked at the machine, then back again. "That's not possible, ma'am."

Amanda caught her hand and pulled her down the hall. "Come and see for yourself."

By this time the other nurse at the station had flagged down the intern on duty and he was hurrying to catch up with them. Amanda went to the side of the bed and picked up Elizabeth's hand. "Do it again. Squeeze my hand!"

"Ms. Wainwright," the nurse began.

The intern nudged her aside. He was new and hadn't read Elizabeth's diagnosis. "She may be coming out of the coma! Prepare an injection of adrenalin. On the double," he barked when the nurse failed to move quickly enough. She ran from the room.

Dakota had heard the increased activity and raced into the room. "What's happening?" he asked.

"I think Mother is waking up!" Amanda said as she went to him. "I was talking to her and she squeezed my hand!"

"Sometimes it happens that suddenly," the intern said as he bent over to read the print out on the monitor. "I've heard of coma cases that did that."

"But she's . . ." Dakota began.

"Hush! What if she's not?" Suddenly Amanda remembered what she had been saying to Elizabeth. If her mother could hear what was said, she would know about Dakota, the baby, and probably Todd as well. Amanda took a step backward. She shouldn't have spoken so freely and wouldn't have if she had thought there was the slightest chance of Elizabeth hearing. Could both Dr. Hastings and Dr. Santon be wrong in declaring her brain dead?

The nurse returned with a syringe and a wickedly long needle on a tray, along with a bottle of medicine. The intern took it and measured out the dose he wanted, then injected it into Elizabeth's chest. For a tense minute everyone stared at the monitor. The recording needle continued on in uninterrupted waves. He made an adjustment on the machine and waited some more. "I think I see a change in the brain waves. I think I see sporadic activity."

He filled the syringe again and tossed the empty bottle into the trash. Again he injected Elizabeth's heart and waited.

"Do you see any change?" Amanda asked.

"I'm not sure." The intern jiggled the knob on the machine again. The nurse left the room, returned with Elizabeth's medical chart and put it in front of him

The intern read the diagnosis, straightened and herded Amanda and Dakota out of the room. "I think you'd better let me work with her. If there's any change, I'll let you know. It could have been a muscle spasm. Don't get your hopes up."

"But she hasn't had a muscle spasm in days," Amanda objected. "I know what I felt! Her fingers tightened on my hand!"

The intern nodded placatingly. "I understand. I'll contact her doctor and he'll probably want to run more tests tomorrow just to be sure. You go on home now and I'll call you myself if there's any change."

Amanda was reluctant to leave but she had spent enough hours in the waiting room to know it wouldn't do any good to remain there. As they drove back to the house, Amanda said, "I know what I felt! I'm not mistaken. I had just told her about us and about the baby. It was as if she was reacting!"

"It had to be a muscle spasm. Dr. Hastings told you that could happen."

"But why would it happen at such a time? It could have happened any other time and I wouldn't have thought anything about it, but it was as if she was trying to tell me she heard!"

"Maybe somehow she did and was trying to tell you it was okay."

"Don't humor me. I'm sure she moved her fingers!"

"I'm not humoring you. But she can't be waking up, and you know that as well as I do."

Amanda stared out the window. Logically she knew he was right but she couldn't get the idea out of her mind that the tests could have been wrong.

When they reached the house, she went straight into the den. "Don't get your hopes up," she said to Grace and Nathan, "but I think Mother moved!"

Grace stared at her for a moment, then leaped to her feet. "She moved! She's waking up?"

"I don't know. The intern on duty is going to contact Dr. Hastings and get back to us. They may have to run more tests."

"You see?" Grace demanded of her brother and sister. "I told you Mother was going to get well."

"You shouldn't read too much into this," Dakota said. "Dr. Hastings said muscle spasms can occur. There's no way she can be waking up."

Grace glared at him. "You are hardly an authority." To Nathan she said, "I want you to drive me to the hospital

mmediately. Todd left in our car. He's never around when
I need him. Amanda, call Dr. Santon and have him meet
us at the hospital."

"I can't call him at this hour. I don't have his home
number."

Grace wrote something on a piece of paper and handed
it to her. "Here it is. Go call him while I get my shoes
on."

"You know his home number?" Amanda asked. "Why
would he give it to you?"

"Just call him."

Amanda was full of questions as she dialed the number.
A sleepy woman answered and she asked for the doctor.
Amanda explained to the man who she was and why she
was calling. There was a pause.

"I'll be right down there," he said.

She hung up and looked at Dakota. "Are you going with
us?"

"No, because I think you're getting your hopes up only
to have them dashed again. No doctor would tell you the
patient is brain dead unless he was absolutely positive.
Certainly two of them wouldn't!"

"Someone should stay here until Todd comes home to
tell him what's happening," Grace said as she slipped her
feet into her shoes. She looked at Dakota and added,
"You're the logical one to do that."

Dakota made a growling sound in his throat and walked
away shaking his head. He didn't know what had happened
in the hospital room, but he did know Elizabeth would
never come out of the coma. It made him angry that
Amanda was willing to believe she might. Even now she
was grasping at anything that would give her a sign her
mother loved her.

He went to the studio and turned on the light. Dr.
Santon or Dr. Hastings would talk sense into Amanda and

they could leave. He wanted to be sure the paintings were dry enough to pack. But whether they were wet or dry, he and Amanda were leaving.

When he looked at the canvases, he couldn't comprehend for a minute what he was seeing. Slowly he walked among them, the canvas hanging in shreds from the frames. Three of his paintings and one of Amanda's had been ruined.

He couldn't breathe. Who would do such a thing!

The answer was obvious.

He left the room and took the stairs two at a time. Amanda was on her way out the door. "Amanda! You've got to come up!"

"For heaven's sake," Grace said to him in the tone she used on Todd. "Whatever it is can wait. We have to meet Dr. Santon at the hospital."

"This can't wait." He caught Amanda's wrist and almost dragged her upstairs and down the hall.

"What's wrong with you?" she demanded, struggling to get free. "What can be this important?"

He took her into the studio. Her protestations died on her lips. As he had, she went to the canvases and stared at them unable to utter a sound. Her horrified eyes met his. "Who?" she whispered.

"Who do you think?"

"Todd isn't home. Grace said he's been out drinking all evening."

"Then she did it."

"No. Grace wouldn't do this." She stared back at the canvases. "The one of the cliff! I loved that one!"

"We're leaving, Amanda. We're leaving tonight! I'm not staying under this roof another minute."

"Tonight! I can't leave now!"

"I've heard that for a month now." He was tired of being understanding and cutting other people slack. Some

f his paintings had been ruined and he wanted to smash
omething. "We're getting out of here!"

She backed away toward the door. Downstairs Grace was
houting for her. "Dakota, don't make me choose. I have
o go. Dr. Santon will be there any minute. We have to go
now."

"You don't have to do anything. It's your choice. Your
mother is dead. Dead, Amanda! That's what 'brain dead'
means. It means she won't wake up and she won't communicate with you and she can't squeeze your hand for any
reason other than because there are chemicals in her
bloodstream that cause muscle contractions!"

"She moved her fingers," Amanda said, her eyes plead-
ing with him to let her believe this. "She did. I felt it
myself."

"Come with me!" he demanded. "I've never asked anything of you, Amanda. Give me this!"

"You're asking too much." Tears were in her eyes. "I
can't choose. I can't."

"You *are* choosing."

She backed into the hall, stared at him for another
second, then turned and ran down the stairs.

Dakota stared after her. He hadn't expected her to go.
But she had. He heard the front door slam. The house
was filled with silence.

He leaned against the doorframe, then straightened.
Without looking at the canvases again, he went to the room
he had shared with Amanda and began to pack.

Late that night when they returned home, Amanda knew
without looking that he was gone. She could sense his
absence.

Grace was full of optimism. Dr. Santon was going to
rerun the tests the next day and she was positive that they

would confirm that Elizabeth was going to recover after all. Nathan was too exhausted to argue with her and was going up to his room.

Amanda stood for a minute in the entryway. She was afraid to go upstairs and confirm what she already knew to be true. But, she had no choice.

The bedroom closet was open and his clothes were missing, as was the suitcase he had brought with him. His shaving kit was gone from the bathroom. She went into the studio and forced herself to look at the destruction again. He had stuck a note to the wet paint of one of the canvases.

"Send the paintings when they're dry. Dakota." Nothing else.

Amanda pulled off the note and wadded it into a ball before throwing it into the trash. She didn't have any tears left. She had lost him. Dakota was the only man she had ever loved and she had lost him by choosing her family over him. That was the most stupid mistake anyone had ever made.

Down the hall she could hear the muffled sound of Grace giving Todd hell for not coming to the hospital. No sounds at all were coming from Nathan's room and she wondered if he had decided to drive to Galveston as late as it was.

She went across the hall and closed herself in her room. How could she have made such a horrible mistake? Dakota had taken a cab to the airport and was probably sitting out there waiting for the next flight. If she went there, she might be able to find him.

And if she did, what would it change? They would only argue again and he would tell her to come with him or else. Amanda considered going to him. Then she realized he had chosen to leave her at a time when she needed

im most. He had decided it was over between them. The
decision was out of her hands now.

It was over.

She lay on her bed and didn't bother to undress. There
was no point in it. She already knew she wouldn't fall sleep.

Chapter Seventeen

"I'm sure you must have some idea what this means," Grace persisted.

The nurse shook her head and tightened her lips stubbornly. "No, Mrs. Hillard, I don't. I wasn't even on duty when it happened."

"A person who is brain dead can't react to words. Right?"

"That's right. That would be impossible. But if I were to speculate with you about a patient's condition it would cost me my job."

Grace gave her a last reproving frown. The woman was too determined to be undermined. She went back to Elizabeth's room and sat beside the bed. Had it been a muscle spasm and nothing else?

She wasn't sure what leeway for error lay in tests such as Dr. Santon had performed on her mother. The results from the second series weren't in yet. It wasn't entirely implausible that something had been missed at first but would now show up. Grace wasn't sure how she felt about this.

On one level, she hoped her mother would recover. On another, she didn't.

Both doctors had been adamant that Elizabeth would never be herself again. Grace had spent enough hours by her bedside to see what lay in store if she didn't. There could be many years ahead of her of caring for an invalid. Grace had tried to prepare herself for this possibility, but until now she hadn't forced herself to see the reality of the situation. Elizabeth wouldn't be a pretty dolllike woman lying more or less permanently asleep. She would look the way she did now—ravaged and ugly. Nurses could be hired, but in the end the responsibility would be Grace's.

Grace had all the responsibility she wanted as it was.

She could move to Elizabeth's house and send Todd commuting back and forth to Dallas, but she would be trapped in the house day in and day out, with an invalid. If Elizabeth remained as she was now, she might as well be dead. If she regained consciousness enough to talk, she might complain constantly and find fault endlessly with the way Grace did everything. Grace would hate that.

She found herself biting her nails, a habit she had thought she had conquered in college. She lowered her hand and clasped both of them in her lap. Elizabeth lay like a lump of flesh, her chest rising in shallow, machine-induced breaths. Had she really responded to Amanda's words?

Hesitantly Grace put her hand in Elizabeth's. Uneasily she said, "Can you hear me?"

Elizabeth's hand lay perfectly still.

"Mother, if you were able to squeeze Amanda's hand, you're able to squeeze mine. Do it." Nothing.

Grace released her hand and sat back in the chair. She

had to find some answers. If Elizabeth's will was in favor of Amanda or Nathan, she might care for her for years, only to have her brother or sister inherit everything in the end. That would never do.

Amanda took the ruined canvases out to the backyard barbecue pit and heaped them into the ashes left from the last cookout. Her father had built the brick pit large enough to accommodate a party. Amanda had always wondered about that since her parents had never given a party where the guests were expected to stay in the yard and cook. Elizabeth's parties were always society affairs with softly modulated conversation and gourmet foods.

She used a stick to press the canvas together, then set fire to it. The flames licked the heavy cloth and curled the paint. She forced herself to watch. It was like seeing a part of her being consumed. Dakota and she had long ago agreed that if a painting were harmed in such a way as to make the canvas unusable, it would be destroyed. That way no one could find it and thus own one of their paintings if their work should become well known. At the time, they had smiled at the possibility and never thought such a thing would become necessary.

Amanda was still stunned at the violence the torn canvases represented. She wouldn't have thought Todd was capable of doing something like this. He had always been more covert in the damage he caused.

With the stick, she pushed the canvas into the hotter part of the fire. The crackle of the flames made the heat from the fire seem more intense. Sweat ran down her forehead and neck. June was sweltering enough without a fire to add to it.

She stayed until the last flame was out and the canvas was a heap of ashes. To be certain, she squirted the ashes with the garden hose and returned to the house. The air-conditioned coolness made her sigh with relief.

In the downstairs bathroom she washed her face and wiped it dry to cool herself more quickly. She had the house to herself. Evelyn had gone to the grocery store and wouldn't return for half an hour. Grace and Todd were at the hospital. The doctors weren't returning Grace's calls and she was hoping to intercept one of them on his rounds.

Amanda walked slowly through the house. So many conflicting emotions were stored here. Anger, resentment, envy, and occasionally happiness. She went to the porcelain cottage and took it off the shelf. Sitting on the couch, she held it in her lap.

Again memories of her father swept over her. She could almost hear his deep voice telling her the endless stories about the pretend family that lived there. A mother, a father, a boy and two girls. But there the resemblance to her own family ended. The cottage's family were happy together and had marvelous adventures.

Her father had had such a talent for telling stories. She wondered if he really had been happy as a businessman. She knew she inherited her artistic bent from him. Elizabeth never told stories or drew or sang or did anything that could be considered creative. Maybe her father had really wanted to be a writer or an actor.

She ran her fingers over the familiar lines of the cottage. She knew its thatched roof and whitewashed walls and shuttered windows as well as if she had actually been inside. Often when she was stinging from a punishment from her mother or an argument with Grace or Nathan, her father had taken her into this room and told her a story about this cottage. Tears filled Amanda's eyes and she thought how strange it was that she still cried over her father but felt only guilt and resentment when she thought about Elizabeth.

Amanda carefully replaced the cottage and picked up the phone. She had tried to call Dakota earlier but there had been no answer. She let it ring until the answering machine started the tape. Leaving no message, she hung up. Had he moved out already? It seemed possible since he hadn't answered her earlier message. He would have taken a break since then and he always answered messages at that time.

The thought of their loft emptied of his belongings made her insides curl. She had thought they would always be together. But then, she would have said it was impossible that he would ever accuse her of encouraging Todd or that he would leave her alone in a place where she wasn't entirely safe.

Without making a sound she went up the stairs. Whenever she was alone here, she always found herself moving silently, as if there were ghosts in the house that were better not awakened. Although it had been her home, Amanda never felt comfortable there.

She went to the studio and looked at the stretcher frames that had held the ruined paintings. At least *they* were salvageable. She took the roll of canvas and carried it to the worktable on the far wall. She measured a length of cloth and was tacking it to the frame when she heard the front door close. For a moment she paused and listened. Evelyn wasn't likely to use that door. If it was Grace and Todd, she would hear them talking. It could be Nathan. He had spent the previous night at his home in Galveston, but he usually came by the house at least once during the day.

Going to the door, she called out, "I'm up here, Nathan." She went back to the canvas and caught the fabric with the metal stretchers to pull it tight. Working from the middle of each side, she pulled the canvas taut and tacked it.

The door opened behind her and she said, "If you're here for lunch, Evelyn hasn't fixed it yet."

"I just thought I would come back to the house," Todd said. "I didn't want you to get lonesome."

Amanda turned and gripped the stretchers as a weapon. "You! I would think you'd never dare set foot in this room again!"

"I don't know what you're talking about," he said with an infuriating grin. "I wasn't the one who ripped up your paintings."

"It had to be you. Grace wouldn't stoop to such a thing."

He shrugged. "We didn't need him. I'm glad he's gone. I'm better for you than he would ever be."

"You don't know what you're talking about. Can't you get it through your head that I don't want you?"

"Because I'm married to Grace. I told you, that can be changed."

"Grace has nothing to do with it. I detest you!"

"Now, Amanda. Remember who you're talking to. I know you too well to believe that. We go back a long way." He started toward her.

"If you don't leave, I'll tell Dakota!"

"He's all the way out in California. I'm not afraid of him." He grinned as if he were enjoying her fear.

"I'll tell Grace then! You know how angry she would be if she thought you were anywhere near me." This time there was no hope that Dakota would come to her rescue. Her fear was mounting.

"No you won't. You never told before and you won't tell now. Remember what good times we had, Amanda?" His hand shot out and he grabbed her by the hair. "Come here, baby."

Amanda blinked against the pain as he pulled her to him but she didn't give him the satisfaction of crying out.

Instead, she stumbled against him, centered herself, and kneed him as hard as she could.

Todd doubled over with a cry. She shoved him aside and ran across the hall to her bedroom. When she was inside, she turned the lock and leaned against the door. She could hear him cursing her in the hall and knew he could break down the door if he tried. The lock was meant more as a safeguard of privacy than as a means of safety. If Todd shoved against it, the door might give way. She sat on the floor, her back against the door and her feet braced against the dresser. At any moment she expected to hear him trying to break down the door.

Instead, she heard him stumble toward the stairs. Then a series of bumps and curses as he fell to the landing. Maybe she had hurt him more badly than she had intended. Or maybe it was a trick to lure her out from the comparatively safe room. She stayed where she was.

In a matter of seconds she heard voices. By putting her ear against the door, she heard Nathan speaking to Todd.

"Are you okay? What happened?" Nathan was asking.

"I fell." Todd sounded as if he were still in pain. "Tripped."

"Give me your hand. I'll help you up. Do you think you broke any bones?"

"No. I'm all right." Todd sounded angry so she knew his pain must be lessening. "Just help me to my room and I'll lie down for a while."

She waited until she heard them walk down the hall, then she opened the door. She felt better with Nathan in the house and she didn't intend to let him leave again.

Nathan came from Todd's room and smiled when he saw her. "I guess you didn't hear Todd. He fell down the stairs."

"I heard him." She tossed a frown at the closed door. "He was bothering me again."

"Again? I hate to say it, but maybe you had better leave. I know it would mean you flying back down soon, but you're not safe here." He matched his steps to hers as they went down the stairs. "I thought Grace would be with him."

"So did I."

"He didn't hurt you, did he?"

"No. Not really. I'm just scared."

"You have to tell Grace. That will put an end to it."

"Only if she believes me. You know how Grace is. She only believes what suits her. Mother's health being a prime example."

"What do you think about Mother? *Was* she aware of what you said?"

"I don't know. At the time, I was positive. And the intern seemed to think it was possible. I just don't know. I'm sure it will give Grace ammunition for weeks. Maybe I should fly home." She bit her lip as she considered the possibility. "I'm just not sure what I'll find when I get there. I've been trying to reach Dakota but he's not answering the phone and he hasn't returned my call."

"All the more reason to go to him."

"Nathan, what am I going to do if he's left me?"

"Would he do that? Move out without saying good-bye?"

"I don't think so, but I also thought he would call me back. It wouldn't be the first time he's surprised me lately."

Nathan was quiet for a minute. "You can make it without him. You're as talented as he is."

"I didn't mean my art. I love him. I don't want to be without him. Of course I would survive, but he's a part of me." She ran her hand over her middle. "We're going to have a baby."

Nathan looked at her in surprise. "Does he know?"

"Certainly he does."

"Dakota doesn't strike me as a man who would run out on his obligations."

"I don't want to be an obligation. That's a terrible thing to say."

"I only meant that I don't think he's left you. Maybe he's just not home today."

"I'm going to leave this afternoon. I should have done this weeks ago. I can't stay in the house with Todd. Eventually he's going to hurt me if I stay here."

Nathan nodded. "I'd feel better if I knew you were in a safer place. Want me to call the airport for you?"

She shook her head. "I'll do it. I have to arrange to send my canvases, too. Will you ship the wet ones to me after they dry?"

"Sure thing."

"Thank you. It's nice to have a brother after all these years." She smiled at him and went into the den to look up the number for Houston Intercontinental Airport.

That afternoon Grace finally found Dr. Santon at the hospital. He didn't look entirely pleased to see her. "I have to talk to you about my mother," she said.

He hesitated, then said, "Come with me."

He preceded her to the consulting room. "Mrs. Hillard, I'm sorry to tell you this, but the latest tests show no signs of improvement. There can't be any. Your mother is brain dead and it's irreversible. What your sister felt was just a muscle spasm, nothing more."

"But the intern . . ."

"He's new. Hasn't been here a month. If he had read the chart instead of running off at the mouth, he wouldn't have given you any hope. He's been reprimanded."

"So you're saying she won't recover? You're positive?"

"Absolutely positive."

Grace was surprised at the amount of relief she felt. Years of being tied to an invalid mother dissolved. "Then I guess there's nothing more to be said."

Santon shook his head. "I'm sorry. I'm particularly sorry that you were given false hope, only to have it taken away."

She stood and shook his hand. "Thank you."

"I suppose you'll want to talk with your brother and sister and we'll meet up here tomorrow. That will give all of you time to say good-bye to her."

"All right." She wasn't listening to him.

She went back to Elizabeth's room and stood at the side of her bed. "You almost won again, Mother. I shaped my life according to your plan. I married a man you approved of, I joined all the right clubs, and I contribute to all your charities. I did everything for you. And you probably didn't leave me a dime." She smiled coolly.

"But I'll come out ahead in the long run. You see, I found your will from last December and I changed the date. Whatever Mr. Bennett has in his safe, I'll contest if I'm not named heir. And I'll win, too. I just hope wherever you are, you know what I'm saying."

Grace bent and unplugged the machine. Straightening, she said, "I even gave up singing for you, Mother. I deserve the inheritance."

For a few more breaths Elizabeth's chest continued to inhale and exhale. Then the breaths became more shallow and finally ceased altogether.

The nurse on duty came hurrying into the room and stared from Grace to Elizabeth and back again.

Grace said, "I talked to Dr. Santon. I acted according to his advice."

"But it's customary . . ." the nurse began.

"I don't give a damn what's customary." Grace brushed past her and walked briskly down the hall.

* * *

When she arrived back at the house, she found Amanda's suitcases in the entryway and ready to be carried to the rental car. "Where are you going?" she asked.

"Home. I'll fly back when it's necessary."

"Unpack. Mother is dead." Grace was gratified to see the shocked look on Amanda's face. "Is Nathan here?"

"In the den. She's dead?" Amanda followed Grace through the house. "What happened? I didn't think that could happen until she was removed from the machine. Grace, answer me!"

Grace found Nathan and said, "Mother has died. We need to contact the funeral home and began preparations."

Nathan looked as shocked as Amanda still felt. "She's dead? What do you mean, she's dead? Did one of the doctors unplug the machine without notifying us first?"

"No, I did it. On the doctor's advice."

Amanda stared at her. "Why didn't you say something to us first? We could have seen her a last time."

"I saw no reason. You've all been eager to do this for weeks. I was the one holding out for a miracle. Not you."

"But she squeezed my hand!"

"Muscle spasm." Grace went to the phone. "It's done now."

Amanda's eyes met Nathan's, then she looked back at Grace. "You unplugged the machine? Not the doctor?"

Grace found the phone number she wanted and quickly punched in the number. "What does it matter who actually did it? Someone had to, so I did." She spoke into the receiver. "This is Grace Hillard. You remember me? Yes, Mother just passed away. All right. Thank you."

"Who was that?" Nathan demanded.

"The funeral home. I chose one last week and told them

Mother was close to death. The preliminary decisions have been made.''

"What!" Amanda stared at her. "You chose a funeral home and made plans? Without consulting us?"

"What difference could it possibly make to you which one I chose?"

"It doesn't, but . . ."

"Someone had to do it and I wanted it to be done right." Grace went to Elizabeth's desk and picked up her address book. "I'll need help in calling all her friends."

"You don't even seem upset." Amanda sat on the arm of the chair. "How can you be so calm?"

"Inside, I'm devastated."

"You sure don't show it," Nathan said. "I can't get over you doing all this without telling us about it first."

"As the eldest, it's my place to see that everything is done properly." She dialed the first name in the book. "Hello, Mrs. Fitzwilliam? This is Grace Hillard, Elizabeth Wainwright's daughter. Not too well, I'm afraid. Mother passed away this afternoon."

Amanda looked at Nathan. "I can't believe it."

"Neither can I. We knew it was inevitable, though." He came to her and awkwardly hugged her.

Amanda hugged him back. It was the first time she could remember him doing such a thing. Realization was sinking in and she felt a rising sadness. "She's gone," she said softly.

He nodded and walked to the window and stared out at the backyard. She wondered if he was trying to hide his tears. She wasn't sure what any of them had really felt about Elizabeth.

Grace finished the phone call and began to dial again.

"You made funeral arrangements?" Amanda asked.

"She will be buried beside Dad, of course. That was decided long ago." Grace got a busy signal and hung up.

As she found the next number, she added, "I want no expenses to be spared. It's the last thing we can do for Mother and we aren't going to skimp."

Nathan turned back. "Are you aware how expensive funerals can be? I hope you didn't let the funeral director talk you into something too extravagant."

Grace glared at him. "We're burying our mother, not comparison shopping! Surely even you won't begrudge her a fine funeral. No one talked me into anything. I'm not a fool."

Amanda wasn't so sure. She had heard horror stories about some funeral homes trying to gouge prospective customers. "One of us should have gone with you. We have a say in the matter, too."

"Then you should have done it." Grace turned back to the phone and her call.

Amanda went to stand beside Nathan. "I guess until now I didn't really think she would die. I mean, I knew she was going to, but it seems amazing to think she won't be here any more."

"I know. I was thinking the same thing."

"I'm glad I couldn't get on the earlier flight. I would have to return as soon as I landed. I have to call Dakota."

"I have to call Cody."

Amanda glanced at him. "Will we lose touch now? Mother won't be here to see to it that we get together on Mother's Day and the other holidays."

"We'll stay in touch. What's more, we may grow closer. I don't want to meet on Mother's Day, however."

"No. Not on Mother's Day." Behind her she could hear the drone of Grace speaking to the people who had known Elizabeth. They could be called friends only in the loosest sense. None of them would cry. Amanda thought that might be saddest fact of all. No one would cry over Elizabeth.

* * *

Hours later Nathan took the phone from Grace and dialed his home number. When Cody answered, he said, "She's gone."

"Oh, no. When did it happen?" Cody was sympathetic and he knew her face would have that worried frown that appeared whenever bad news arrived.

"This afternoon. Grace has been on the phone or I would have called sooner. She's made arrangements with the funeral home and the service will be tomorrow."

"So soon?"

"Grace says they have a busy schedule this week and it's tomorrow or not until Friday."

"Yes. Tomorrow would probably be better. All of you are there so you don't have to wait for anyone else to arrive. It's not as if it wasn't expected."

"I want you to come, too."

There was a silence. "You want me there?"

"Yes. And Nate as well. Go buy yourself a new dress."

"I don't need one. Are you sure this is the best time? At your mother's funeral?"

"It's the only time that's left. When it's over, we'll go our separate ways. I want my sisters to meet my family."

"We'll be there. Do you think the funeral will upset Nate?"

"I don't think he's old enough to understand what's going on. He never knew her, of course."

"How about you? Are you all right?"

Nathan thought for a minute. "I'm okay. I guess. I thought I was more prepared than I was. I'm going to stay here tonight. There are things that need to be done."

"I understand. "What time is the funeral?"

"Three o'clock."

"Nate and I will come to the house. I'm sure I can find
t."

"I wish I could be with you right now."

"I could come up tonight."

Nathan glanced at his watch. "No, it's almost Nate's
bedtime and I want him to be rested when he meets everyone. You'd better wait until tomorrow."

After he hung up he sat in the den, thinking what the
next day would bring. It was all happening so fast. Like an
avalanche, it was going faster and faster and nothing could
stop the inevitable. It was over, but the ending could be
as traumatic as the waiting had been.

Amanda dressed to go to the funeral home. It was late,
but the director had called to say Elizabeth's body was
ready for viewing. She dreaded going. Amanda had hated
and feared funerals since her father died.

Before going downstairs, she lifted the receiver on the
hall phone. She was slightly surprised to find the line was
open. She dialed her home number and when the answering machine began, she said, "Dakota, Mother is dead.
The funeral is tomorrow at three. I'll be home as soon as
I can."

She hung up and paused to compose herself before
going down the hall.

The ride to the funeral home was too short. Amanda
wanted it to last for hours so she could get better control
of her feelings. It would have taken that long because the
depth of her emotions were threatening to overwhelm her.
There was sadness over losing her mother, but it was laced
with anger as well, and a heavy amount of frustration. Now
Elizabeth would never approve of her, never love her. That
brought a keen pain and disappointment.

Todd parked at the funeral home and Amanda got out

with the others. The colonial building looked out of place with the neighboring buildings that were distinctly commercial in design.

When Amanda went through the door, a cloying calm eddied around her. It was as if sounds were swallowed by the thick carpet, the enormous vases of silk flowers, the heavy draperies. A man came to meet them and offered his deepest sympathy. Grace burst into tears. Amanda watched her as if she were a stranger acting the part in some incomprehensible play. Grace's display of sorrow didn't touch Amanda, who had seen her perfectly composed in the car.

Amanda hung back as the funeral director showed them to a room off the main one. Soft music was being piped from speakers set discreetly in the wall. A casket stood across the room, its lid raised, the body inside exposed from the hips up. The lower part of the coffin was closed and covered with a huge spray of pink roses. Grace had been busy on the phone that afternoon.

With barely controlled sobs, Grace approached the casket, leaning heavily on Todd's arm. Nathan was behind her, his face a mask of painful resolve. Amanda stayed near the door. She didn't want to look in the casket.

Grace touched Elizabeth's hand and burst into fresh sobs. Todd offered to help her to a chair but she swatted him away. The funeral director stepped to her side then and she allowed him to seat her.

Nathan was paying no attention to Grace. Amanda watched him stand there gazing down at their mother, his expression unreadable. She wondered what he was feeling.

When he stepped to one side, she had nothing to block her view of Elizabeth. She looked remarkably the way she had in life.

The director's art had transformed Elizabeth's gaunt features into the bloom of health. Her makeup was impeccable. He had even had someone come in to dye and set

...er hair in its usual style. Except for the complete stillness
of her body, Elizabeth could have been taken for someone
asleep.

"She's beautiful," Grace sobbed from her chair. "You
made her beautiful again."

"It's how you'd want to remember her," the director
said soothingly. "I followed your instructions exactly."

Amanda wondered how detailed those directions had
been. Nothing here had the look of having been done in
haste.

She forced herself to step closer. Elizabeth's eyelashes
lay against her skin in undisturbed stillness, but it was all
too easy to imagine them snapping open and her turning
her fury upon them all for staring down at her. Her rouged
lips were closed firmly and the director had managed to
coax a faint smile at the corners. Smiles had been one of
Elizabeth's best weapons. She had used them to get her
way with everyone outside the family. Within the family,
she was more apt to use rapier sarcasm. Amanda hated
herself for remembering at such a time.

She looked at Elizabeth's hands. They looked fake. The
long fingers were folded together like the wax petals of a
flower. Her hands seemed more dead than her face. The
mortician's makeup hadn't adjusted to the subtle shadings
of color normally found between nail, skin and vein. Her
hands had a slightly orange cast that had never been there
in life.

Although it was difficult to be in the room, Amanda was
glad she had come. Now she could see Elizabeth was really
dead. Another emotion and a more surprising one crept
over her. Relief. She couldn't hurt Amanda anymore.

Amanda turned away so no one could guess what she
was feeling and went to sit in a chair near the door. Death
was in the room and she wanted to be as far from it as
possible. She wasn't feeling any of the things she had

expected to feel and she wondered if Nathan and Grace were experiencing the same odd reactions. Grace was still playing up the part of bereaved daughter but Nathan was sitting to one side and staring into space. There was no discerning what he might be thinking or feeling.

Amanda just wanted to go home.

Chapter Eighteen

"I've ordered two limousines to take us to the funeral," Grace said as she dabbed at her swollen face. She dropped her purse on the table in the entryway beside the front door.

"Why go to that expense?" Nathan said. "We can drive ourselves."

"I won't have you questioning everything I've done," Grace snapped at him. "The plans have been made and I'm not going to change them at the last minute."

Amanda followed the others into the den and sat in the nearest chair. She was too tired to care about Grace's plans. Grace went to the desk and checked the messages on the answering machine. All were condolence calls, none was from Dakota. She closed her eyes.

"Nathan is right," Todd said carefully. "Limos are too expensive."

Grace turned on him. "My mother is dead and you have the gall to talk to me about expenses? It's none of your business anyway. The estate will cover what the life insurance won't pay."

"You went over that amount?" Nathan asked. "Why did you plan something so expensive?"

"I picked a top-of-the-line casket. It was the least I could do for her. She would be proud of the arrangements I've made."

Nathan looked as if he were about to challenge her, but thought better of it. Todd went to the wet bar and poured himself a generous drink.

"You never shed a single tear," Grace said accusingly to Amanda. "Not a single one! Don't you have any feelings?"

"Of course I do." Amanda curled her legs under her in the chair and tried to settle more comfortably. Her body ached as if she had been doing strenuous exercise. "You've always cried easily. I don't. Not in public."

"Well, I hope you don't embarrass me tomorrow. I expect everyone who is anyone in Houston to turn out for this funeral. Mother was so fortunate to live in River Oaks. I've always loved this house."

"That's good because I guess it will be yours now," Todd said after a hefty swallow of bourbon. "When will the will be read? Day after tomorrow?"

Grace glared at him. "Mother isn't even in her grave yet and you can talk about the inheritance?"

Todd folded and turned away.

"I'm exhausted," Amanda said. "I'm going to bed. Nathan, are you staying here tonight?"

"Of course he is," Grace answered for him. "We're all going to stay together. This is all the family we have left." She dabbed at her eyes again as if she were preparing to let loose a fresh stream of tears.

"Not entirely," Nathan said.

"Okay, so there a few cousins here and there," Grace said in exasperation. "They don't count. Most of them aren't even coming to the funeral. We aren't close to them."

Nathan didn't answer.

Amanda stood up and Grace stopped her. "I don't want you to go. We're going to stay down here and have a wake."

"A what? A wake? Why on earth would we do that?" Amanda asked. "Mother's body isn't here. Wakes are held where the body is."

"Are you all going to fight me every step of the way?" Grace exclaimed. "How can you just go off to bed as if this were an ordinary day?"

"This has been a difficult day. I'm more than ready to see it end."

"It's not right to go to bed as if we weren't upset," Grace said. "If anyone asks me tomorrow, I'm going to tell them I couldn't sleep at all."

"Go ahead. Personally, I'm going to bed." Amanda left them and went through the silent house.

Time seemed to be hanging in place. Amanda had the sensation of being trapped between moments. Just hours before, Elizabeth had been alive, at least technically. Tomorrow she would be buried and strangers would throng to the house. By the next day, the house would belong to one of them, probably Grace, and it would never be their home again. Amanda had as many mixed emotions about that as she did about her mother's death.

She went up to her room and closed the door. After turning the lock, she opened her suitcase and took out her toothbrush. By now she had expected to be home. Hopefully with Dakota.

He hadn't even returned her call about the funeral.

Amanda sat on the edge of the bed and tried to tell herself there could be reasons why he wasn't at home and why he hadn't checked his messages. But there wasn't one that she believed.

* * *

The following morning Amanda felt as if she hadn't closed her eyes all night. In spite of Grace's insistence on a wake, she had heard them all come upstairs not long after she had gone to bed.

Nathan had reverted to his silent and closed-off self. Amanda thought he must be defending himself against the same withering emotions that were warring inside her. Grace was still in her role of stricken mourner and had come downstairs dressed in black from head to toe.

Todd, on the other hand, was behaving like a man who had received good news. The reason for his lifted spirits wasn't difficult for Amanda to determine. Todd, like Grace, assumed the Wainwright fortune had been left to them.

When they went into the living room to wait for whatever callers might happen to drop by, Amanda noticed the shelf beside the clock was empty. "The cottage is gone," she exclaimed without thinking.

All eyes went to the shelf. Grace leaped to her feet. "Someone stole the cottage! Evelyn!"

The housekeeper came to see what Grace wanted.

Grace pointed accusingly at the empty shelf. "Has anyone been in this house?"

"No, I don't look for anyone to come by until after the funeral. Why, where did the cottage go?" Evelyn came into the room and peered more closely at the shelf.

"That's what I'm trying to find out!" Grace glared at them all. "One of you took it. Who was it?"

"I didn't take it," Nathan said. "I wouldn't do something like that."

"Neither would I," Amanda added. "None of us would. Evelyn, could you have moved it when you were dusting and forgot to put it back?"

"I've been dusting this house for nigh on to forty years

and I've never once moved it away to a new place. I didn't do it this time."

"It's easy to see why someone would want it," Grace said angrily. "It's a signed piece and worth a great deal of money."

"Are you accusing anyone in this room of stealing?" Nathan asked with rising anger of his own. "You're the only one who attaches a monetary value to it."

"I do nothing of the kind. I simply know what it's worth. My interest in it is purely sentimental." She cut her narrowed eyes at Amanda. "Dad used to tell me stories about that cottage and I have fond memories of it. I don't want it to go to the wrong person."

Amanda bit her lip. She couldn't remember her father ever singling Grace out for special attention, but Grace was ten years older. When she was small, he might have told her the same stories he later told to Amanda. And maybe he told them to Nathan, too. Grace had claimed that he had. A part of Amanda grew ever sadder. Until this visit, she had thought she had known a small part of her father that none of the others had. That for a brief time she had been the favorite of someone.

"This isn't the time to argue about it," Nathan said.

That was enough to spark Grace's temper. She launched into a tirade and refused to let the issue die. It occurred to Amanda that she was protesting too much. Quietly Amanda left the room and went upstairs.

She had seldom been in Grace's room, even when they were girls. Grace had been grown by the time Amanda was old enough to care about her companionship. Standing in the room gave her an odd feeling, as if she had barged into a stranger's house.

The decorator had finished the job as Grace had wanted. The result was a sickly sweet cocoon of rose and pink and cream. The curtains were held to one side by silver cherubs with pudgy legs and sappy smiles. The bedspread was a confection of pink and rose trimmed in Battenberg lace. "At least I don't have to sleep in here," Amanda muttered to herself.

She looked around, not wanting to touch anything. There was the outside chance that she was wrong and she wasn't one to poke through other people's belongings. Still, she had to know. She went to the closet and opened the door. Grace's dresses took up the overwhelming majority of the closet. Todd's clothes were stuffed into the back corner. Amanda looked up at the shelf. There sat the cottage.

She was able to reach it by tiptoeing. She held it gently in her arms, the memories flooding back. How had Grace been so selfish as to take it? She knew this was the only thing in the entire house that Amanda wanted. Worse, she had accused the others of stealing it.

Amanda closed the closet door and took the cottage to her room. This was one time Grace wasn't going to win. She opened her suitcase, wrapped the cottage in a sweater so it wouldn't be broken, and closed the suitcase again. Grace would certainly know it was missing from her closet, but unless she admitted it had been there all along, she couldn't accuse Amanda of having taken it. She put her suitcase with the other case beside her door.

Grace went up to lie down after lunch. She was tired and cross. Todd had been following her around all day and she had hoped he would stay with Nathan if he thought she was going to take a nap. She stepped out of her shoes and opened the closet door to put them away.

Instantly she saw the cottage was missing. At first she couldn't believe her eyes. Someone had come into her room and taken it!

Her anger flared again. It had to have been Amanda.
She was constantly saying their father had promised the
cottage to her and how he had told her stories about it.
He had never done anything like that with Grace and she
was consumed with jealousy every time Amanda mentioned
it. That had been one reason she wanted the cottage; the
other was its monetary value. Not that she would ever sell
it, but she liked to have nice things about her.

Her first reaction was to go to her sister and demand it
be returned, but better sense prevailed. She didn't want
the others to know she had taken it since she had made
such a production out of saying one of them had stolen
it. She felt justified in her action because she would be
the one to inherit everything as soon as the will was read.
Hiding it had been an assurance that no one else would
take it when she wasn't looking, or in case someone else's
claim to the estate seemed stronger than hers.

She heard footsteps in the hall and knew Todd was
coming to the bedroom. She went to the bed and lay down
fully clothed. If she pretended to be asleep, perhaps he
would go away again.

Todd came into the room, stood there for a minute,
then said, "There's something we need to discuss."

"For heaven's sake, Todd. Can't you see I'm trying to
rest before the funeral?" She refused to open her eyes.

"This is something important."

"And Mother's funeral isn't?" She opened her eyes and
frowned up at him. "Change into that darker tie. That
one looks ridiculous for a funeral."

Todd began to removed the offending tie. "There's
something we need to decide in the near future. Like
today."

"What could possibly be so important that I have to talk
about it today? Why can't you be more understanding?"
She sat up and patted her hair to be sure it wasn't out of

place. "I hope you're happy. You've chased all possibility of a nap right out of me. I'm going back downstairs. When you get your tie changed, buff your shoes. You can't go anywhere looking like that."

She left Todd staring down at his shoes. He was such a fool, she thought. Why had her mother wanted her to marry such a man? The answer was obvious. Todd was like clay in her hands. She could make anything she wanted out of him, and she had. A more uncomfortable idea was that Elizabeth had married their father for exactly the same reason. Grace preferred to think of their father as having been perfect.

As she passed the front door, the bell rang. Grace opened it, a sad smile pasted on her lips. Instead of one of Elizabeth's friends, a black woman and small boy stood on the porch. "Yes?" Grace asked suspiciously. She had heard stories of houses being burglarized while families were at funerals. For this reason she had insisted that the time for the service not be printed in the newspaper.

"I'm looking for Nathan Wainwright." The woman seemed a bit nervous, but she didn't falter under Grace's frown.

"What business do you have with Mr. Wainwright? The family is in deep mourning and he can't be disturbed." She immediately wished she hadn't said that. Now the woman knew the newspaper obituary was accurate. Grace looked past her to see if other black people were in the vintage car parked by the curb. It appeared to be empty.

"Would you tell him that Cody is here?" the woman asked.

The name was vaguely familiar to Grace but she didn't make the connection. "As I said, this is a bad time. If you're applying for work, you'll have to go through the proper channels."

"I'm not applying for work." Cody's voice was as firm as Grace's.

Grace was about to put the woman in her place when Nathan came to the door. He stepped past her and embraced the woman. The little boy grabbed him around the legs and hugged him fiercely. Grace was so astonished her mouth dropped open. Cody. No, it wasn't possible.

Nathan turned, his arm still around the woman. "Grace, I'd like you to meet my wife. This is Cody and the boy is Nate. Nathaniel Redmond Wainwright IV, to be exact." He lifted the boy and tickled his middle.

"No. That can't be true." Grace stared at them "These people are . . ."

"Black. Yes, I know." Nathan kept Cody safely in his embrace and pushed past her and into the house.

Grace shut the door and hurried after them.

Amanda looked up when they came in. She had heard someone at the door and assumed it was one of Elizabeth's friends dropping by to pay her respects. She did a double take when she realized Nathan had his arm around the woman. Understanding dawned. By the time she got up, she was smiling. "You must be Cody." She held out her hand and when Cody took it, she noticed the other woman's fingers were icy. She might look calm but clearly she was nervous. "I'm Amanda." She touched the little boy. "You're something of a surprise."

Nathan grinned. "This is Nate."

"Magic couldn't come," the little boy said seriously. "She had to stay home."

"Magic is his dog," Cody said. "He didn't understand having to leave her behind."

Nate was looking around the room with great interest. "Do we know these people, Mommy? Are there any kids here?"

Amanda smiled. "There aren't any children, but there's

a playhouse out back. Would you like to see it?" She smiled at Cody. "Come on. I'll show you." She wanted to get Nathan's wife out of the house before Grace found her tongue again.

"I guess we're quite a shock," Cody said carefully as Nate raced over the grass to explore the playhouse.

"Not entirely. He told me about you. Well," she said with a smile. "He told me your name."

Cody smiled cautiously. "He said none of you would accept me. He asked me to come today, but I almost backed out a dozen times. I don't mind for myself—I think Nathan needs me this afternoon—but I don't want Nate to be hurt."

"The only one you have to worry about is Grace. Her mind is as closed as they come. Her husband Todd, just parrots whatever she says." She watched Nate look out one of the windows and she waved at him. "So I'm an aunt and he never told me."

"You aren't the way I expected you to be."

Amanda laughed. "Neither are you. Grace and Mother thought you were a man. A white man, I might add."

"Now that's *really* funny," Cody said with a more genuine smile. "You'd think they would know Nathan better than that."

"Until this visit, none of us really knew the others. Not in the ways that count. How long have you been married?"

"Four years. Nate is two, almost three."

Amanda shook her head in amazement. "My brother sure can keep a secret. Especially considering Mother lives—lived—in the next town. How did he keep her from finding out?"

Cody shrugged. "He showed up when he was supposed to and nobody asked the right questions, I guess. If this hadn't happened, he might have kept us hidden forever."

She glanced at Amanda. "I'm sorry about your mother. I should have said that right away."

"Thank you. I'm just glad it will be over soon." She saw Nathan coming across the yard to join them.

"I guess you've figured out why I was reluctant to tell Mother and Grace about my family," he said, taking Cody's hand in his.

"Yes, but you could have told me. Especially after you met Dakota."

"I wanted to, but the time had to be right." He waved at his son in the playhouse. "Grace and Todd are in a state."

"Good. Maybe she'll stop speaking to us."

"I wouldn't count on a blessing of that magnitude." He gestured back at the house. "She wants to talk to you, by the way."

Amanda crossed her arms. "I don't want to discuss anything with Grace."

"Go ahead. I want her to get it out of her system and maybe she won't say anything in front of Nate."

"If she does, I'll help you gag her." Amanda gave in to the inevitable and went back into the house.

Grace was lying on the sofa with Todd was standing over her. Amanda sighed. This was going to be a bad one.

"Did you know about this!" Grace demanded, pushing Todd aside. "Did Nathan tell you he was married to a black woman? His son is black!"

"Actually Nate is only a bit darker than we are. Cody isn't that dark, either. She's beautiful, isn't she? I wonder if she used to be a model."

"Who cares about that? What are we going to tell everyone? I can't allow them to go to the funeral with us!"

"If they don't go, neither will Nathan and I. Besides, we have two limos to drive us. It's not as if we're short on space." She added, "And if you say anything to hurt her feelings, or Nate's, I'll go straight to the airport and not go to the funeral at all. I mean it, Grace. You're not going to cause a scene."

"I can't believe you're talking to me like this," Grace gasped. "My own sister . . ."

"Sister? You and I haven't been close in so long I don't remember when we were. And we certainly don't agree on this. Just remember what I said." She looked at Todd. "That goes for you, too. One false step and I walk out on the funeral and you can explain that to everyone." She paused to let her threat sink in. Then she went to the window and looked out.

Nathan and Cody were in deep conversation beneath the oak tree. Nate was running in circles on the grass. She thought they made a nice family. When Nathan and Cody looked at each other, anyone could tell they were in love. If she were in Nathan's place, she wouldn't have told the secret, either.

The doorbell interrupted her thoughts.

"I'm not answering the door," Grace stated. "I don't want any of Mother's friends coming in with them in the backyard. Just ignore it and they'll go away."

Amanda went to the door and opened it. Dakota stood on the porch. For a moment they studied each other uncertainly, then Amanda threw herself into his arms. Without speaking, they held each other tightly. She never wanted to let him go.

"I wasn't sure if you'd want me to come," he said, his voice muffled against her neck.

"I was afraid you wouldn't." She blinked back the tears of happiness that were forming in her eyes. She released him and stepped back. "You're wearing a suit. I didn't know you owned one."

He laughed. "Just one. It lives in the very back of the closet and almost never sees the light of day." The navy

uit fit him perfectly and the pale cream shirt was a striking
ontrast. His hair was pulled back in a thong that echoed
he colors in his tie and the earring he wore was small
nough to be almost unnoticeable.

"You look almost civilized," she teased. "Grace will be
o glad."

He grimaced.

"I'm glad you're here." She stepped aside. "Come in.
want you to meet Nathan's family."

He caught her hand and pulled her back out to the
orch. "Not yet. There's something we have to settle first."

As always when there was a possibility of unpleasantness,
Amanda felt a curling in her middle. "What?"

"I want you to marry me as soon as we get back to L.A.
don't ever want to go through what I went through these
ast few days. We're going to be together and I don't ever
vant to be away from you again."

"Wait. What was that first part?"

"I want to marry you."

She stared up at him. "Are you sure? I mean, we said
ve weren't ever going to tie each other down."

"Does that mean no?"

"That means yes." She hugged him again. "I was afraid
ou didn't want to marry me."

"I love you and you're going to have my baby. I thought
you had to know we would get married. Then we had that
oig argument and all of a sudden I wasn't sure if you loved
ne any more."

"You're the one who went tearing off to California!"

"I expected you to come, too. When you didn't, I was
oo hurt to stay."

Amanda swatted at his arm. "Don't you ever do that to
ne again! If we have an argument, we're both going to
stay put until we work it out. Agreed?"

"Yes." He touched her face and trailed his hand over

the curve of her cheek. "I've missed you like hell." He
pulled her close again. "I thought I had screwed up royall
and had lost you."

"Why didn't you return my calls?" she demanded. "
kept getting the answering machine!"

"I've been busy." He grinned. "It's a surprise."

"God, not another one!" she groaned. "This family ha
enough surprises up its sleeve to supply the nation."

"What did you mean by wanting me to meet Nathan'
family?"

Amanda took his hand and led him into the house. She
was sure the surprise he had mentioned would be a new
canvas that he was particularly proud of. He must have
been too busy painting to answer the phone or return
calls. She was looking forward to seeing it. "You're not the
only one with a surprise." She took his arm and led him
through the house, ignoring Grace and Todd's hostile
looks at Dakota's presence.

She took him to the window that looked out onto the
backyard and said nothing as she looked at his face to see
his response.

"Well, I'll be damned! Cody, I take it? And their son
I'll bet Grace—"

"Yep. As predictable as any bigot there ever was."

"Well, come on. Introduce me."

"With pleasure." And she knew it would be a pleasure.
With certainty she knew they would all become good
friends. Family she could be proud of, at last.

Chapter Nineteen

The silence in the living room was strained as the family waited for the limousines to arrive. Even Nate was subdued and sat quietly on Nathan's lap. Grace looked around at them all and wondered how she could possibly explain Dakota's long hair and Nathan's black wife. As she was checking her watch for the fourth time, the limos arrived.

Grace was careful to put everyone but Todd in the second car. She was determined that her family wasn't going to ruin this day for her.

On the way to the funeral home, Todd said, "When does Bennett intend to read the will?"

"I told him I want it done tomorrow. I asked him to do it today, but he said that usually doesn't happen the day of the funeral. He'll be at the house at ten tomorrow morning." She gave him a suspicious look. "You're certainly quiet today. Why is that?"

"I have a lot on my mind."

"Not that business about the mall again. Don't you ever think about anything but work?"

"I have a call in to Fred Willis. I hope he doesn't try to reach me while we're at the funeral."

"We're on the way to Mother's funeral and you're worrying about missing a business call? That's just like you! Thoroughly insensitive." She touched her hair. "I wonder if I should have worn a hat. No one does these days, but at a time like this it seems improper to go without one."

Todd gave her a confused look, then went back to staring out the window.

Something odd was happening with him and Grace didn't like it. He had been quiet all day and that wasn't like Todd. He could usually be counted on to strike up a conversation even if it was a boring one. Maybe he was still in shock from meeting Cody and Nate, or from Dakota returning. "At least all that hair is pulled back and his earring is small."

"Who?"

"Dakota, of course. Who else would I be talking about?"

Todd only looked more confused. "Dakota who?"

"Have you been drinking this early in the day?"

"I haven't been drinking. I don't know what you're talking about."

"All right. Be difficult. Just don't embarrass me."

"There's something we have to discuss," he said as if he was trying to remember just what it was. "Something important."

"Not now, Todd. This is no time for a discussion." She could see the funeral home ahead and was gratified to see the parking lot was full of cars. "Mother was so well loved by everyone. Look how many people have turned out to say good-bye."

In the second car Nathan said to Nate, "You're to be

especially good until we get back to the house. Do you understand?''

Nate nodded solemnly. "I like this car, Daddy. Can we get one like it?"

Nathan smiled. "No, it wouldn't fit in our driveway." He covered Cody's hand with his and asked her, "Still hanging in there?"

She nodded as solemnly as Nate had. "I just wish it were over."

"Don't worry. Grace won't do anything to cause a scene in public." He hoped he was right.

"I never pleased Mother," Amanda said softly to Dakota. "No matter what I did, it was never good enough. I don't want to remember that today."

He squeezed her hand. "I'm right here. We can get through anything together."

They pulled into the parking lot and circled around to the back of the building to line up the limos behind the hearse. Men in dark suits and somber expressions opened the limo doors and escorted the family into the building.

Amanda was glad they didn't have to make their way through the group of people who had come to pay their last respects to Elizabeth. Her emotions were at war again and she wasn't sure she could have responded appropriately to a conversation. At times she felt as if this were a dream. That couldn't be Elizabeth lying over there in that pink coffin with the spray of pink roses almost engulfing it. She looked more like a wax doll than the woman Amanda had known and feared.

Reverend Emmett stepped up to the podium and the service began.

Amanda heard only parts of it. Her mind kept flickering back to her childhood, to her father's funeral in this same building. Had Grace remembered or was it a coincidence?

She held Dakota's hand and hoped the preacher wouldn't be long-winded.

Grace's thoughts weren't on the service, either. She was mentally going over lists in her mind. On Grace's instructions, Evelyn had stayed at the house to oversee the plates of food that friends had sent for the gathering after the funeral. Another woman had been hired for the day to help her, and Grace was nervous about the stranger being left in the vicinity of the sterling silver.

On the pretext of dabbing a tissue at her eyes, Grace touched her hair to be sure it was in place. She had gone to the beauty shop early that morning and the woman who had done Elizabeth's hair for years had styled Grace's. She had an image to uphold even in her time of sorrow. That was how she liked to think of it—her time of sorrow. It had a Victorian sound to it that was appropriate for the day.

Grace glanced around at the other pews. So much had needed to be done so quickly. She was still angry with the funeral home for having the service so soon after Elizabeth's death. Rushing seemed so inappropriate. Mentally she ticked off the names of the people she had called to tell about Elizabeth's death. Surely she had notified everyone who was important—to have forgotten someone would be so embarrassing.

Nathan was sitting beside her and Cody was on his other side, with the little boy in the middle. Grace could see him out of the corner of her eye. Since he was staring at her it was hard to overlook him. She gave him a warning look and he sat back against Nathan's side. Grace sighed and leaned against Todd as if she were overcome by grief. Of all the times for Nathan to introduce his wife and son, he had picked the worst. Grace imagined the speculation that must be going on. It was a terrible shame that their mother hadn't known about Cody and Nate. Nathan would have been disowned instantly and Grace would have one less sibling to battle over the inheritance.

Reverend Emmett finished with a prayer and the funeral director motioned for the family to file past the casket. Amanda almost rebelled. Grace poked her from behind and she steeled herself. She could feel the eyes of all the other mourners on her as she walked past and looked at Elizabeth one last time. When she thought she was going to falter, Dakota put his hand on her shoulder. She felt stronger for his support.

The graveside service was mercifully short. The day was blistering hot and no breezes stirred the tall cedar trees. The family was seated under a dark green awning, but it was only slightly cooler than the sunlight. Most of the people who had been at the church had skipped the cemetery and the ones who hadn't looked distinctly uncomfortable in the heat.

Amanda stared at the casket, now closed and fastened shut for all time. It was startling to think of Elizabeth sealed up in there, her hair beautifully combed, her dress immaculate, her hands folded over her stomach.

When the service was finished, Amanda shook hands first with the minister, then with everyone else. Their faces were a blur to her. She knew a few of the people, but for the most part they were strangers She saw three workmen standing at a distance and knew they were waiting for everyone to leave so they could lower the coffin into the ground and cover it with dirt. Again the thought of Elizabeth lying in frozen perfection inside the box struck Amanda and her skin prickled.

After they left the cemetery, the limos deposited the family at the house and Amanda braced herself to get through the next few hours. Acquaintances of Elizabeth who considered themselves close friends began arriving. Soon the house was full of people, all talking in the carefully modulated voices considered correct for such an occasion. Occasionally someone laughed out loud or exclaimed without thinking, but they quickly were quiet again.

Amanda watched Nate threading his way through the forest of legs and skirts until he reached the back door. Then he ran from the house toward the playhouse. He had already discarded the clip-on tie he had worn to the funeral and was clearly glad to be away from the press of people. She wished she had that same freedom.

Grace was managing to look mournfully helpless while expertly overseeing the well-stocked table. Evelyn and her assistant saw to it the bowls were kept full and that used plates were cleared away. Amanda wondered how they would ever be able to return all the pie plates and casserole pots to the correct owners. She decided that could be Grace's chore since she was the one who was determined to live here afterward. Amanda only wanted to go home.

"Our family will be different," Dakota said at her side.

She turned to look at him. "I didn't know my thoughts were showing."

"Only to me. We'll raise our babies to love us and to respect us through love, not fear."

"My relationship to my family has been like a moth to a flame," she said, thinking out loud. "No matter how often I got burned, I flew back again."

"They raised the dysfunctional family to an art form."

She smiled. "Wait here. I'll be right back."

She threaded her way to the stairs and went up. It was quiet on the second floor and she was relieved to be away from people for even a short time. She went to her room and put her suitcase on the bed, opened it, and took out the cottage. For a while she sat on the bed and looked at the porcelain house and remembered. Then she carried it back to Grace's room and returned it to the shelf in the closet. Love couldn't be proven by tangible things. She knew her father had loved her and she didn't need the cottage to remind her.

Todd saw Amanda come downstairs and move close to Dakota. He was confused in the extreme. When Dakota had left, he had assumed that he was out of Amanda's life forever. Todd tried to clear his thoughts. Wasn't she still planning to leave with him after the reading of the will? Something was wrong with that picture but he couldn't remember what it was.

And why was Amanda holding Dakota's hand when she was in love with Todd? He would have to tell her later that the time for making him jealous was past.

Todd had experienced these jumbled thoughts since awakening that morning. He couldn't understand why he wasn't thinking clearly, but this wasn't the first time it had happened to him. Once several years ago he had gone to work and had forgotten how to get home again. The doctor had diagnosed him as having arteriosclerosis and cautioned him that similar bouts could occur. But this wasn't one, he was certain. He knew exactly where he was and could recognize everyone. No, he was only confused.

That reminded him. He had to make a greater effort to tell Grace that he was leaving her for Amanda. He had tried two other times, the most recent being in the limo on the way to the funeral home, but Grace had changed the subject each time. He considered finding her and telling her now, but the crowd was too confusing. He would remember to tell her later. And he also had to remember to propose to Amanda. Everything had to be done in the right order if he was to get part of Grace's inheritance and a share of Amanda's as well.

Amanda felt someone watching her and she looked up to see Todd staring at her. He had a drink in his hand but he didn't seem to be drunk. He was only staring. She put her hand in Dakota's and didn't move from his side.

* * *

The morning after the funeral was anticlimactic. Todd was still experiencing the disconnected sensation but his thoughts were clearer than they had been the day before. He knew he would have to make a doctor's appointment as soon as he returned to Dallas and that Amanda had agreed to marry him. He didn't recall exactly when he had proposed, but there was no doubt in his mind that he had.

This was the perfect time to tell Grace about his plans for the future.

She was sitting on the foot of the bed putting on her shoes. She was wearing a navy dress and a strand of pearls he didn't recall having seen before. Grace often went shopping without showing him what she had bought so he thought nothing of it.

"We need to talk," he said as he stepped in front of her.

"For goodness' sake, Todd. You sound like a broken record. What can we possibly have to discuss right now?"

"I'm leaving you."

Grace's head shot up. "What?"

"I'm going to divorce you. I thought you should know about it." He smiled to show that he wasn't doing this out of anger but from careful consideration.

"You're not that big of a fool. If you divorce me you won't get a penny of the Wainwright money."

"Yes, I will, because we're still married and you've already inherited it. Half of everything you have is mine." He remembered not to gloat, but to say it simply. He could gloat later.

"You stupid idiot! Inheritances aren't part of community property. What's mine is mine!"

"Not if my lawyer is smarter than your lawyer." He

stepped aside. "I hear the doorbell. Bennett must be here to read the will. Let's go downstairs."

For a moment she sat there staring at him. Then she sprang to her feet and stalked from the room.

Todd followed her with a smile. She was angry but he didn't care. It occurred to him that he had forgotten to tell her that he was leaving her for Amanda, but there was time for that later. Maybe he and Amanda would make the announcement to everyone after the reading of the will. That would be a good time.

Grace was furious. It had never occurred to her that Todd might divorce her. If anyone was filing for divorce, it was her! She no longer needed him. Of course the divorce would have to be done in Dallas so no one in Houston would know. In time, perhaps a couple of years or more, she would let it to be known that she was divorced. No one ever would realize it had happened on the heels of her mother's funeral.

In spite of Todd's statement, she knew Texas law considered an inheritance to be personal property and not part of the marital property. Todd was going to be in for a rude awakening. She would be the one to come out a winner because she would have her mother's money, half of everything Todd was worth, and maybe alimony as well.

"I'm going to be glad to be rid of you," she hissed at him in an undertone as they went down the stairs. "You've been a hindrance to me for much too long."

"By the way," he said as they moved to join the others sitting with Bennett in the living room. "I'm leaving you for another woman."

Grace stared at him. Todd had another woman? How could he be in love with someone else? He hadn't been out of her sight for a month. Then she remembered the flights to Dallas. Maybe he hadn't been going up on business at all. And maybe all those phone calls to Fred Willis had been to that woman. She was seething inside as she took her place.

Amanda felt Todd staring at her again and turned to speak sharply to him. He motioned for her to step into the dining room with him. She hesitated, then reasoned he could hardly try anything with the entire family and Clay Bennett just around the corner. "What is it?" she asked impatiently when they were out of sight.

"I've told Grace that I'm divorcing her."

"You did what?" she exclaimed. "When?"

"Just now. I knew you'd be excited."

Amanda stared at him. "I don't believe this. You and Grace are getting a divorce?"

"I haven't told her about us, but I'm going to after the will is read. All she knows is that I'm leaving her for another woman. She doesn't have any idea that it's you."

"Whoa! Wait a minute. What are you talking about?"

"You and me. This means that we can be together. I've got it all planned. I'll get Grace's share because we're still married and she inherits it today. Then you and I will contest the will and I'll see to it that you get the rest of the money. We'll live on easy street from now on." He smiled at her as if he was positive she would go along with his scheme. "It's taken me a long time to get us to this place, but I did it. I wish you could have seen Grace's face when I told her."

"I'm not going to run away with you! Is that what you think?" She was having trouble assimilating all this. "Where did you get an idea like that?"

Todd's smile faltered. "Don't play games with me, Amanda. You know you love me."

"I don't even like you! I'm in love with Dakota. We're going to be married as soon as we go home. I'm going to have his baby."

"You can have my baby instead," he said in a wheedling tone.

"Todd, I love Dakota and I'm pregnant. I'm going to marry Dakota." She glared up at him.

"No," he said in a confused voice. "That's not right."

Nathan stepped into the dining room and took Amanda's arm. "Mr. Bennett is waiting for you."

She went with him. She was glad Todd didn't follow them. Where had he gotten the idea she would leave Dakota for him? She glanced at Grace. That explained why she seemed so angry. Grace looked as if she were about ready to explode as it was.

Bennett opened his briefcase and took out a legal document backed in blue paper. As he unfolded it, he said, "It's always with regret that I have to read a will. I'm sorry to have to read it so soon after the funeral, but I understand that all of you have other lives that have been disrupted for too long as it is. So without further ado I'll tell you what it says." He began to read.

Amanda concentrated to understand the legal terms. It wasn't that difficult. Everything went to Nathan.

Grace leaped to her feet. "That's not possible. I was her favorite child!" She glared at Nathan as if she thought he had taken the inheritance from her by design. "There's a more recent will in the wall safe in the den. I happen to know it names me as beneficiary, not Nathan!"

"I'd like to see that document," Bennett said.

Grace swept from the room on her mission.

Bennett shifted uncomfortably. "I'm sure you know your mother was rather eccentric in some ways. One of her quirks was that she frequently changed her will. I don't, however, know of another will having been made and it's unlikely that she had time to execute one. As you know, her accident occurred the day after she signed this one."

He handed it to Nathan and showed him the date and notary seal.

Grace came back into the room with another document in her hand. "Here!" she said triumphantly. "Here's the most recent one." She thrust it at Bennett.

He unfolded it and read, then shook his head. "No, I'm familiar with this will. I drafted it myself. It was done in December."

"Look at the date," Grace demanded. "Look at the date!"

Bennett frowned. "This document has been tampered with. I hope you're not going to insist on pursuing this." He fixed Grace with a stare that held no humor in it. "That would be very serious indeed."

Grace faltered. "I found it in the safe. The date was like you see it. Mother must have changed it herself. Doesn't that prove she changed her mind after she drew up the one you have?"

"It doesn't seem likely to me. As I said, she changed her will frequently but not from one day to the next. No, the one in my possession is the valid one. No judge would disagree and would question why the date on this one has been changed to the day of the accident. A judge would suspect the beneficiary of such a will to be guilty of forging it in her interest."

Grace's mouth snapped shut. She looked furious but she was too smart to make matters worse.

Bennett settled back in the chair. "It really is a moot point anyway. Over the past years, Mrs. Wainwright's investments haven't paid off the way they should have and her savings account has dwindled accordingly."

"How would you know that?" Grace demanded suspiciously.

"I handled all her financial matters."

"Mother didn't do that herself?" Amanda asked in surprise.

Bennett shook his head. "She never had a head for numbers. When your father was alive, he kept track of everything, of course, but after he passed away, she turned it all over to me. I even paid the bills and balanced her checkbook. The investment choices were, of course, always hers. Even over my occasional advice to the contrary."

"That's not possible!" Grace exclaimed. "Mother was a financial genius!"

"No, Mrs. Hillard, I'm afraid not."

Amanda had to suppress the urge to laugh. Elizabeth, regal and awe-inspiring, hadn't balanced her own checkbook. "She had her own secret!"

Grace silenced her with a glare. "Exactly what are you trying to say to us, Mr. Bennett?"

"Mrs. Wainwright had little left in savings or investments at the time of her death. The cost of her medical expenses and the funeral will have used it all up. You almost certainly will, in fact, be forced to liquidate the rest of the estate to pay them off."

"Liquidate?" Grace asked.

"He's saying we may have to sell the house," Nathan spoke up at last.

"I'm afraid so," Bennett confirmed. "I'm sorry. If any of you have any questions, I'll do my best to answer them."

In the den Todd was on the phone to Fred Willis. In the space of a minute, he'd learned that the all the investors for the partially completed mall had backed out and the project was dead.

Todd held the receiver for a moment. He could hear Willis calling his name over the wire but it didn't matter anymore. Nothing mattered. Ironically his mind seemed clear for the first time in days and the reality was staggering.

He went into the hall and heard Grace berating the lawyer. That meant someone else had inherited his mother-in-law's money and that Grace's ploy with the faked will hadn't worked. Who had inherited the money didn't matter. Amanda was lost to him. He could see her from where he stood, her hand in Dakota's. He had lost everything.

He went upstairs and found the bottle of sleeping pills the doctor had prescribed for Grace. She had recently refilled the prescription, so the bottle was almost full. He ran water in a glass and took all the pills, swallowing as many at a time as he could.

Then he went into the bedroom and sat down on the bed. He detested the room. It looked like Grace. He took a pencil and a pad of paper from the nightstand and wrote Grace a note, telling her why he was taking his life. He didn't want to go without having been the one to tell her they were bankrupt. When it was finished, he lay on the bed and closed his eyes.

It took longer for the pills to take effect than he had expected but at last a deep drowsiness crept over him. He tried to open his eyes but the effort was too much. He let sleep envelop him.

Downstairs Amanda nudged Dakota. "Let's go. There's no reason to sit around and listen to Grace."

He stood and followed her out of the living room and up the stairs.

"There's not much left to pack. I was all ready to go before Mother died. Just let me get my things out of the bathroom." She left him fastening suitcases and went to get her toothbrush and toiletries.

The door to Grace's room was open and she saw Todd

lying on the bed. She hadn't known he was upstairs and was startled at first, but hurried on by. The last thing she wanted was a confrontation with Todd.

Her belongings were together beside the sink just as she had left them. The only object out of place was a bottle of pills. Amanda picked up the bottle to put it away and noticed it was empty. She unscrewed the top and looked in. She thought Grace had reordered some sleep medication the day before. In fact, she had insisted that Todd stop what he was doing and go to the pharmacy and get it for her. It shouldn't be empty.

With a frown Amanda put the bottle back on the cabinet, then picked up her belongings and went back to her room.

She put the things away and looked around the room. "I guess I won't be back here again," she said to Dakota. "That seems so odd. I thought I would be in and out of this house all my life."

"Did we leave anything in the studio? Better double check. I'll start carrying the bags down to the car."

Amanda went to the studio and opened the door one last time. A faint smell of turpentine and linseed oil met her like old friends. The room was empty. Because she never intended to return for any length of time, Dakota had broken down all the easels and shipped them by bus to Los Angeles the day before.

She went inside and walked around the room for the last time. This room, more than her bedroom, had been home to Amanda. Her happiest times had been spent here. Her father had taken up the carpet and enlarged the windows just so she would have a good place to paint. She looked out the window and saw Dakota carrying the suitcases to the car. Her future was much rosier than her past had been.

As she left, she pulled the door shut with a click. She was ready to leave.

When she passed Grace's room she again thought Todd
had picked an odd time to take a nap. He hadn't been in
the living room to hear the outcome of the will and that
had seemed strange to her as well. She had expected him
to be hovering over the lawyer as much as Grace had been.

Hesitantly she went to the door. "Todd?" she called
out. He didn't move. She stepped in. "Todd, are you
asleep?" She reached out and gingerly shook his foot.
Then she saw the note beside him.

Understanding began to dawn on her. She grabbed up
the note and read the first few words. Then she threw it
back on the bed and ran out into the hall. "Nathan! Grace!
Call 911!" She ran back to the bedroom.

She hauled Todd to a sitting position and began slapping
his face to wake him. He groaned but didn't open his eyes.
"Todd! Wake up. Todd!"

By this time Nathan had run into the room. He stared
at her.

"Call 911! He's taken sleeping pills!"

Grace was near enough to hear this and she pushed into
the bedroom as Nathan was running out to make the call.
"What's going on here?"

"Sleeping pills!" Amanda didn't stop slapping Todd
and trying to wake him.

Grace ran to the bathroom and came back with the
empty bottle in her hand. "Why would he do this to me?"
she wailed. "Todd, why did you do this?"

Amanda let Todd fall back onto the bed. She pressed
her ear to his chest. "He's stopped breathing!" She knelt
on the bed and ripped his collar open. Tilting his head
back and pulling his jaw open, she breathed into Todd's
mouth. Grace was screaming in what sounded like actual
hysteria.

Dakota hurried into the room. "What's happening?"

Amanda could hear Bennett and Evelyn talking loudly

the hall. "He's stopped breathing." She clasped her
ands and began pumping on his chest. She felt his ster-
um give way and heard a crack as it broke, but she didn't
top the heart massage. "Breathe, damn it!" she shouted
t Todd.

Dakota knelt beside her and felt for a pulse in Todd's
eck. "Keep it up. I don't feel anything."

Amanda breathed into him and shoved against his chest
ntil she was exhausted, then Dakota took over for her.
n the distance she could hear the ambulance sirens. Grace
ad stopped crying and was standing against the wall beside
velyn and Bennett. Nathan was nowhere in sight and she
new he must have gone downstairs to let in the EMTs
nd to keep Nate from seeing what was happening with
odd.

There was the sound of running feet on the stairs and
hree men in white came hurrying into the room. Dakota
noved aside and let them take over. He put his arm around
Amanda and held her close.

As two of the men set up the stretcher, the third was
vorking on Todd. "I'm getting a pulse!" he announced.
The stretcher was shoved beside the bed and they lifted
Todd onto it. "Clear the way," he said, brushing Bennett
and the others aside. "Let us get through!"

Amanda put her arm around Grace and helped her out
of the room. She seemed to be in shock. Grace had read
the note and Amanda had seen enough of it to know
what had driven Todd to attempt suicide. Grace was self-
centered enough for part of her shock to be over the
prospect of having lost everything they had.

Dakota drove them to the hospital. Nathan and Cody
followed in his car. By the time they reached the emergency
room, the doctor on duty told them that Todd's stomach
had already been pumped. He was breathing regularly and
his vital signs had stabilized. He was going to survive. Grace

went with the doctor to see Todd, leaving the others in the waiting room.

"I'm going to stay a while," Nathan said to Cody. "You take Nate and go on home. I'll be there as soon as I know Grace won't need me."

"I can stay," Amanda said reluctantly.

"No, I think she'll be more comfortable with me. You and Dakota have a plane to catch." He smiled at them. "Todd will be all right."

"How about you?" Amanda asked.

"I'm fine. I never expected Mother to leave me anything, so I'm not disappointed. I'll put the house on the market as Mr. Bennett suggested. Cody and I don't want to live there and it should pay off Mother's debts."

"Let me know if I can help you," Amanda said. She stepped close and gave him a hug. "Call me soon."

"I will," he promised. As Amanda hugged Cody and Nate, he shook hands with Dakota. "We want you to stay with us when you're in town for the exhibit."

"You bet," Dakota said with a grin. He winked at Nate. "I want to get to know my nephew and to meet Magic the wonder dog."

As Amanda and Dakota walked to the car, he said, "Your family sure knows how to throw a homecoming."

"I'm glad this is the last one I'll ever have to face." She looked back at the hospital. "I wonder if Grace will be all right. She barely said good-bye to me."

"She'll be fine. Nathan will hang around until Todd is settled in a room and I'm sure he'll check on them until they head back to Dallas."

They drove onto the busy street and headed for the airport. "You aren't as curious as you used to be," he commented. "You haven't asked me about the surprise."

"It's a painting, right? I'm looking forward to seeing it."

"It's not a painting."

She gave him a puzzled look. "What is it? Don't just grin at me—tell me what it is."

"Then it wouldn't be a surprise," he teased. "Okay, okay. It's a house."

Amanda shook her head. "I don't think I heard you correctly. It's a what?"

"I bought a house." He chuckled as he drove expertly onto the freeway. "Or at least I bought it if you like it. I haven't signed any papers yet."

"A house! We can't afford a house!"

"Yes, we can. Your angels sold and they sold big." He reached into his shirt pocket. "Look at this."

It was a xeroxed copy of the check. Amanda's mouth dropped open. "You're kidding! Tell me this is a joke! My angel sketches sold for this kind of money?"

"Yep."

"I've been working my rear end off for years on important oil paintings and I sold some sketches for this much?" She had to remember to breathe.

"You're going to love the house. I found one that was a steal. It's in a valley, not too far from L.A. for us to visit our friends but definitely out of town. There's a pool, room for children, puppies, kittens, any kind of pet you can mention. There's even room for horses."

"Really?" she whispered.

"Really. So see? You have to marry me because I'm going to be living in your house and riding your horses and making all those babies to play with all those pets."

Amanda threw her arms around him and kissed him on the neck. "I love you, Dakota!"

"Careful, honey. You're going to love me to pieces." But he kept his arm around her long enough to kiss her cheek.

Amanda refastened her seat belt and stared at the copy

of the check. "It's really going to happen. All our dreams are going to come true."

He nodded. "You'd better start planning some new ones fast."

She smiled. "I will."